Walla Walla
County Libraries

Love Finds You™

━━ IN ━━
GROOM
TEXAS

D0973192

Love Finds You™

IN
GROOM
TEXAS

BY JANICE HANNA

FJC
HANNA
2011

summerside
PRESS™

Summerside Press™
Minneapolis 55438
www.summersidepress.com

Love Finds You in Groom, Texas
© 2011 by Janice Hanna

ISBN 978-1-60936-006-1
All rights reserved. No part of this publication may be reproduced
in any form, except for brief quotations in printed reviews, without
written permission of the publisher.

The Holy Bible, New International Version®, NIV®. Copyright © 1973,
1978, 1984 by Biblica, Inc.™ Used by permission of Zondervan. All rights
reserved worldwide.

The town depicted in this book is a real place, but all characters are
fictional. Any resemblances to actual people or events are purely
coincidental.

Cover Design by Koechel Peterson & Associates | www.kpadesign.com

Interior design by Müllerhaus Publishing Group | www.mullerhaus.net

Cover and interior photos of Groom, Texas, by Dale Shawgo,
www.wix.com/awesomephotography/awesomephotography.
Used by permission.

*Summerside Press™ is an inspirational publisher offering fresh,
irresistible books to uplift the heart and engage the mind.*

Printed in USA.

Dedication
....

To my 2010 *Johnny Be Good* codirector, Kathy Deitz.
As the cowardly lion would say:
"If it hadn't been for you, I wouldn't have found my courage."
Your help as codirector freed me up
to write this quirky tale. I'm eternally grateful.

GROOM
1914
TX

*Anyone who does not take his cross and
follow me is not worthy of me.
Whoever finds his life will lose it, and
whoever loses his life for my sake will find it.*

MATTHEW 10:38–39 NIV

Groom, Texas

GROOM
1914
TX

GROOM, TEXAS, IS LOCATED IN THE TEXAS PANHANDLE, JUST EAST of Amarillo. There, against the backdrop of ranch lands and canyons, you can find tumbleweeds, open plains, and some of the finest cattle in the country.

Groom was once known for its ranches. In fact, Colonel B. B. Groom owned one of the largest ranches in the area. These days, Groom is known for something else—the tallest cross in the world. The cross, which is nineteen stories high, can be seen from twenty miles away. Of course, it was built long after the action in this book takes place. Because I couldn't use the cross in my story, I opted to allude to it. You will notice that Anne wears a cross necklace at all times. The Lord uses it to bring healing to her heart and draw her to Him. In the same way, the cross in modern-day Groom offers hope and healing to all who pass by.

Groom, Texas, is not a fairy-tale place. It is very real. And while it may not be known for its single fellas, it is known as a place where people can find healing and hope for their lives. I pray this story reflects the spirit of the people in that fine town.

Janice Hanna

Chapter One

....

Amarillo, Texas, 1914

> *Looking for some of the best ranch land in the country? Look no farther than the plains of the Texas Panhandle. The pioneers of yesterday saw the possibilities and arrived in record numbers. Famed cattlemen settled the area, building some of the most impressive ranches the state has ever known. Why not join them? If you have a hankerin' to rustle cattle or build fences, c'mon out to the Texas Panhandle. Join hundreds of other cattlemen in their quest to make Texas the beef capital of the world.* —"Tex" Morgan, reporting for the *Panhandle Primer*

"How does it feel, being the last single fella in town?"

"S'cuse me?" Jake turned to face his best friend. "What did you say?"

"You heard me." Cody laughed, and his eyes sparkled with mischief. "When I get married a week from now, you'll be the only fella in Groom who isn't hitched. Don't tell me it hasn't occurred to you. Everyone's talking about it."

"Ugh." Jake raked his fingers through his hair. Of course it had occurred to him. He just hadn't planned on taking it up with anyone other than the Lord. And as for everyone in town gabbing about it, that only made the situation more uncomfortable. Why did folks always have to go nosing in where they didn't belong? He'd already had his fill of family members prodding into his nonexistent love life. Take Mama, for instance. And his older brothers—and their wives. Why couldn't everyone just leave him alone? What was the problem with being single, anyway?

Jake continued walking down the railroad track toward home, hoping his friend would take his silence as a hint to change the direction of the conversation.

Unfortunately, Cody had other ideas. He slapped Jake on the back and chuckled. "I guess being single and male makes you something of an oddity in these parts. You can't blame folks for talking, now, can you?"

"Actually, I can." Jake felt his jaw tighten as he spoke. "Gossip is gossip. So let's just call it what it is." He drew in a deep breath to calm himself and focused on the train track under his feet. *Just keep walking. Don't let 'em get to you.*

"Ah." Cody's eyebrows elevated. "Taking this pretty seriously, are you?"

"You betcha." Jake stopped walking and turned to look at his friend, willing his temper not to flare. "I'm the laughingstock of the town, according to all my brothers. And you know how they are."

"I do know how they are." Cody laughed. "The O'Farrell brothers are a force to be reckoned with, especially once they get their minds made up about something. Present company excluded, of course."

"They're having a field day with this." Jake paused and shook his head. "And as for being an oddity, it's always been that way. I'm the only one in the family who thinks that working for the railroad holds more interest than branding cattle or building fences. That alone makes me strange in their eyes." He paused to think about how true those words were. Nothing like being the odd man out, especially in your own family. Then again, he'd always been fodder for jokes for his older brothers. In that respect, nothing much had changed—only the type of jokes.

"Your brothers are competitive, that's all." Cody shrugged and gave him a thoughtful look. "They want to prove that your family's ranch is the finest in Carson County. No shame in that. Just a hefty dose of family pride."

"I don't care anything about having the largest herd or the finest piece of land." Jake paused to think about what he'd just said. "Well, let me restate that I do care, because my father cared. It meant a lot to him, and anything that was important to my father is important to me. But I see my work with the railroad as a way to help my brothers accomplish their goals on the ranch. To carry on my father's legacy. So I guess you could say we're working hand in hand to achieve the same things. They just don't see it that way. Or if they do, they're not sayin'."

Cody's expression grew more serious. "They'll catch on before long, Jake. With the railroad so accessible, a lot of things will be changing. For the better, I mean."

He shook his head. "Maybe. I just have different ideas from most around here, even my own brothers. Can't help that. Ma says I was cut from a different piece of cloth."

"Well, if we could find you a bride who liked to sew, that would be just the ticket, now, wouldn't it?" Cody bent over and slapped his knee, his laughter reverberating through the air.

Jake did his best not to groan aloud. "I really don't think you need to be trying to find me a bride. Honestly, I—" Off in the distance a train whistle pierced the air. He paused and stepped off the track, knowing the 5:35 train to Amarillo would be through momentarily.

"Don't give up just yet." Cody stood aright and gave him a pensive stare. "I'm going to find you a bride if it's the last thing I do. Consider it my life's mission."

"I really wish you would stop this ridiculous—"

"The Widow Baker is lookin' for a husband." Cody gave him a knowing look. "She told my mama just last Sunday after church that she's itchin' to be hitched."

Jake kept walking. "She's in her fifties. And do we really have to talk about this? I'm very happy being single."

"Of course you are." The look on Cody's face shifted to one of sympathy. "What about Cassie Martin? She's always taken a shine to you. Remember how she used to tease you back in school? And if I remember right, you played along. 'Course, she's not as easy on the eyes as my Virginia, but if a fella squinted, I'm sure she'd be near to tolerable. I hear she's a great cook. That has to work in her favor. Just focus on the circumference of her flapjacks, not her waistline."

Jake groaned and continued walking away from the tracks. This was getting worse by the moment. "You and I both know that Cassie's mama has been trying to marry her off to any fella who would look her way. And I'm not saying she's not pretty, that's not it. She's just not..."

"Your type?" Cody hollered over the clacking of the approaching train. "Well maybe that's the problem. Maybe you're too picky. To hear your sisters-in-law tell it, they've brought dozens of girls around over the past couple years and you've turned up your nose at every one."

"I'd like to change the subject now," Jake called out.

Thankfully, the locomotive came barreling through, making so much racket that Cody's response couldn't be heard. Only when the caboose finally slipped off in the distance could Jake make out his words.

"No doubt you're content to stay single. Still livin' at home with Mama doin' all the cookin' and cleanin'. Sounds mighty tempting, I'll admit."

Ugh. Those were fighting words.

Only one problem—Jake didn't have it in him right now to fight. What could he say in his own defense, anyway? His mother did cook and clean for him. She wouldn't have it any other way. And sure, he'd talked about moving out of the main house for years, but every time he'd brought it up, her tears convinced him to stay. He didn't blame her. Not really. Ever since Papa's death two years ago, she'd been more dependent on Jake than ever. Much as he wanted to, if he started working on his own place, she would surely crumble. No, he'd stay put for now to make sure she was all right.

"Nothing wrong with being a mama's boy." Cody grinned. "You're the youngest of five brothers and the last to leave the nest. Can't blame her for doting on you." Off he went on a tangent, talking about the pros and cons of a grown man living at home with his mother.

Jake bit his tongue and willed himself not to respond. If his best friend saw him as being tied to his mother's apron strings, no doubt everyone else in town did too. Once again, he wished everyone in Groom would keep their thoughts and opinions to themselves.

"One of these days, a pretty gal's gonna come along and convince you there's a whole new world out there just waiting for you." Cody paused and appeared to be thinking. "I speak from experience. Until I met Virginia, I had no plans to marry and settle down. You of all people should remember how much I loved playing the rowdy bachelor."

Jake remembered, all right. And the fact that Cody had been won over by the love of a well-bred girl from the East was nothing short of miraculous. The older ladies in town had pretty much written him off as husband material because of his wild and woolly ways. Virginia Harrison had calmed him down and then some. Cody hadn't missed a Sunday service in nearly four months now. Talk about a changed man.

"Speaking of my bride-to-be, I hear she stopped by your place this morning with her maid of honor in tow." Cody grinned. "What did you think of Amaryllis, anyway? She's a pretty girl, isn't she? And she came all the way from New York to be in the wedding. What do you make of that highfalutin way she talks? I can't make heads 'ner tails of it, but I hear tell it's citified."

"Very." Jake shrugged. "And to answer your question, she seemed nice enough. Didn't really pay much attention to her, to be honest."

"So I heard. Virginia said you slipped out the back door just minutes after they arrived. What was so important down at the station that you couldn't wait five minutes to meet a pretty lady who came all that way?"

Jake shook his head. Looked like this conversation wouldn't be ending anytime soon. And what could he say to turn things around, really? That he wasn't interested in any of the girls he'd met thus far, or that matchmaking was a primeval form of entertainment for the town's married women? That God was going to have to split the heavens open and add the backdrop of a heavenly choir when the right gal happened by?

It sounded ludicrous, but Jake couldn't help how he felt about the matter. Besides, what would be the point of marrying some woman who didn't suit him just because folks talked him into it? Likely he'd get fifty-plus years of agony out of the deal. Or worse, a pretense of a relationship. No thank you. He'd seen that happen with his uncle Leo and aunt Bets. He'd wait for the real deal, thank you very much.

And if the real deal never came along...well, that would be all right too.

Chapter Two

....

Searching for the perfect place to settle down and raise a family? Look no further than the scenic Texas Panhandle. In this breathtaking slice of heaven on earth, night skies are so clear and bright you can practically reach out and snatch the stars with your hand. Majestic canyons run so deep they'll draw the breath right out of you as you gaze down at the rivers running through them. And those wide-open plains! Why, there's no greater spot in the modern-day Wild West for an adventurer to settle down and kick off his boots. Folks from Dalhart to Amarillo to Wichita Falls will welcome you with open arms and a genuine "Howdy." So, what's keepin' you away, friends? Head to the far northwestern tip of Texas today for the adventure of a lifetime. Tell 'em Tex sent you.
—"Tex" Morgan, reporting for the *Panhandle Primer*

Anne smoothed her gloves between her fingers, agonizing over how stained they'd gotten between Denver and Amarillo. So much for propriety. A proper Denver socialite would never be seen in public with soiled gloves.

"Denver socialite, indeed," she whispered as she gave the once-white gloves a final glance. Those days were long gone, and she'd better get used to it.

Looking out the grimy train window at the miles and miles of barren plains did little to lift her mood. "Thank goodness we'll be in Dallas by tomorrow afternoon. I'm going a little stir-crazy." Anne flashed what she hoped would look like a comforting smile in the direction of her two younger sisters. "I feel like I've eaten nothing but soot for the past forty-eight hours. It's going to be the death of me."

Little Kate looked up from the book she'd been reading, her precious blue eyes brimming as she appeared to be pondering that last phrase. "W–what did you say, Annie?" the youngster whispered, a lone tear trickling over the edge of her lashes. "Something about dying?"

At once Anne wished she could take back her words. How careless they'd been. "I'm sorry, honey. I didn't mean it like that. It's just a silly expression."

"I see." The seven-year-old rubbed the back of her hand across her cheek and turned her attention to the train window, whispering, "It's just a silly expression."

Anne released a slow breath, wishing she knew a way to make this right. Her younger sisters had been through enough pain already. Why did she add to it with such thoughtless words? Anne turned her attention to ten-year-old Emily. "Still reading that tourist paper you picked up at the train station in Amarillo?"

"Yes, and it's wonderful!" Emily's eyes widened as she clutched the paper to her chest. "Oh, Annie, do we *have* to go to Dallas? Can't we stay in the Panhandle forever?"

"Whyever would we want to do that?" Anne pointed through the dirty glass. "As you can see, there is not much to recommend this area to those of us accustomed to Denver's beautiful snowcapped mountains. Best I can tell, no one settles here anyway. I've never seen such barrenness."

"Oh, but you're not seeing all of it." Emily rose and handed Anne the newspaper then wriggled her way into the spot next to her. "At least, not the way Tex Morgan describes it in this tourist paper."

"Tex Morgan?" Anne stifled a laugh. What sort of fellow called himself Tex?

"He's a reporter, and a really good one too. Read this and then you'll know what you're missing. It sounds…breathtaking!"

"Breathtaking, eh?" Anne took the paper and began to read. Several lines into the over-the-top description of the Texas Panhandle, she looked up and sighed. "Wild West, indeed. How do folks come up with such nonsense?"

"It's not nonsense," Emily said. "And I would give my left arm to write for the paper like Tex Morgan does. To be a reporter for a Texas newspaper would be…splendiferous."

"Splendiferous?" Anne chuckled. "Have you taken to memorizing the dictionary now?"

"Yes." Emily sighed, and a dreamy-eyed expression took over. "I need to learn all the words I can if I'm going to be a famous writer. My vocabulary needs to grow expo…exponen…"

"Exponentially?"

"Yes." Emily grinned. "Exponentially."

"Well, I must say, your stories are much better written than this…." Anne wanted to add "piece of drivel" but didn't. Instead, she continued reading until she finished the article then folded the paper and handed it back to her sister. "These Texans are mighty proud of their state, aren't they? And it's clear they love a tall tale."

"I love them too." Emily sighed and a faraway look came over her. "Papa used to tell the best stories, didn't he, Annie? I miss him so much." The youngster's eyes filled with tears and she turned her face to the window.

Anne did her best not to sigh aloud. Their father had told some rather majestic tales over the years. He'd whisked away his three daughters on a whimsical cloud with some of those fanciful stories of his. Then again, she'd needed to be whisked away. Ever since Mama's death five years ago, those make-believe stories had brought comfort, offering a form of escape. And now that Papa was gone, too...

No. She wouldn't think about sad things today. Who had time, anyway? Better to think practically. Someone had to, and she was the only logical choice. No point in keeping her head in the clouds like Emily tended to do. Not when there was so much work to be done right here on earth.

Anne fussed with the tiny gold cross she wore on a chain around her neck. It was the only piece of her mother that she could still touch with her own hands. And though Anne struggled to hang onto the faith she'd once held dear, at least the little cross brought some degree of comfort.

Another glance out the window revealed a couple of tumbleweeds rolling across the plains. Anne watched them, feeling like a kindred spirit. She knew what it felt like to be tossed around by an invisible wind. And she also knew the sense of desperation in not knowing where one might end up.

Lord, I trust You, but...

She didn't finish the sentence. Papa used to say the only "buts" were the ones left behind when a man finished a good cigar. She could almost picture him now, seated in the drawing room, smoking one of his favorite El Rey del Mundo cigars and sipping a glass of brandy. Or two. Or three.

There's no brandy in heaven.

The words flitted through her mind, followed by, *You don't even know Papa's in heaven anyway, so what does it matter?*

Just as quickly, she chided herself for dwelling on the negative. No doubt Papa was standing at the pearly gates this very moment, sharing one of his tall tales in an attempt to get Saint Peter to open them up. One day she would know for sure if he'd made it inside. Papa usually managed to get what he wanted. For now, the possibility brought some comfort.

Thankfully, Kate's voice rang out, interrupting her thoughts. "Do we really have to stay with Uncle Bertrand?" The youngster's nose wrinkled, signifying her disgust with the idea.

Emily looked up from her paper, and her eyes narrowed into slits. She tossed back her dark curls with exaggerated flair. "I would rather be shackled in chains in a dank and dreary prison cell with no food or water than to live in a mansion with that hideous man." She released an exaggerated sigh. "Toss me in a dungeon and throw away the key, but please do *not* make me go to Dallas, Annie!"

"I do believe you missed your calling on the stage, Emily." Anne stifled a laugh. "But as for Uncle Bertrand, we truly have no other choice." She bit back the rest of the words. Anne had never cared for her father's brother, but who else would take them in? Life in her uncle's home might not be comfortable, but it would be a sure sight better than living in the poorhouse in Denver.

"He's so mean." Kate shivered. "Remember that last time he came to see Papa? He got angry at me for playing hide-and-go-seek in the library while they were talking in the next room."

Anne remembered the incident clearly. How Uncle Bertrand had stormed into the room, insisting that the girls receive lashes for their childish noise. Papa had not gone along with him, naturally. Of course, Papa was full to the brim with whiskey that night. He could barely walk, let alone fuss at a child. But Uncle Bertrand's harsh words had served as a cruel enough punishment and left a lasting impression.

"Maybe our uncle has softened with age," Anne said. *One can hope, anyway.*

"Uncle Bertrand said Papa was a *gambler*." Emily emphasized the words, her eyes widening. "Do you think it was true, Annie? Did Papa really gamble away all our money like Wild Eyed Joe?"

"Who in heaven's name is Wild Eyed Joe?"

"He's a gambler from a story I read in a magazine. Best card cheat in the Wild West. He made a marvelous villain." Her expression softened. "Not that I'm calling Papa a villain. Just wonderin' if that's what Uncle Bertrand meant."

The woman seated across from them looked up with curiosity etched on her brow. Just as quickly, her gaze shifted back to the needlepoint in her lap.

Anne bit back the words that threatened to escape. "We don't speak ill of the dead, Emily," she whispered at last. "Papa was a fine man." *A fine man with a serious gambling problem. And a drinking problem, to boot. But you are far too young to know about such things.*

"I'll bet the Texas Panhandle is filled with gamblers and such." Emily giggled, and her face came alive with excitement. "Ruffians and renegades."

"Ruffians and renegades?" *Where does she come up with these things?*

GROOM
1914
TX

"Yes, bad guys—and good guys too. My story is going to feature the handsomest good guy you ever saw—a cowboy set on protecting the frontier against lawlessness and crime." A happy sigh followed. "Sounds fantastical, doesn't it!"

"Hmph. Not sure 'fantastical' is the right word, but I can see you've located plenty of fodder for your story. Get busy writing," Anne said. "I'll read it when you're done and offer my critique."

"Marvelous!" Emily reached for her bag and pulled out her tablet and pencil. "Oh, it's going to be a terrific story, Annie. The hero is going to save damsels in distress from a fate worse than death." She turned to her little sister and whispered, "I'm sorry, Kate. I didn't mean to say death."

"What kind of distress will he save them from?" Kate asked, her eyes widening.

"Oh, I don't know." Emily shrugged and rolled her pencil between her fingers. Her voice grew more animated as she offered a suggestion. "What do you think? An Indian attack?"

"No, you used Indians in your last story, remember?" Kate paused and appeared to be thinking.

"I've been contemplating bubonic plague or maybe dysentery." Emily wrinkled her nose. "But neither of those is very romantic. Besides, if the heroine has an illness, she's going to need a medical doctor, not a handsome Texas cowboy."

"Unless the cowboy happens to be delivering the medicine she needs," Anne offered. "What do you think of that idea?"

Emily shrugged. "I suppose that could work. But if she's suffering from some sort of terrible malady, she won't look beautiful to him, now, will she? I was thinking she should be exquisitely beautiful."

"True beauty is internal," Anne added. "So keep that in mind, if you please."

"I suppose." Emily's eyes took on that dreamy look again. "She can be beautiful on the inside, then. But he's going to be handsome inside and out."

"Is he now?" Anne couldn't help but chuckle.

"Yes. I can't abide an ugly hero. He's got to be a rugged cowboy with a six-shooter who rides the most beautiful stallion in all of the state of Texas. I'm calling him Copper."

"The cowboy?" Anne asked.

"No, silly." Emily giggled. "The stallion. I'm calling him Copper because that's his color. I haven't given the cowboy a name yet, but it has to be something that suits him. Something dashing and adventurous—appropriate to the handsomest man who ever drew a gun."

"What about Tex Morgan, the name of the man who wrote that tourist paper?" Anne suggested. "That's a romantic name. And rather fanciful, if I do say so myself."

"Ooh, great idea." Emily began to scribble on her tablet with Kate looking on. "I do hope it's not considered plagiarism to use a real person's name."

"I cannot imagine that's his real name," Anne said. "I would be more concerned about slander than plagiarism, anyway."

"What do you mean?"

"I mean, your stories are so fanciful, Mr. Tex Morgan might come looking for you. If you make him out to be a villain or something, I mean."

"Oh no. Tex is going to be my hero, remember? I'll think of a name for the villain." She leaned over her tablet then suddenly looked up, her eyes brighter than ever. "Ooh. Bertrand. That's my villain."

Emily and Kate began to carry on a conversation about the cowboy in the story. Anne couldn't help but think about their father. Despite his flaws, he'd done his best to play the role of the hero in his daughters' lives. He'd worked hard to give them a home—and life—they could be proud of. Most of that had unraveled in the end, but at least he'd tried. And the illusion of having a fine home and clothes had gotten her through those rough years after Mama's death.

Anne's thoughts shifted to Uncle Bertrand. No doubt Emily found it easy to name him as the villain in her novel. He came across as such, both in manner and in appearance.

Anne had done her best over the years not to be put off by the way he looked. His protruding chin and long, thin nose made it difficult, of course. One couldn't help but stare—at least when he wasn't looking. Of course, being the gentleman, he always wore a proper suit and hat and spoke with an exaggerated air. Beneath that handlebar mustache, however, was a mouth that could rip a person to shreds. She'd experienced his hurtful words firsthand on many occasions.

Then again, he was their only living relative, and he *had* sent for them upon their father's death. Surely he wouldn't bring three girls into his home without careful thought and preparation.

She relaxed against the seat. Yes, likely he had softened upon hearing the news of his younger brother's death. And caring for his three nieces was the penance he would pay for the cruelty he had bestowed upon others in years past. Perhaps Uncle Bertrand would turn out to be like one of the heroes in Emily's story—a fine man with a good heart who rescued damsels in distress.

One could hope, anyway.

* * * * *

As Jake entered the house, his mother's voice rang out in singsong fashion. "Take off those muddy boots, Jakey O'Farrell. Don't want to make a mess of my rugs. I spent this morning mopping up the mud you dragged in last night."

He bit back a response and pulled off the boots as instructed.

"I've made your favorite meal, son." She entered the room, wiping her hands on her embroidered apron. "Chicken and dumplings. And blackberry pie for dessert. I know how much you love my blackberry pie." She flashed a bright smile and opened her arms in anticipation of a hug, which he promptly delivered.

"I daresay this season's blackberries are the best we've ever had. Those little nieces and nephews of yours have been picking buckets and buckets. Don't know what I'm going to do with so many." She straightened a wayward hair on his forehead. "Guess we'll have to eat a lot of pie. And jam." She pinched him on the cheek. "I know how much my boy loves his mama's homemade jam!"

He could almost taste it now. Still, Jake couldn't get Cody's words out of his mind. Did folks really see him as being a mama's boy?

"You don't have to cook for me every night, Mama," he said at last. "I'm a grown man. I can—"

Her smile faded at once. "But I love cooking for you, son. It's one of the few remaining joys in my life." She paused and lifted the hem of her apron to dab her eyes. "Ever since your father passed away..."

Jake managed a weak smile. *Say no more.* "Can't wait to taste that blackberry pie."

"Now, there's my boy." She paused to glance in the large mirror above the buffet. "Gracious, this red hair of mine is as unruly as a tomcat after a brawl. I'll need to tend to it before supper. But first I'd better get back in the kitchen. Those dumplings are going to overcook if I'm not careful. And we can't have that, now, can we? No sir, only the best for my Jakey." With a nod, she disappeared into the kitchen.

For a moment or two, Jake contemplated throwing himself off a cliff. He finally decided a bowl of chicken and dumplings sounded more appealing. There would be plenty of time to fret over his "mama's boy" status later.

And, indeed, there was. No sooner were the dumplings consumed and the dishes washed than Mama busied herself with some needlework in the parlor. That left Jake free to take a stroll and think about a potential solution to his problem. He made his way to the edge of the fenced portion of the yard and gazed out over O'Farrell's Honor, the ranch his father had worked so hard to build.

Hundreds of acres of the nicest ranch land in Carson County beckoned him. Off in the distance, a half dozen workhorses grazed. His favorite, a mare he'd named Frances, stamped her foot, as if willing him to come and dress her for a ride out into the pasture. No time for that right now, though the idea of riding off into the sunset did hold some appeal, in light of his earlier conversation with Cody. And besides, with Frances due to deliver in the next couple of weeks, she needed the rest.

Jake tipped his hat and wiped the sweat from his hair. As he did, the majestic sunset captivated him, the reds, oranges, and yellows all melding together. He squinted and glanced to his right, making out John and Ruth's place. His brother Joseph had taken up residence in the home just beyond it with his wife. And behind both of those, Jeremiah had constructed a home for his wife and their children. Of course, the newest addition to the ranch sat to the left of the others—Jedediah and Pauline had lived there for only four months, since their Christmas wedding.

Jake stood for a moment, the quiet stillness wrapping him in a warm embrace. The 7:55 train to Dallas was due to pass by at any moment. Most evenings he stood here until it passed and then created stories in his head of what life would be like in a big city like Dallas or Houston or even New York. Maybe one day he would climb aboard one of the passenger cars and find out for himself. He would travel to places unseen and see how other folks lived.

Maybe. Right now, however, something else sounded far more appealing. Jake had a hankerin' to head back inside the house and swallow down a big piece of his Mama's homemade blackberry pie.

Chapter Three

....

*The famed Fort Worth and Denver City Railway Company
(FW&DC) has merged forces with Rock Island and Santa Fe,
providing a rail network throughout the Texas Panhandle.
The lines come together in the town of Amarillo. In that
opportunistic place, folks can experience the very best the
Panhandle has to offer—culture, a rich social life, and plenty
of commerce and trade. Perhaps you're not interested in living so close to town. You prefer ranching or farming. Well,
look no farther! When you choose a piece of land in the Panhandle, nearby rail lines provide easy access to markets. Talk
about having the best of both worlds! I guess you could say
the Texas Panhandle is perched on the "track" for success!*
—"Tex" Morgan, reporting for the *Panhandle Primer*

After dozing off in the uncomfortable train seat, Anne awoke
to a screeching sound, followed by a scream from Kate. Something
jerked her forward, nearly causing her to tumble onto the floor. The
piercing sound of the train's brakes reached a deafening level then
subsided. The noise was quickly followed by a thick round of black
soot filling the air.

Anne took a moment to get her bearings once the train stopped
moving. At once the smell of soot nearly choked her. She began to

cough then reached for her hankie and covered her nose until the odor dissipated. Finally convinced that the worst had passed, she stretched every aching muscle in her body.

"Why did we stop, Anne?" Kate looked her way, clearly frightened.

"I don't know, honey." She slipped her left arm around her sister and pulled her into a comforting embrace. "I'm sure we'll find out soon enough. Go back to sleep if you can."

Kate nuzzled against her and dozed off again in no time.

To her right, Emily stirred awake. "I was having the most marvelous dream. We were under attack and a handsome cowboy rescued us." The youngster yawned and extended her arms in a lengthy stretch. "Why did we stop? Are we in Dallas already?"

"No, sweetie. We're not to arrive in Dallas until tomorrow afternoon. This is probably just a routine stop. Perhaps we're taking on more cars."

"Oh, I see." Emily leaned against Anne and closed her eyes. Anne kissed the top of her sister's head and prayed she would go back to sleep.

Moments later the porter appeared, his brow wrinkling as he spoke. "Folks, we've received word that a section of track is out up ahead due to a derailment earlier this afternoon. We'll be stopping for the night."

"All night long?" At once, panic overtook Anne. She hadn't planned for this. "But we're due to arrive in Dallas tomorrow afternoon."

"Not anymore, ma'am." He shook his head. "Not until they get that track fixed. Railroad workers will assess the damage in the morning and give us a time frame for when we can leave. In the meantime, we've sent for help from the town of Groom."

"Groom?" She'd never heard of such a place.

"Yes'm. It's a town about nine miles from here."

Emily's face lit with excitement. "We're staying in a town called Groom?" She glanced at Anne and giggled. "I'm going to add that to my story, Annie. How perfectly wonderful! I couldn't have given it a better name if I'd tried!"

"It's not much of a town, really," the porter said, "but they've got a hotel of sorts. Nothing very grand but certainly more comfortable than sleeping on the train."

"I see." Several thoughts went through Anne's head at once. The train might be uncomfortable, but she couldn't afford a room in a hotel. Uncle Bertrand had grudgingly paid for the train fare but hadn't sent anything in the way of spending money. They'd been fortunate to have food to eat on the journey, thanks to her best friend Charlotte back in Denver.

Kate stirred then rubbed her eyes and peered out the window. "What's happening, Annie?"

"The train is stopping for the night, honey. Just go back to sleep and don't fret. We'll be fine." She patted her on the arm.

The woman seated across from them stopped fussing with her handbags long enough to look Anne's way. "You're staying on the train?"

"We don't have any choice. I…" How could she say the words aloud, that they had no money? "We'll be fine, I'm sure."

"Hmm." The woman brow wrinkled a bit as she appeared to be thinking about Anne's response.

Over the next few minutes, Anne saw lights from a host of lanterns as people from the other train cars made their way outside. Minutes later, she made out the sound of wagons approaching and the chatter of voices.

The porter reappeared and tipped his hat in her direction. "Miss, the railroad has sent a couple of company trucks and a wagon as well. We've emptied out the train cars ahead of you. We'll be taking you to town now."

"No sir," she said. "I...well, I do believe my sisters and I will be fine. We'd like to stay aboard." Her heart twisted as she contemplated her dilemma. What would she do if he gave her no choice but to leave?

The fellow lifted the lantern as if trying to get a better look at Emily and Kate. "Are you sure?"

"Y–yes." Anne nodded and tried to look confident. Truth be told, the very idea of staying alone on this train made her feel sick inside. Still, she forced a smile. "Besides, I'm sure they'll have the track repaired in no time."

The woman across from her rose and placed a hand on Anne's shoulder. "I do hope so, for your sake," she said, offering a sympathetic smile. "But if you change your mind, look me up at the hotel. I would like to help...if you would allow me to."

"Oh, I, well..." Anne shook her head. "That's very kind, but my sisters and I will be fine. We're on an adventure, you see. Just ask Emily. She's writing a story about it."

"We're going to be rescued by a cowboy with a six-shooter strapped to his side." Emily's voice and expression grew more animated. "It's going to be the most thrilling scene you've ever read, I can promise you that."

"Indeed? Well, then, I might just wait with you." The woman gave her a wink. "Sounds like a lovely ending to a story."

"Oh, it's just the beginning," Emily said. "I haven't decided on the ending yet."

CHOOM
1914
TX

The woman leaned over and whispered, "Well, when you do, stop by the hotel and tell me. I'd love to hear all about it." Then she turned her attention back to Anne. "My offer still stands. I would be honored if you would allow me the privilege of looking out for you until the track is repaired." She ran her hands along the fine green linen in her skirt, trying to smooth out the wrinkles.

"If we don't hear anything by morning, we'll come to town," Anne said.

"Promise?" The woman stopped fussing with her skirt and focused on the girls.

"Yes." Anne nodded.

"When you get to the hotel, ask for Mrs. Witherspoon." With a nod, she disappeared into the darkness.

Anne stared out the window, trying to find the woman amongst the evening's shadows but not succeeding. A somber feeling came over her, and for a moment she thought about following on Mrs. Witherspoon's heels all the way to the hotel.

"We are not beggars," she whispered. "Not yet, anyway."

"What did you say, Annie?" Kate asked.

"Oh, nothing, honey." She offered a smile. "Isn't this exciting? We're living out one of Emily's adventures firsthand."

"Thank goodness there are no Indians." Kate shivered.

"Not yet, anyway." Emily turned to them, her eyes sparkling. "But there's still plenty of time for them to appear and threaten our lives. I do hope a whole band of them will come at once, riding on horses and carrying bows and arrows. Can you imagine how exciting that would be? Maybe they'll carry us off—far, far away from Dallas and Uncle Bertrand. Wouldn't that be the very best sort of adventure?"

"I'm not sure 'adventure' is the correct word," Anne said. "And I daresay, your imagination has run away with you once again. You'd better go and catch it."

"What would be the purpose of having an imagination and not using it?" Emily's gaze narrowed. "That would make me too much like everyone else in the family." On and on she went, talking about the various complications to the scene she planned to write.

Anne finally managed to get a word in edgewise when her sister paused for breath. "Well, enough about how you would have written this scene, Emily. We're not in one of your books. Not yet, anyway."

She leaned back against the seat and offered up a rushed, silent prayer for their safety. *Lord, You see the three of us. We're like those Texas tumbleweeds. We don't know where we are or where we're headed, at least not tonight. But You do. And I trust You, Lord. Oh, and if there are any Indians out there*—she shuddered—*please keep them at a distance!*

The porter entered their train car a few minutes later, after the voices outside disappeared on the evening wind. "Only a handful of passengers decided to stay onboard," he said. "Most have gone to town. Would you follow me, please?"

Anne hesitated. "We have to move?"

"Yes, please. We would like our remaining passengers to stay in one area, at least for now. Follow me, miss." He led them from one car to the other until they arrived at the dining car.

"Oh, I'm afraid I couldn't..." Anne shook her head. The room smelled delicious, but she knew she couldn't afford to feed her sisters. She had just enough hardtack and cheese to get them through the next twenty-four hours. If they shared.

"I've been given special instructions from the woman who was seated across from you to make sure you're well-fed." He smiled. "And when we leave here, you're headed to one of our empty sleeper berths."

"A sleeper berth?" Anne could hardly believe her ears. "But I don't... I mean, we couldn't possibly..."

"It's all taken care of." He nodded. "You three must have an angel looking out for you tonight, that's all I can say about it."

"An angel?" Kate's eyes widened.

A theatrical sigh from Emily followed. "I was counting on a handsome cowboy with a six-shooter, but I guess an angel will have to do."

"Indeed, an angel will do." Anne smiled.

"I suppose you're right." The edges of Emily's lips curled up in a delicious fashion. "I'll just envision the angel with stupendous wings riding across the skies on a stallion."

Anne did her best not to roll her eyes.

The girls enjoyed a lovely dinner with the handful of passengers who remained. Afterward, bellies full, they followed the porter to a sleeping car. While nothing could rival Anne's bed back home in Denver, her berth did provide a spot to lie down and sleep. Or, try to sleep, rather.

When she eventually dozed, visions of a handsome cowboy with a six-shooter strapped to his side flitted through Anne's mind. He rode a copper-colored horse with a mane that flew in the breeze as they raced across the plain.

The whole thing made for a lovely dream. A lovely dream, indeed.

* * * * *

Jake awoke to the sound of someone rapping on his bedroom door.

"Jakey," his mother called out. "Something's happened and you're needed at the station. No dillydallying. They said it was important."

Jake stumbled out of bed, still half-asleep, then crossed the bedroom and cracked open the door. "What is it?"

His mother stood before him, dressed in her housecoat, her hair tied up in rags. "There's been a derailment several miles east of here."

"Derailment?" At once, alarm shot through him.

"Yes, but no one was hurt. It was a freight train. Coal. But it made a mess of things, as you might imagine. So they've had to stop a train coming through from Amarillo." She pulled one of the rags out of her hair, then another. "And you've been asked to transport passengers to town. Most will need a place to stay, from what I was told, so feel free to bring a handful here. I'll cook up a feast tonight."

"All right." He dressed as quickly as he could and then swallowed a biscuit as he sprinted toward the door.

Jake made the journey to the station on foot as always…but traveled a lot faster than usual. Off in the east the early morning sun rose, casting a pinkish haze over the town. He took a shortcut, sprinting down the main street with his hat tipped forward. Hopefully folks would take it as a sign that he wasn't in a talking mood. Unfortunately, it didn't appear to be working.

"Howdy, Jake," Reverend Johnson called out from the porch steps as he ran by. "How are things at O'Farrell's Honor this fine day?"

"Fine, but I can't talk right now, Reverend." Jake paused to catch his breath. "We've got a situation east of town. Urgent. Folks will be needing a place to stay, so spread the word."

"Will do. I'll get right on it." The reverend tipped his hat.

"Thanks."

Seconds later, as Jake passed through the heart of town, the butcher stuck his head through the opening of his shop. "How's life treatin' you these days, Jake?"

"Oh, fair to middlin'." Jake slowed his pace to a fast walk. "But I've really got to—"

"Speaking of Midland, I've got a sister over in Midland who's had a little trouble finding a husband." He wiped his hands on his bloody apron and offered a crooked grin. "Want me to send for her? I think she'd be perfect for you. Of course, she's got a little temper. But I daresay you can tame her in no time. She needs a strong fella like you, if I do say so."

Jake swallowed hard and kept on going.

Off in the distance he could make out the mercantile. Unfortunately, Cassie Martin stepped out onto the front porch as he sprinted by. "Well, hello there, stranger." She ran her fingers through her long brown locks of hair and took a couple of steps in his direction, her broad physique causing her to lag a bit behind him. He slowed to a walk. "I looked for you in church last Sunday but couldn't find you."

"Oh, well, I was there. I was sitting with my mother, as always. But I really can't talk right now. I—"

"Are you getting excited about your best friend's wedding this comin' Saturday night?" She sighed. "Everyone in town is talking about it. It's going to be the most beautiful ceremony the folks in Groom have ever seen." Then she added the words, "For the time being, anyway."

Jake turned back to give her a quick glance. "Yes, but as I said, I really can't talk right now," he tried to explain. "See, there's been a derail—"

"I just love weddings." Cassie's blue eyes sparkled. "Virginia is going to be a beautiful bride, and there's nothing lovelier than a bride, now, is there?"

"I don't suppose so." He shrugged but kept walking.

Cassie's mother stepped off the mercantile porch, her eyes brightening as she looked Jake's way. "'Course, there are plenty of girls around here, should a man be looking for a beautiful bride," she called out loud enough for everyone in town to hear. "Problem is, some fellas can't see the forest for the trees."

Jake glanced to his right and his left, seeing nothing but wide-open plains and a few scattered buildings. "Yes, well, I—"

Falling into step behind him, Mrs. Martin lit into a list of all the reasons he needed a good woman in his life, singing the praises of her daughter along the way. Cassie began to puff and pant, clearly struggling to keep up.

"I've really gotta go," Jake managed at last. "I'm needed up at the station."

He gave the Martin women a little wave and then took off sprinting, far more concerned about the condition of the train track than the condition of his love life.

Chapter Four
....

From time to time, we at the Panhandle Primer highlight one of our fair towns. This week I've chosen to focus on the tiny town of Groom, incorporated three years ago in 1911. Located about sixty miles east of Amarillo, this small town might look like just a dot on the map to some, but it has served as home to some of the most famous cattlemen in Panhandle history. Chief among them was the late Colonel B. B. Groom, for whom the town was named. He purchased thirteen hundred head of cattle back in '82 and never looked back. Unfortunately, his dreams of having the largest ranch in the country didn't pan out. Still, you can't blame a fella for trying. And that go-get-'em spirit lives on in the modern-day ranchers of Groom. Ask any one of them to show you his patch of land and he'll flash a smile so bright it'll light up the Panhandle on even the darkest day. —"Tex" Morgan, reporting for the *Panhandle Primer*

Anne awoke to the sound of horses' hooves. She yawned and stretched, trying to get her bearings. *Where am I again?* Ah yes, a sleeper berth on the train. Thanks to her angelic benefactor. Anne eased herself into a sitting position, careful not to awaken Kate, who slept soundly to her right. And Emily...

Turned out Emily was already wide-awake and staring out the window. "Ooh, look, Anne. You're not going to believe it!"

"What is it?" Anne followed her little sister's pointed finger and looked at a cluster of young men standing outside the train. Bunched together in a group like that, she could barely make out their faces.

"Do you think they're thieves, come to rob us blind?" Emily pressed her nose against the glass. "Oh, I do hope they are. I can only imagine the stories I will one day tell my children and grandchildren about the time I barely escaped with my life."

Anne began to fan herself. "They're just local men, silly. Don't be so dramatic."

"Humph. Well, if they're not thieves, then they must be cowboys." Emily giggled. "A couple of them are wearing hats. And they are rugged and handsome, just like the fellas in my story." She glanced out of the window once again. "Most of them, anyway. But I don't see any six-shooters." She looked at Anne with a shrug. "How are they going to rescue us without guns? It won't be nearly as exciting."

"We're hardly in need of rescuing." Anne yawned. "I slept really well in this berth. You?"

Emily groaned. "I want to get off this train. They could come aboard at any time and rescue me and I wouldn't fuss one little bit."

The porter's voice rang out, awakening Kate, who startled. The youngster glanced up then rolled back over.

Anne cracked open the door of the train car to respond to his call. "Yes?"

The porter tipped his cap. "Miss, we've received news that the damage to the track is more severe than expected."

"What does that mean?" She fussed with the door to keep her body hidden behind it.

"From what I've been told, we'll be in Groom for the better part of a week."

"A *week*?" Anne, Emily, and Kate spoke in unison.

Anne had barely managed, "Whatever will we do?" when Emily began to cheer.

"Oh, it's perfect! See, I told you we were on an adventure, Anne! One more week to do as we please without Uncle Bertrand around!"

"If the people here don't know us, they can't possibly tattle to Uncle Bertrand when we're naughty." Kate mumbled, still half-asleep.

"When, or if?" Anne asked.

"When." Kate let out an exaggerated yawn.

"You're forgetting one very important thing." Anne popped her head back inside the car, her thoughts a jumbled mess. "We have no place to stay in this godforsaken place."

"And no food to eat." Kate sat up, now frowning.

"Those problems have been solved for you, miss." The porter's voice sounded from outside the door. "Several of the local families have offered to open their homes to folks in need of a place to stay. I do believe that would offer the best possible alternative to this otherwise uncomfortable situation."

Anne peeked her head back around the door. "I don't know how I feel about that." She shook her head. "Staying with strangers seems so...unsettling."

"You're such a scaredy-cat." Emily plopped down on her bed and crossed her arms at her chest. "We're having an adventure, remember?"

"Yes, I remember." And what an adventure it was turning out

to be. Anne could never have predicted any of this. She turned back to the porter. "Can we telephone our uncle to let him know of the delay?"

"Of course. As soon as you get settled. Or we can wire him from the station in Groom for you."

"That's fine, I suppose. Though I do have to wonder what he will think when we don't arrive at the station in Dallas this afternoon." *He's bound to be angry. Very angry.*

"The folks at the station will let him know. But if you would feel better contacting him personally, that can certainly be arranged."

"Thank you."

"My pleasure. I'll go fetch your luggage while you get dressed. Then some of the nice local gentlemen will assist you fine ladies down from the train and drive you on to your destination."

"That would be fine." Anne turned back to the window, glancing down at the handsome cowboys standing alongside the track. Her gaze shifted to one in particular. He didn't look like the others—not quite as rugged, maybe. And he had a welcoming face. For a moment, he glanced her way. She could read the interest in his eyes as their gaze met. Just as quickly she turned away, her heart rate skipping to double-time.

Yes, indeed. It looked as if staying in Groom might be very unsettling indeed.

* * * * *

Jake stood outside the train, his gaze shifting from the beautiful young woman at the window to the porter, who approached with luggage in hand.

"How many of you fellas can help transport these folks to town?"

Cody raised his hand. "I brought the Model T. It can hold five, counting you and me. Where are we taking them, though? The hotel is full."

"It's my understanding that several families in town have offered to help house them for a few days," the porter said.

It took Jake only a couple seconds to respond with, "I'll take a handful back to our place." Who else in the county had a home with so many bedrooms? Yes, they could surely take at least one family.

"Very nice." The porter pulled out his pocket watch and gave it a glance. "Would you mind helping some of the ladies down from the train?" the fellow asked. "We've got quite a few who need assistance in the next car."

"I'd be happy to help." Jake shifted his thoughts from the young woman at the window and climbed aboard the train behind Cody, ready to get to work.

First to exit the train was an elderly couple. Cody helped them down the steps and led them to the first truck. Next came a ragtag lot of men who looked as if they'd just been awakened. These fellas didn't require much assistance, though one nearly tumbled down the steps to the ground below.

One by one they came, young and old—about twenty in all.

"Might I ask for your assistance?" A genteel voice rang out from the doorway.

Jake did his best not to gasp aloud as he saw the dark-haired beauty in the lavender dress. He'd caught a glimpse of her through the window minutes before, but seeing her in person could not compare. Those beautiful blue eyes. That lily-white skin with dark hair tumbling over her shoulders. Her slender physique. Those perfect lips.

She looked for all the world like that woman he'd read about in school, the one in that King Arthur story. What was her name again?

Guinevere. Her name was Guinevere.

Jake rushed to her aid, for the first time noticing the young girls standing behind her. She extended her white-gloved hand his way, and he felt her hand trembling in his as she took the first step down.

Jake felt himself tongue-tied. "C–careful, ma'am," he finally managed.

Fine lines appeared between her brows as she gazed his way. "*Ma'am?*" Her emphasis of the word made him wonder if he'd some- how offended her. She stepped down onto the ground, the younger girls following.

"Well, sure." He grinned. "You're a lady. That would make you a 'ma'am.' Least around these here parts."

"Would it now." The woman's once-somber expression shifted, and Jake thought for a moment he saw a hint of a smile cross those perfectly shaped lips. "I daresay this is the first time I've been called 'ma'am.' I felt sure that expression was reserved for older women. Still, there's something about it that's rather…"

"Silly?" the little girl behind her spoke up, ruining a perfectly good moment.

"I was going to say 'quaint,'" the dark-haired beauty said. "It's so…Southern." Her eyelashes took to fluttering, and Jake focused on those captivating blue eyes. Boy howdy, a fella could get lost in eyes like that. And that fancy dress…definitely store-bought. Guinevere was a big-city gal, no doubt about it. How she'd come to land in a place like this was nothing short of a miracle.

"Well, we Southern boys are polite," Cody spouted off from behind him. "Our mamas raised us right."

At once the woman's smile faded and her eyes clouded over. Jake wanted to elbow Cody but really couldn't find just cause. Nothing unusual had been said—had it?

The youngest of the three girls shook her head and gave Cody a pointed look. "Our mama is *dead*."

"I–I'm so sorry," Jake managed.

"Sorry, little miss." Cody removed his hat. "I had no idea."

"Papa's dead too," the youngster added, her eyes filling with tears. "He died six weeks ago." She turned and flung herself into fair Guinevere's arms.

Cody knelt next to the little girl and patted her on the shoulder. "Please forgive me. Shouldn't have been so careless with my words. And just so you know, I lost my mama last year. She was the finest woman I ever knew, and she worked really hard to raise me right, though I strayed a time or two."

A time or two? Jake chuckled then found himself distracted by someone pulling on his sleeve. He looked down to see the youngest of the girls staring up at him.

"'Scuse me, sir," she said.

"Yes, miss?" He couldn't help but smile at the innocent face and bright blue eyes.

"Sir, are you a real Texas cowboy?" She pointed to his hat.

"Well, now, I hardly think you could call me a cowboy." Jake shook his head. He pulled off his hat and raked his fingers through his hair. "Though I do live on a ranch."

"Do you wear a six-shooter?" The other girl—the one with the inquisitive face—asked as she pulled out a writing tablet.

"A six-shooter?" He fought to hide the smile as he shoved his hat back into place. "Nah. I work for the railroad. We don't carry guns." This girl certainly had an imagination.

"The railroad?" The middle girl's nose wrinkled and she closed her writing tablet. "How can I possibly interview you for my story if you don't carry a gun? There's nothing romantic about that."

"Romantic?" He and Cody spoke the word in unison.

"Yes." The youngster batted her lashes. "Don't you see? I'm a writer. And the story I'm writing is about a handsome cowboy who rescues females in distress. When I looked out the train window and saw you…"

"You thought I was the hero in your story?"

"Well, of course." She giggled. "Don't you believe in stories coming true?"

Cody snorted.

Jake looked at the little girl and shrugged. "Never thought much about it, to be honest. I'm usually too busy working to read any fanciful stories like the one you're describing." *Though I surely might be interested in rescuing this fair female in distress.* His gaze landed on fair Guinevere, whose cheeks turned pink.

"Please excuse my little sister." Guinevere nudged the youngster. "She's got quite an imagination."

"Annie, you're just jealous because I come up with great stories and you're so boring." The youngster stuck out her tongue.

Annie, eh? So, Guinevere had a real name, one that wasn't fictional. Jake gave her another quick glance, deciding she looked like an Annie.

"Emily, if I've told you once, I've told you a thousand times, you need to get your head out of the clouds," Annie said. "Plant your feet on earth for a change."

"Nothing wrong with having your head in the clouds," Jake said. "I've been accused of the very same thing."

"Yep, Jake's a dreamer, all right." Cody grinned. "You should hear some of his big ideas."

Jake gave Cody a warning look. Then he glanced at the little girl who'd riddled him with questions. "If it makes you feel any better about my current lack of weaponry, I've been known to carry a rifle during hunting season. My aim's not very good, though."

"What he's trying to say is that he couldn't hit the broad side of a barn," Cody threw in.

Jake elbowed him but tried not to lose his composure. Why did everyone feel like he deserved to be the brunt of every joke? A sigh threatened to erupt, but he shoved it back. No point in getting riled up. Better to just play along.

The little girl turned her attention to Cody. "Ooh, I'll bet you're a real cowboy."

"Nah, I work for the railroad too," he said.

Her expression soured.

"Don't fret," Jake said. "Where we're taking you, there are cowboys aplenty. More than enough for any of your stories. And all their names start with J."

"They do?" The little girl's eyes brightened.

"Yep." He grinned. "The O'Farrell brothers: John, Joseph, Jeremiah, Jedediah...and then there's me—Jake."

"And trust me when I say that all of Jake's brothers will be perfectly willing to tell you why they should be the hero in your story," Cody threw in and then laughed.

"Yes, my brothers love to play the role of hero." The words didn't sit well on Jake's tongue, and he wished he could take them back. His brothers did enjoy getting the attention for their good deeds. Saving the ranch after their father's death, for instance. And having the largest herd of cattle in Groom.

Thankfully the youngsters took to chatting again, freeing Jake to think about the beautiful dark-haired distraction next to him—Annie. From what he could gather, she was the older sister to the two younger ones. She seemed to be doing a fine job of tending to them, too, though she certainly had her hands full. Jake couldn't help but feel sad about her recent loss. To think these girls had parted with both mother and father...

He suddenly felt very protective of the ladies—one in particular. And the sooner he got them back to O'Farrell's Honor, the better.

Chapter Five

....

Wondering where all the good, neighborly folk have gone? Why, they're living in the Texas Panhandle, of course. The men and women in this area are ruggedly independent but always seem to wear a smile, even in the toughest of times. Their determination hasn't kept them from helping folks who are new to the area. Indeed, they tend to newcomers with a gentle spirit that puts folks at ease. Need a new barn? No problem. Your Panhandle neighbors will lend a helping hand. Pining for a tall tale but don't know where to find one? Visit any of the ranchers who've been around awhile. They'll tickle your ears with exaggerated stories. Best of all, these friendships can be had at no cost. Link arms with your neighbors today...in the Texas Panhandle. —"Tex" Morgan, reporting for the *Panhandle Primer*

Most of the passengers from the train were loaded onto company trucks, but Jake helped the beautiful young woman and her sisters board Cody's Model T. He sent up a prayer of thanksgiving when Guinevere accepted his offer to take the seat up front. Jake coaxed Cody into letting him take the wheel so that he could settle into the spot next to her, and Cody slipped into the backseat with the two younger girls.

"I don't mean to seem ungrateful," Anne said, with her eyes fixed on the train, "but would you mind telling me where we're going exactly?"

"To my family's ranch—O'Farrell's Honor. I hope that settles well with you."

"A real Texas ranch?" Emily's voice sounded from behind him. "Oh, this is perfect. I can study the ranch for my story. What a lovely interruption! Simply serendipitous."

"That's a mighty big word for such a small girl," Cody said. "You must've had quite an education in…where are you from, again?"

"We're from Denver," she explained. "And besides, a true writer is a wordsmith. My schoolteacher said I have the vocabulary of a collegiate."

Anne turned to look back at her sister, her gaze first lingering on Jake for a moment. "If only her humility matched the level of her vocabulary. Now *that* would be something."

"Maybe they were so busy teaching her to be a collegiate that they left out the lessons on humility." Jake quirked a brow and tried not to chuckle aloud.

Emily leaned forward between Anne and Jake and stuck out her tongue. "For your information, I'm ten times smarter than the both of you put together. And I'll prove it too. Ask me anything you like about history or mathematics and I'll answer."

"See what I mean?" Anne looked at Jake and shook her head. "She could stand an extra portion of humble pie."

"My mother's the best pie baker in the county," Jake said with a smile. "She's a shoo-in at the county fair each fall. We'll have to ask her to pack up her best humble pie and serve it in hefty slices."

"It's a real pie?" the youngest child's voice rang out from the backseat.

"He's just teasing you, honey." Annie turned back to face her littlest sister. "There's no such thing as humble pie. At least, not that you can actually eat."

Kate lit into a story about pie, which led Emily to a story about a chef in London who murdered people for fun on the side. Jake tried not to chuckle as Emily's story grew more animated. Cody played along by coming up with a story equally as dramatic.

Jake turned his attention to the beautiful young woman seated next to him, thankful Cody was keeping the sisters occupied. "So, your name is Annie, then?"

"It's Anne, but my sisters have nicknamed me Annie. My father called me Anne. And my friends…" She paused and shook her head, making him wonder what words might've come next.

"I'm Jake O'Farrell," he said. "Should've made proper introductions earlier. My mama would be embarrassed that I swooped you up without so much as a how-do-you-do."

"This whole thing has been rather startling." Anne began to fan herself with her hand. "One minute we were on our way to Dallas, the next we're detained in…" She paused and looked out at the fields. "What did you say this place is called?"

"Groom." Jake deliberately slowed the car's pace so the drive would take longer. "Pride of the Panhandle."

"I read a story about the Panhandle while we were aboard the train," Anne said. "Seemed a bit exaggerated, if I do say so myself."

"Must've been Tex Morgan's column." Jake grinned. "He's a reporter from Amarillo. Comes through Groom every now and again when he's working on a story. Seems nice enough, and I hear he has a wonderful family."

From behind them, Emily's voice rang out. "I'm going to be a writer too, Annie. Tell him."

Anne turned to Jake and shrugged. "My sister is of the firm opinion that her stories are going to make her famous."

"Yes, I recall hearing something about handsome cowboys," Cody said.

"The story I'm writing now is going to be the best one ever." Emily paused. "Just out of curiosity, are there Indians in this part of the country?"

"Indians?" Jake shrugged. "Well, there's a Tonkawa reservation a ways east of here. And every now and again you'll see an Indian come through."

"Are they wild?" Her voiced sounded animated. "Do they attack when you least suspect it?"

"Attack?" He chuckled. "Well, the last time I was attacked by an Indian, I was six years old and my older brothers had dressed themselves up and put war paint on their faces. They converged on me when I was eating my oatmeal at the breakfast table. As you can plainly see, I lived to tell about it." He glanced back at her.

"Oh." Her shoulders slumped forward. "That's too bad." She looked at the littlest girl. "Guess an Indian attack is out of the question."

"You were hoping for one?" he asked.

"Well, sure." Her voice grew more animated. "There's nothing like a good Indian attack. 'Cause then the cowboys can come to the rescue."

"I'm tired of Indian stories," the youngest sister chimed in. "I told Emily that the heroine in this story should have dysmentary."

"Dysmentary?" Cody laughed.

"She means dysentery," Anne said.

Kate rolled her eyes. "Yes, but Emily says dysmentary isn't romantic enough."

"Ah. So I should be on the lookout for a romantic disease, then?" Cody asked.

"Yes, please." Emily began yet another story, this one involving bubonic plague.

Jake tried to listen but found himself distracted. He could hardly wait to introduce these three to his mother. The youngest was a cute as a pixie with her dark curls. And Emily...well, he'd never met anyone quite like her. The oldest one, Anne, was the most beautiful thing he'd ever clapped eyes on. His thoughts drifted to her, and he wondered why she and her younger sisters were aboard the train to Dallas in the first place.

From behind him, Emily's story slowed. She tapped him on the shoulder and he turned his head a bit.

"Want me to teach you how to cheat at cards?"

"You're a card cheat?" Cody sounded a bit taken aback by this revelation.

Jake glanced over at Anne, who rolled her eyes.

"The best in Denver County." Emily released a dramatic sigh. "Not that I live in Denver County anymore."

"And who, pray tell, taught you to cheat at cards?" Jake asked.

"Wild Eyed Joe."

Jake shrugged. "Never heard of him."

"You don't read 'Wild West Adventures' in *The Spirit of Colorado* magazine?"

"Nope. Guess we don't get that one around here."

"Well, you don't know what you're missing. Wild Eyed Joe goes from town to town, making hundreds of dollars off unsuspecting card players. He's very good at what he does." She paused. "I don't think Papa was a very good card player. He gambled away all our money. Least, that's what Uncle Bertrand says. So I figure if I practice, I can win it all back in a poker game." She paused. "Do you play poker?"

"No, ma'am." He shook his head, trying to hold back a laugh. "My father was never one for card playing, so I've never been taught."

"Just leave it to me, then." She leaned over and whispered, "I have a deck of cards in my handbag. Wait till you see how I shuffle. I'm the fastest you've ever seen."

"Merciful heavens." Anne fanned herself. "How you do go on. Jake, please ignore my little sister. She's never played poker and wouldn't know the first thing about cheating at cards. This is all part of some story she's writing."

"That's what she thinks." Emily giggled. "Just wait till later when she's gone to bed and I'll show you the cards. I'll teach you to play too. And then I'll win every hand. Watch and see. I'll rob you blind."

"I'll have to be on my guard, then." Jake nodded. "Wouldn't want to be taken by a child."

"I'm not a child." She grunted. "I just turned ten three months ago—March 18."

Jake bit back a chuckle and tried to keep his voice steady. "So, tell me more about this Wild Eyed Joe character and why he's your hero."

As the youngster dove into another of her stories, Jake turned his attention back to the road. Well, mostly to the road. Out of the corner of his eye he kept a watchful eye on the beautiful woman to his right. Her gaze rarely shifted from the plains surrounding them. Likely she was enraptured by the beauty of the area. Or maybe she was just too shy to glance his way. Either way, he planned to garner her attention before the day was over. And there would be no card cheating or Indian attacks to accomplish the feat, either. No, he would go about it the old-fashioned way. He would work double-time to catch her eye. If he could just figure out how, exactly, that was done.

* * * * *

Anne tried to keep her gaze on the terrain, particularly when they turned off onto a road that led away from town. Still, their handsome driver captivated her thoughts every time she looked to her right. Before long, Anne found herself looking for excuses to glance his way.

Their rescuer might not be a cowboy with a six-shooter strapped to his side, but he was mighty handsome. He almost had what she liked to call a 'mama's boy' face—soft, with kind eyes. But those broad shoulders spoke of hard work...and the strength in his arms as he'd lifted their luggage proved this was no child.

Anne listened in as her sister carried on about cheating at cards. Likely Jake thought they were all a bunch of hooligans out to cause trouble. Maybe he wouldn't even want to take them to his family's ranch. What would she and her sisters do then?

No, thankfully he appeared to be set on getting them to their destination. And if the expression on his face was any indication of things to come, she could hardly wait to meet the rest of the family.

"My mother's going to think she's died and gone to heaven when she claps eyes on the three of you," Jake said.

Anne turned to Kate to make sure she didn't overreact to his words. Thank goodness, the youngster didn't appear to notice his reference to heaven, instead listening to Emily chatter nonstop.

They'd no sooner pulled the car up to the front of the house than a robust woman with the wildest head of red hair Anne had ever seen bounded from the front door. She stood with hands clasped at her ample bosom as she waited for everyone to get out of the car. Then she drew near.

"Have you brought me visitors, Jakey?" Her voice was laced with excitement.

"Sure have, and they're of the female variety. These fine ladies are in need of a room for a few days."

"Oh, girls!" His mother laughed and extended her arms in their direction. "The good Lord blessed me with sons. Looks like I've got some adopted daughters now." She pulled Anne into a soft embrace and planted a tender kiss on her cheek. "Welcome to O'Farrell's Honor. I'm Maggie O'Farrell."

"Headmistress and mother to all," Jake added with a nod.

"Mother to all?" Emily's eyes sparkled at this news. "Really?"

"It's an expression, honey." Anne gave her sister a warning look. No point in stirring up wishful thinking on Emily's part.

"Oh. Another expression." The youngster sighed.

"I'm so blessed that you'll be staying a few days, and I hope you'll feel the same." Maggie fussed with her apron strings. "You've come to the right place. There's plenty of room for all of you."

"Oh, we won't require much room," Anne said. "I'm sure we can all bunk together."

"Oh." Maggie's bright smile faded. "Well, I suppose that would be all right. But let me show you around. Might make more sense for each of you to choose a room of your own."

She led the way up the porch steps, where a large dog—something of the collie variety—met them.

"Oh, look! A dog." Emily extended her hand, and the dog licked it. Then the animal jumped up and put both paws on Emily's chest.

"That seals the deal," Jake said. "Ginger is smitten with you."

"Ginger?"

"Yes, I think she likes you."

Kate hid behind Anne's skirts. "You can come out, Kate," Anne said. "She's a nice dog. She won't hurt you."

"Are you sure?"

As if to prove the point, Ginger took a few cautious steps in Kate's direction. The dog's tail wagged merrily all the way.

"Don't get too attached to that pooch or she'll follow you everywhere," Maggie said. "Just this morning I had to shoo her out of my kitchen. She'd gotten ahold of a slab of bacon and was going to town. I lost that fight, by the way. Ginger's the fastest eater around."

Kate looked stunned. "I've never heard of a dog being inside a house before."

"Well, around here folks are pretty relaxed about such things, though you would rarely find one in a kitchen. Dogs are part of the family. Horses too, but I don't imagine you'll ever find a horse in my house. Hope not, anyway." Maggie laughed until tears filled her eyes. She dabbed at them with the corner of her apron. "Oh, that's a good one. A horse in the house. Can you imagine?"

Anne couldn't. But then again, she couldn't picture a dog in the house, either. And she could only imagine what Uncle Bertrand would say about such a thing. As the cheerful conversation continued, Anne found herself overcome with emotion. Something about being in a situation this homey touched a part of her she'd worked hard to bury. And for the life of her, she couldn't keep the lump from rising in her throat.

Hopefully it would pass. In the meantime, she would do her best to enjoy her stay in Groom with this remarkable family. And though she hadn't prayed much during the past few weeks, she might offer up a short thank-you to the Almighty for giving her a few extra days away from Uncle Bertrand. Perhaps this whole thing was part of some heavenly plan.

No. She'd given up on thinking the Lord wanted to save her from pain ages ago. This visit to the town of Groom was just a fluke. But she might as well enjoy it as long as she could.

Swallowing the lump in her throat, Anne turned to Maggie and offered a smile. Maggie responded by wrapping Anne in her arms and giving her another warm hug. Strange… Though she'd never met the woman until today, it felt as if they'd been friends forever. And as Maggie whispered, "So happy to share my home with you, sweet girl," Anne found her eyes filled with tears once again. She swiped them away, forced a smile, and followed the others into the house.

Chapter Six

....

Beef, chicken, fish…what's your pleasure? You name it, we've got it in abundance in the Texas Panhandle. I've had the rare privilege of traveling north to south, east to west, in search of some of the greatest food this corner of Texas has to offer. In Amarillo I dined on buffalo steak. It was fried catfish in Cisco. The sirloin couldn't be beat in Groom, and the home-made chili left me begging for more in Abilene. Still, nothing compares to the luscious banana pudding lovingly made by a certain pretty gal I eventually asked to marry me over in Carson County. She takes the prize, at least in my book. And speaking of the prize, keep an eye out for those ladies in Dumas. I hear they're cooking up something special for this year's county fair. —"Tex" Morgan, reporting for the Panhandle Primer

Maggie talked a mile a minute as she stepped inside the ranch house. Anne followed her, gasping as she took in the beautiful home. Though a bit more rustic in design, its size rivaled their house in Denver. And she'd never seen such beautiful woodwork.

"Jake, just leave their bags here for now," Maggie instructed, her words coming faster now. "I'll show these precious girls around, and they can decide on their rooms." She led them from one bedroom to the next, chattering all the way. Anne liked the feel of the place. Maggie's fingerprints were all over this house.

The strangest sense of nostalgia came over Anne as she took in her new surroundings. She felt the sting of tears in her eyes. In the years since Mama's death, she'd been strong in nearly every sense of the word. What other choice did she have? But in this moment, walking from room to room with a total stranger, Anne felt more vulnerable than she had in years. How could a place she'd never seen until today feel like home? And how could she stop the emotions that threatened to barrel over her as she considered that possibility?

Anne squared her shoulders and kept walking, determined to keep things under control.

"This first bedroom was where the twins slept when they were young." Maggie flashed a smile as she glanced Anne's way. "Since you're the oldest, maybe you would like this space. It's a bit larger than the other rooms."

"That would be lovely."

"Jakey, c'mon in here with the bags, please." Maggie placed her hands on her ample waist as she hollered out the instructions. "This is where..." She paused and shook her head. "Land sakes, I didn't even ask your name."

"Anne. I'm Anne Denning, and these are my sisters, Emily and Kate."

"Pleased to meet you." Maggie turned back to the door. "Jakey, bring Anne's bags in here. She's the pretty one with the beautiful brown curls."

At once Anne felt her face turn hot. Gracious. Were people in Texas really this forward? Besides, she'd never thought of herself as pretty, so that woman's words didn't even fit.

Jake arrived a few seconds later, carrying her bag. As their eyes met, she shifted her gaze back to the room to keep from staring at him. Why she hadn't noticed his boyish dimples before? Likely because he hadn't flashed such an appealing smile till now.

"Let's keep moving," Maggie said. "Plenty of house left to see." She led the way to another bedroom. As soon as they opened the door, Emily came to life.

"Oh, I like this one. It's perfect for me!"

"Perhaps, but it's not very feminine, is it?" Maggie chuckled. "My oldest, John, slept here. I never could get that boy to keep his room straight when he was young."

"Is that a writing desk?" Emily pointed to a rolltop desk.

"Yes." Maggie stepped inside the room and ran her fingers along the curved top. "It belonged to my father. It was left to me after he passed. Truly one of my most cherished possessions."

"Your papa died too?" Kate looked at her, wide-eyed.

"He did, honey." Maggie's eyes misted over. "Not a day goes by that I don't think of him. Sometimes I imagine he's up in heaven sitting at a desk just like this one, writing me a letter. Oh, he was a wonder with words. Maybe I can show you some of his poetry."

"That would be lovely," Anne said, nodding.

"Could I—I mean, would it be all right if I used this desk?" Emily asked. She squared her shoulders. "I'm a writer too."

"You are?" Maggie looked pleased at this news.

"Yes, and I'm writing the most thrilling book about a Texas cowboy."

"Don't get her started on that, Mama." Jake's voice sounded from outside the door. "She'll fill your head with tales of card cheats and Indian attacks."

Maggie chuckled. "I do love a child with an imagination. Jake was always the same way as a youngster."

"I'm not a child."

Emily's expression tightened, and Anne sighed. How would she ever turn this sister of hers into a young lady? It would take a miracle.

Maggie patted Emily on the shoulder. "No, you're not a child, are you? A big grown-up girl you are, one who deserves a rolltop desk for her writing. Yes, I do believe this was all meant to be. This will be your room for the next several nights, Emily, though it's not very girlish, I'm afraid."

"Oh, I don't mind. Who needs girlie stuff?" Emily lunged onto the bed then turned and faced a large painting on the far wall of the room. She rose and walked toward it, her mouth agape.

"What is it, Emily?" Anne asked.

"A sign! First the writing desk, and now the painting of a cowboy."

"Ah, I see." Anne stared at the painting, marveling at the colors of the sunset and the detail in the cowboy's weathered face.

Maggie took a few steps toward them and ran her finger along the edge of the frame. "Jakey was only sixteen when he painted this picture of his father. Isn't it something else?"

"Mama, it's not right to brag." Jake stepped into the room, holding Emily's bag.

"How can I help but brag?" Maggie asked. "When your child is talented, you have no choice but to recognize it."

"I'm not sure 'talented' is the right word." He placed Emily's bag on the end of the bed. "It's just a hobby."

"I've never seen anything like it." Anne couldn't take her eyes off it, in fact. She turned to Jake. "You're an artist?"

He shrugged. "It's not a very good likeness, to be honest."

"It's exquisite." Emily ran her finger over the painting. "And I'm sure it will provide the perfect inspiration for my story." She gave him a coy smile. "Among other things."

Why, you little flirt! Anne took hold of Emily's upper arm and gave it a little pinch.

"Ouch!" Emily turned to glare at her. "What was that for?"

"You know." Anne gave her a warning look.

"Now, where shall we put the little miss, here?" Maggie knelt down and brushed Kate's hair behind her ears.

"I want to stay with Emily." Kate's lip began to quiver. "P–please?"

"Of course, honey."

Jake brought Kate's bag to the room as well and then mumbled something about having to get cleaned up for supper.

Not that Anne had had time to think about it—or him. Maggie led the way to the kitchen, still talking nonstop. "I do hope you're hungry. I'm making enough food to feed half the folks in the Panhandle. The whole family's coming for supper."

"The whole family?" Emily grinned. "All of the cowboys?"

"And their wives and children," Maggie added. "My boys have the most wonderful wives. I can't wait for you to meet them. There's Ruth—she's married to John. Oh, and Cora, married to Jeremiah. Then there's Milly, Joseph's wife. I really think you're going to like her, Anne. You remind me a lot of her. Oh, and I almost left out Pauline. She's Jedediah's bride." Maggie chattered a mile a minute about her family.

Anne stood off to the side of the kitchen with her sisters, listening to every word.

"Can I be of any help?" she asked when Maggie reached for a bowl filled with potatoes.

The older woman looked up, never missing a beat as the potato peels started flying. "Oh, honey, you just sit right down and make yourself at home while I fix supper. You're my guest."

"Are you sure? I don't mind a bit."

Maggie turned to face her. The older woman's eyes glistened with tears. "Sweetie, I don't expect you to understand this, but I'm accustomed to waiting on folks. It's what I do, and I love it. These past few years..." She gestured around the kitchen. "Well, ever since my husband James passed away, God rest his soul, the house has been pretty empty, as you can see." She paused and dabbed her eyes with the hem of her apron. "Jakey's here for dinner at night, and the other boys bring their families by at least one or two nights a week. Other than that, I'm pretty much on my own all day. It's taken some getting used to, I must say. When one is accustomed to a bustling house, the stillness can drive a body a bit mad."

"I see." Anne wasn't sure what to say next. Being alone in a wonderful home like this wouldn't be so bad. It sounded far more appealing than staying at Uncle Bertrand's place, which she imagined as stiff and cold. Anne had a feeling they would never experience true peace and quiet there. Not the kind she longed for, anyway. "Still, it hardly seems fair that you're having to work so hard to make our dinner. Helping is the least I can do. Besides, it will make me feel more at home."

"Then, for heaven's sake, come over here and help me cook. I want you to feel at home." Maggie's smile warmed her heart. "And if there's anything I love to do, it's working in a kitchen with a friend."

Interesting, that she should choose the word "friend." After all, they'd only known each other a short time. Still, the idea of working alongside Maggie did give Anne something to do, and right now she needed to feel useful.

"Have you eaten chicken-fried steak before?" Maggie asked, reaching for a slab of meat. "It's a staple 'round these parts."

Anne shook her head. "I don't believe so. It's steak fried like chicken?"

"Ah, watch and see. And prepare yourself to fall in love with the most delicious Texas treat of all. But first let me put this sister of yours to work at peeling potatoes; then you can help me with the meat."

Emily wrinkled her nose as the potatoes were placed in front of her, but she began to peel them just the same. Kate stood next to her, looking on.

"My mother used to tell me that if I could peel an entire potato in one long strand without breaking the peel, I could have an extra-large slice of pie for dessert." Maggie's eyes twinkled. "How does that sound to you, honey? I've got blackberry cobbler."

"Sounds delectable!" Emily focused on the potato, peeling with careful precision.

"Now, then." Maggie went to work, pounding down the steak. Heavens, the woman was strong. She worked the meat until it was tender. Then she dipped it in egg and coated it with flour. Then back in the egg it went, then once more in the flour. "This is the best part." She took the battered steak and dropped it into the cast-iron skillet. It sizzled when it hit the hot lard. Minutes later, the most delicious smell filled the house.

Anne could hardly wait to taste it. "Oh my. It smells wonderful!"

"Thank you." Maggie's cheeks flushed. "We're beef eaters, as you might well imagine. Most of us who live on ranches depend on our cattle, not just for our income but also for our daily meals. And trust me when I say you've never had such tender meat in all your born days." She paused. "I take no credit for that, by the way. My boys know just when to slaughter a cow to give us the most tender meat."

"Ooh, I want to help slaughter a cow." Emily looked up from the potato, breaking the long strand of peel. "Oh, bother." She sighed. "If I keep this up, I won't get any cobbler at all."

"And you won't get to slaughter any cows, either!" Kate giggled.

"That's okay, honey." Maggie grinned and handed Emily a second potato. "You'll have another opportunity to get that extra-large piece of cobbler—and in response to what you just said, I'm afraid there won't be any slaughtering around here for a while. We've got enough meat to keep us fed for months."

"That's a shame." The edges of Emily's lips curled down. "I would have loved slaughtering a cow."

Anne did her best not to roll her eyes.

"Now it's your turn, Anne." Maggie led her through the process of breading the meat and dropping it in the skillet. Before long, she almost had the hang of it.

Emily seemed to be doing pretty well with the potatoes too. Within a few minutes, most of the ones in the bowl were peeled. Mostly peeled, anyway. Anne still noticed a few smidges of peeling, but Maggie was gracious enough not to mention it. Instead, she went to work, chopping the potatoes and putting them on to boil.

As she worked, Maggie started another conversation about life on the ranch, her every word holding the littler girls spellbound. Anne, however, found herself distracted with unhappy thoughts of Uncle Bertrand.

When Maggie paused for air, Anne dove in. "I need to reach my uncle," she explained, her words a bit rushed. "He is expecting us this afternoon, so I'm sure he's going to be quite startled that we're not arriving."

"Hmm." Maggie leaned against the countertop. "Surely when he goes to the station to fetch you he'll get word about what's happened. I wouldn't worry too much if I were you."

"Still, I would feel better if we could reach him. Do you know where I could find a telephone?"

"Why, we have one right here in our home." Maggie grinned and gave her a playful wink. "My older sister Bets is green with envy. Has been ever since we had the phone put in a couple of months back. Don't know why she's always bothered by such things. I've tried to tell her that jealousy is a sin, but she doesn't seem to believe it. Then again, Bets has always been the jealous sort." She finally paused for air. "What was your question again, honey?"

"Oh. I was just asking... Hmm." Anne shook her head. She couldn't seem to remember.

"She asked if we had a telephone." Jake's voice rang out from behind her. "She wants to call her uncle in Dallas."

"Yes, that's right." Anne turned, her heart gravitating to her throat as she took in the cleaned-up version of Jake. He'd combed his hair, and she found the new style very appealing. It really accentuated his green eyes. And the plaid shirt showed off his broad shoulders, as well. My goodness, if that boy didn't clean up nice.

He flashed her a boyish smile. "Ma'am, I took the liberty of asking the folks at the station to send your uncle a telegram. I hope you don't think I'm out of line. Just wanted to give him your whereabouts."

"But how did you... I mean, however did you know how to reach him?"

"Oh, easy." He leaned against the wall, his gaze shifting to Emily. "Our young reporter over there gave me all the facts. She also gave me a lesson in Texas Panhandle history too. She's quite a pistol."

"Oh, she's a pistol, all right." Anne chuckled. "Let's just hope she never gets her hands on one!"

"Ooh, I wish I *could* shoot a gun." Emily extended her hand, pointing her index finger in gun-like fashion. "Wouldn't that be something? I'd wear boots and a ten-gallon hat and shoot anyone who looked at me cross-eyed."

"That's my concern," Anne said. "What if someone you loved accidentally looked at you cross-eyed? Then what? They would go to an early grave." Anne wished at once she could take back her words. Why did the conversation always go back to death? She glanced at Kate, who sat on the floor playing with the dog. Thankfully the youngster didn't seem to notice her choice of wording.

At this point, Maggie took over the cooking of the meat. Before long, the platter on the counter was filled with thick, steaming slices of fried steak. The smell was almost enough to drive Anne to her knees. Still, they couldn't eat until the others arrived. Besides, Maggie needed her help with the gravy and the biscuits. Oh, what a heavenly meal this was turning out to be!

Minutes later the grandfather clock chimed six times. What happened next caught Anne completely off guard. The door to the house swung open, and a passel of children raced inside. The two in front—both redheads—were boys. They were followed by a little one, maybe three, in a darling yellow-checked dress. Behind her came a young woman not much older than Anne. Must be the mama.

Within minutes, the house was full, side-to-side, top-to-bottom, with family. Anne had never seen so many people crowded into a kitchen before. And the voices! They overlapped, one on top of the other. Laughter rang out, along with slaps on the back and lots of chatter about how good the meat smelled.

Through the crowd, she made out Jake's smiling face. He grabbed one of the littlest children and swept her into his arms, giving her a tender kiss on the cheek. One by one he embraced them, laughing and talking as if they were his own.

Introductions were made, but Anne felt sure she'd never keep all the names straight, especially since all the boys—little ones included—had J names. Thankfully, the females were a little easier. There was Pauline and Milly, Cora, and Ruth. Still, with so many, Anne hoped she wouldn't be quizzed on the names later. And which one was it Maggie had said reminded her of Anne? Was it Cora? No, maybe it was Ruth. Or was it Pauline, the newlywed?

Oh, bother. She couldn't remember. Not that it mattered tonight. No, all that mattered now was sitting down to dinner with this amazing group of new friends.

Maggie clapped her hands together, getting everyone's attention. "Let's gather around and pray before we dish up this meal. My chicken-fried steak tastes even better once it's been blessed." She nodded in her oldest son's direction after everyone stood around the table. "John, would you do the honors?"

"A-course." He nodded then removed his hat and bowed his head. The other brothers followed suit, one after the other. Jake wasn't wearing a hat, but he did bow his head...after flashing a smile Anne's way.

She tried to focus on the prayer. Truly, she did. But Jake's smile, along with those dimples and gorgeous green eyes, drew her attention instead. Indeed, once John stopped praying, Anne was still deep in thought about Jake.

"Annie!" Emily nudged her, and she startled to attention. "Don't fall asleep just yet. We might never get another meal like this as long as we live. We need to enjoy it."

Anne tried not to let her embarrassment get the best of her as she took her seat alongside the others. She fussed with her napkin to avoid looking at Jake once more. *I'm going to enjoy it all right.*

"Oh, I daresay if you stay on at O'Farrell's Honor, you'll see plenty of meals like this," Milly said. "We eat like this nearly every day." She told the girls about the different types of food Maggie was known for, and the older woman's cheeks turned pink.

"Oh, go on with you." Maggie fussed with her hair. "I just do what every other woman in these parts does. I care for my family. That's a woman's greatest joy."

Anne found herself feeling that strange feeling again, this time a tightening in her chest adding a bit of physical pain to the emotional. Why did she find herself so affected by Maggie's mothering skills? Why, she'd known dozens of great mothers in Denver, including Charlotte's precious mother. None had caused this kind of reaction.

Anne found herself so caught up in her thoughts that she almost missed a joke one of the children was telling. She managed to catch the tail end of it and offered a smile, just in case anyone happened to look her way.

Yes, someone happened to be looking her way. Out of the corner of her eye, she caught a glimpse of Jake offering her another boyish grin. Gracious, a girl could get used to that.

"If you think this is delicious, you should see what Maggie cooks up for Christmas!" Ruth said. "There's ham and turkey and the best sweet-potato casserole you ever tasted."

"Then I want to stay till Christmas!" Kate licked her lips and everyone laughed.

Still, Anne could see the potential for disaster with this situation. In spite of the overwhelming welcome, she needed to stay focused. In just a few days, O'Farrell's Honor would be nothing but a distant memory. She and her sisters would be living in Dallas at Uncle Bertrand's home. Likely the only Christmas dinner to be served there was one around a painfully quiet table with servants spooning out the food.

Oh, but when she smelled that chicken-fried steak, when she heard the laughter of the children, Anne could almost picture herself one of the O'Farrell's Honor brides.

She stifled a laugh. How funny would that be—to be a bride in a town called Groom?

Gazing across the room at Jake, she had to conclude that there were worse fates to befall a female in distress.

Chapter Seven

....

If you've traveled from state to state, you've likely witnessed hundreds of sunsets. The colors of the setting sun over the Grand Canyon are magnificent, to be sure. And the snow-capped Rockies are quite a sight to behold in the evening's afterglow, as well. But there's nothing like the north Texas plains, springing to life under the colors of the near-night sky, to capture the imagination. There simply are no words to describe the variety of vivid reds, golds, and purples as the vibrant day gives herself over to the shadows of night. No matter where you travel, where you roam, you'll never find a sunset like the one you'll find at home...in the Texas Panhandle. —"Tex" Morgan, reporting for the Panhandle Primer

After supper, Anne helped Maggie and the other women clear the table. She offered to wash the dishes, but Maggie wouldn't hear of it. Likely because Anne couldn't stop yawning.

"Go on outside and take a walk," Maggie said. "Feast your eyes on that gorgeous Texas sunset. Then get on back in here and tuck yourself into bed for the night."

The idea sounded simply delicious. Anne gazed up at Maggie, wanting to pour out her thanks but unwilling to speak even a word. What was it about this place? This woman?

She knew, of course. The overwhelming sense of family. The laughter of children, coupled with the disciplining they received from loving parents.

"Yes, you go on outside and soak up that sunset, Anne," Maggie said. The older woman fussed with Kate's disheveled curls. "I do believe this young lady could stand to have her hair washed." Maggie glanced Anne's way. "Would it be all right with you if I took care of that?"

"Why, of course." Anne nodded.

Maggie's eyes filled with tears. "Must sound silly, but it's been years since I've helped a little one with her hair." She clasped her hands together and looked at Kate. "Oh, I know! Let's put your hair in pin curls tonight. Would you like that?"

Kate's expression hardened. "Will it hurt?"

"Oh, no. I'll be as gentle as a lamb, I promise. You won't even know you're sleeping on them. And while we're pinning up your curls, I'll tell you a story about the day I first arrived in Texas as a young woman."

Suddenly Anne found herself intrigued. "You're not from Texas?"

"No, my folks lived in Missouri. My father, God rest his soul, came down to the Panhandle on business and fell in love with the place. He took one look at this magnificent land and..." Maggie giggled. "Anyway, I'm getting ahead of myself. Let me get Kate's hair washed and then I'll tell the story." She and Kate disappeared into the bathroom and Anne glanced at the front door, wondering if she could really slip outside for a few moments of alone time. Off in the other room, she heard Kate's voice ring out alongside Maggie's in a rousing rendition of "Camptown Races." Before long, she found herself humming it too.

Just about the time she'd opened her mouth to sing a few of the words, a gentle voice rang out from behind her. "So, the fair Guinevere sings too."

Anne turned, her cheeks suddenly feeling as if they were on fire. "Excuse me? What did you call me?"

He grinned. "Oh, sorry about that. Just a slip."

"Did you say Guinevere?" She took a seat. "Like the one in the legend of King Arthur?"

"That's the one. From the minute I first met you, I felt you resembled her. Or at least the image of her I'd painted in my head after reading the story."

"That's a lovely compliment." Anne found herself embarrassed by such flattery. "Thank you."

"You're welcome." He paused and gave her a tender look. "Did I hear you say you were going outside for a walk?"

"Yes."

"You'll catch the sunset if you hurry. I've got to head out to pen up the goats and then tend to my mare, Frances."

"You named your mare?" For whatever reason, this got her tickled.

"Well, sure. Don't you name your animals?"

"Yes." She chuckled. "I call them Emily and Kate."

He seemed to get great pleasure out of that. Before long they were both laughing.

"I'll be in the barn a few minutes, but I'll join you when I'm done." Jake gave her a second glance. "If that's all right."

"Of course." She offered him a shy smile, her heart skipping to double-time as he returned it. Oh, those dimples. How they captured her imagination.

Before heading outside, Anne peeked in on Kate, who was

singing a song in the bathtub while Maggie scrubbed her hair. Since when did Kate sit still for a hair scrubbing? Why, the youngster was really going to town, singing that song. And where was Emily? She'd disappeared. She glanced into the youngster's room and was surprised to find her seated at the rolltop desk. As Anne entered the room, Emily looked up.

"Aren't you too tired to write tonight?" Anne asked.

"Not at all." Emily looked at her, clearly stunned. "This has been the most amazing day. Loaded with fodder for my story. If I don't capture it right away, I'll go to sleep and forget. I need to put the words down while they're fresh."

"I see." Anne chuckled. She didn't really understand her sister's enthusiasm for stories but knew that writing brought some sense of comfort. "Well, I'm headed outside for a little walk. I'll be back in before long."

"Mm-hmm." Emily turned back to her tablet, her pencil moving fast across the page.

Anne slipped through the front door and stood on the porch for a moment. She thought about sitting in the swing to enjoy the sunset but decided that a walk sounded more appealing.

She made her way down the stairs and across the lawn, going west so she could see the sunset in all its glory. In all her nineteen years, she'd never seen such a large property before. Their home in Denver had been situated just yards away from the house next door. Most houses in the city were built so close you could practically reach out and touch your neighbors. But here, in this wide, expansive place, a person could walk for hours and never cross a neighbor's property line.

Perhaps she would have to do that tomorrow. Walk for hours,

GROOM
1914
TX

that is. How glorious it sounded. Of course, if she got to choose, she would continue walking west, as far away from Dallas—and her future life with Uncle Bertrand—as possible.

Anne strolled across the yard and out into the field, enjoying the sunset. Off in the distance, she heard the voices of John and his children. Before long, the chatter of young voices gave way to the silence of the wide-open plains.

She tried to picture her mother just beyond that sunset. Her wonderful, kind mother—who'd been so good to everyone. She'd slipped off to heaven without so much as a real good-bye, leaving behind only memories and the little cross, a small symbol of her very large faith.

Anne fingered the necklace, hoping to stir up some degree of faith to see her through this current problem. A thousand thoughts ran through her mind. Though her prayers of late felt as if they weren't going much higher than the clouds, she decided to give it another try. Perhaps this time the Lord would give her an answer she could live with...if she could only think of a way to voice the question.

"Lord, is this some sort of sign?" She looked to the skies but saw nothing. Heard nothing—nothing but the sound of a whip-poor-will in the distance. "Maybe we're not supposed to go to Dallas. Am I supposed to turn back around and return to Colorado?"

Across the field, the sun dipped below the trees, casting ribbons of color across the field. The grass, once golden, now looked almost red. If she stood here awhile longer, would it drift to shades of gray? Likely. Hadn't her life moved in that direction already?

Pushing back the tears, she forced herself to pray.

* * * * *

Jake finished his work in the barn then headed to the fence, to the spot where he'd seen Anne walking. From a distance, he watched as she stood beneath the glow of the setting sun, her beautiful black hair shimming under a red-orange sky. He could tell from her posture that she felt relaxed. He hated to interrupt her but felt himself drawn in much the same way he'd been drawn to work for the railroad three years ago. Some things were just unavoidable. He drew near and cleared his throat.

She turned, and he could see at once that her eyes brimmed with tears.

"Oh, I'm sorry. I—I didn't know you were..." Jake reached inside his pocket and came out with a handkerchief, which he passed her way. "Would you like me to go? I don't mind."

"No, it's fine." She dabbed at her eyes with the handkerchief. "I'm just being silly, I guess."

He took another step in her direction. "Missing Colorado?"

"Yes. Missing a great many things."

He hoped she would elaborate, but she did not. He had so many questions—about the life she'd left behind and why she and her sisters were on their way to their uncle's house.

He opted to say nothing at all. Maybe it would be better to leave things as they were for a moment. He stood alongside her, gazing out over the pasture. From time to time, he heard what sounded like a contented sigh as she took in the sight before them.

Off in the distance, the family's collie rested in the yard. "From what I hear, Ginger worked hard today," Jake said. "John said she was worth her weight in gold. They rounded up the cattle on the back twenty."

"Aw. Poor Ginger."

"Yes. It looks like she's tuckered out."

"I'm a little tired myself."

"Should we go back inside?"

"Not just yet." She turned and offered up the sweetest smile he'd ever seen.

"What do you think of O'Farrell's Honor?" Jake gestured to the acreage before them. "It's really something, isn't it?"

"I've never seen anything quite like it."

"Keep your eyes on that field over there." He pointed to the west. "Every few minutes the sunset changes and you see something new. If you stand here long enough, you can see literally dozens of different colors. It's like a kaleidoscope."

A few minutes later, she gasped. "Oh, I see what you mean. First it was red, and now it's sort of a purple color."

"Yes, and that will eventually fade to pink and gray, so keep watching."

They stood in silence as the sun slipped over the horizon and left behind heavy gray skies. Still neither of them moved.

After a while Anne yawned, and Jake fought the temptation to slip his arm across her shoulder so that she could rest against him. "Sounds like we need to get you back inside. You've got to be exhausted."

"I am tired, but it's so beautiful here, even in the dark. So peaceful and quiet." She offered another sweet smile, which he could barely make out in the hazy shadows of the evening. "Just a couple more minutes?"

"Of course."

"You're very blessed to live in such a wide-open space," she said after a few moments of silence. "Do you ever feel...lost?"

"Lost?" He shook his head. "Not that I can remember. Of course, I'm surrounded on every side by family. It's hard to feel lost when the people you love are all nearby."

He paused, realizing the pain his words must be causing her since she'd just lost a parent. How insensitive could he be?

She sniffled and he reached for his handkerchief once again.

"I'm sorry." She turned his way, her voice as soft as lamb's wool. "I think I'm just exhausted. I'm not usually this emotional. I try to be the strong one for my sisters. Ever since Papa died..." Her words drifted off.

"You don't have to say anything else. And I'm sorry if I hurt you with what I said a minute ago, about having family surrounding me on every side. I don't ever want anyone to think I dislike having family nearby. They're wonderful. Chaotic, but wonderful. I love every single person and would give my life for any one of them. So it's not that I feel crowded. I'm just..." He found himself unable to continue. How could he explain what he really felt? That he couldn't live up to what others expected of him? That no matter how long he tried, folks would go on seeing him as nothing but the baby brother?

"There's plenty of room for everyone here." She gestured to the open field. "I've never seen so much land." She paused, her eyes widening. "Oh, look!" She pointed heavenward. "I can actually see the stars here."

"Well, of course." He chuckled. "They're as bright as candles. It's like this every night."

"Not in Denver. With all the tall buildings, I rarely caught a glimpse of the stars. But out here, it's magnificent."

"Mama always says you can reach out and touch the stars. That's one of the things that drew her father to the Panhandle." He chuck-led. "When I was a kid, my grandfather used to tell me to snatch 'em in my hand and put 'em in my pocket."

"In your pocket? Why?"

"So I wouldn't lose them." He laughed. "I can't tell you how old I was when I finally figured out that the stars were too big to be able to reach out and grab with my hand. It was quite a letdown, let me tell you."

A contented sigh followed from Anne…and then a yawn. After-ward, she turned his way. "I guess it's time to get back inside. It's been a long day."

"Mm-hmm." He wanted to add, "It's been a wonderful day," but didn't. Instead, he offered her his arm so they could walk together across the field toward the house. Maybe, if he took small steps, he could snatch a few extra moments alone with Guinevere.

No, not so. From the porch, he heard Kate's voice. "Annie, are you coming in? It's getting late, and I want you to tuck me into bed."

Anne picked up her pace, and he followed suit. Hopefully there would be plenty of time to spend with her tomorrow. And the next day. And the day after that.

* * * * *

Anne couldn't get Jake's words out of her mind as she settled into bed that night. She rested her head against the pillow and tried to sleep but could not. Through the open window, a beam of moonlight cast a silvery glow across the room. The sound of the cattle lowing in the nearby field served as a beautiful backdrop. She'd never found herself so content. Or so conflicted.

Anne closed her eyes, and a vivid picture of her mother flashed through her mind. The image was so startling that Anne's eyes flew open. Her heart raced. She reached for the tiny cross necklace, rubbing it between her thumb and index finger. As always, it brought comfort, and before long, she began to relax.

Just as she started to doze off, a noise at the bedroom door startled her.

"W–who is it?"

"Annie, it's us." Kate's voice rang out. "Can we come in?"

Anne sprang up from the bed, turned on the bedside lamp, and opened the door. Emily and Kate stood outside the room.

Emily stood with her arms crossed at her chest and a sour expression on her face. "Kate couldn't sleep, so I told her she had to stay in here with you."

"Emily told me a scary story—that's why I couldn't go to sleep." Kate turned and stuck out her tongue at her older sister.

"You asked for it. How was I to know you would be such a scaredy-cat?"

'Well, come and get in bed with me for a few minutes, Kate," Anne instructed. "If you doze off, you can stay here and Emily can go back to her room."

Then Anne heard a suspicious panting sound coming from the hallway.

"Emily, is that dog with you?"

"Yes. I couldn't help it, Annie. Ginger was really lonely and needed someone who understands."

"Tell me you did not allow that dog in your bed."

"Well, I…" Emily climbed into Anne's bed, and the dog followed suit.

Anne waved her arms, trying to shoo Ginger away, but the contented pooch was having none of it. She weaseled her way under the covers and collapsed at Anne's feet.

"Now look what you've done. Maggie's going to be mortified if she finds out."

"No, she won't. I know her. She's so sweet, Anne. She won't care one whit. And besides, Ginger is a great guard dog. Out here in the wilderness we need a good watchdog."

"Well, all right. Just this once. But we can't make it a habit."

The girls—and Ginger—settled into the bed, and Anne pulled the covers up to Kate's chin.

"Annie..." Kate pulled her hand out from under the covers and touched Anne's arm. "Do we have to go to Uncle Bertrand's?"

All the questions she'd asked the Lord earlier this evening washed over her. Anne struggled to find the right words to say. "Honey, if I could change our situation, I would. I've thought about this from every angle, but there just doesn't seem to be any other way. We will stay with Uncle Bertrand, and I will find work. Perhaps once I've made a little money, we can get a place of our own."

"Find work?" Emily sounded stunned. "Doing what?"

"Perhaps I can work as a nanny. I've had a lot of experience in caring for the two of you."

"Humph. We don't need caring for."

"Or maybe..." An idea took hold. "Maybe I could ask Maggie to teach me to cook. Then I could get hired on as a cook or a waitress. Maybe even one of those Harvey Girls."

"Ooh, a Harvey Girl?" Emily's eyes shimmered. "How romantic. I've heard such wonderful stories about them. Harvey Girls meet so many interesting people."

"Surely there's a Harvey House hotel in Dallas," Anne said. "If so, that would be just the ticket." She chuckled at her choice of words. Ticket. Railroad. Funny.

Still, there was nothing funny or romantic about the idea of being on her feet all day serving customers or slaving away in a hot kitchen. Suddenly the idea of working didn't sound as appealing.

Emily yawned and curled up next to her. "I daresay Uncle Bertrand won't like the idea of you working. He will marry you off to some rich banker friend of his as quickly as possible. Of course, he won't be much to look at, but his wealth will blind you to that fact."

"You and your silly notions." Anne laughed. "I daresay Uncle Bertrand's well-to-do friends won't be interested in the slightest in a girl with no money and no family position. So you can put that thought right out of your pretty little head. Besides, I plan to marry for love, not money."

"Oh, but to marry a wealthy man would mean that Kate and I could live with you and your new husband. We wouldn't have to stay with Uncle Bertrand." Emily's eyes filled with tears. "We won't, will we? If you leave, I mean."

"Not if I have anything to do with it." Anne crawled under the quilt and beckoned Kate to her side. "But let's put this conversation to bed, shall we? I have no intentions of marrying anytime soon."

"Speaking of weddings..." Emily's voice grew more animated. "Did you know that Cody is getting married one week from tonight? I heard Maggie talking about it."

"Is he, now?"

"And guess what? I heard Maggie say that Jake is going to be the last single fellow in the town of Groom after Cody gets married." Emily giggled. "Isn't that funny?"

"I'm sure Jake doesn't think so." She paused to think about that news. No doubt he felt more than a little awkward about it, especially if folks were making a big to-do over his situation. How would she feel if she were the last single woman in a town?

Well, she wouldn't mention it. No point in pouring salt on an open wound.

With the moon's glow hovering over the room, she found herself caught up in a story-like frame of mind. Her thoughts settled on Jake. His warm smile. Those cute dimples. His handsome face. Those broad shoulders.

Careful, Anne. You're not Emily. This isn't some story you're writing.

Oh, but if it was, she'd give it a happily-ever-after sort of ending. Any story with a hero this perfect called for nothing less.

GROOM 1914 TX

Chapter Eight

....

Summertime is upon us, and you know what that means... church socials. Grab your partner and a picnic basket and head outdoors to the church lawn after a rousing Sunday morning service. Spread out that hand-stitched quilt lovingly made by your mama or grandma, and settle down for some afternoon fellowship with other parishioners. Surrounded by mountain-mahogany and mesquite trees, you'll dine on fried chicken and homemade bread with jam and will drink cold glasses of pink lemonade. Panhandle socials are by far the best way to get to know your neighbors. And when the pie auctions get going, watch out! You'll find yourself paying top dollar for your sweetheart's apple pie! —"Tex" Morgan, reporting for the *Panhandle Primer*

Anne awoke bright and early on Sunday morning to the smell of bacon. She rolled over in the bed, and Kate let out a squeal.

"Oh, sorry, honey." Anne giggled. "I forgot you were here." She sat up and stretched. "Guess Emily went back to her room."

"Mm-hmm." Kate rolled over. Then she too sat up. "Is that bacon I smell?"

"Yes. Heavenly, isn't it?"

"Yes." Kate stretched and released a contented sigh. "Can't we just stay here forever, Annie? Please?"

Anne almost let "Don't I wish we could!" slip between her lips but chose to remain silent. No point in letting Kate get too carried away.

Minutes later they were dressed and headed to the kitchen, where Maggie greeted them with a smile. "Happy Lord's Day. I'm hoping you ladies will join us in church this morning. Our Sunday morning services are wonderful."

Anne nodded. "I would love to." She looked down the table, which was loaded with platters of scrambled eggs, bacon, and biscuits. Was the whole family coming back for breakfast, or did Maggie always serve up such a large spread?

Jake entered the room dressed in his Sunday finest. Anne couldn't help but gawk as she saw him in the blue button-up shirt and slacks. He did look like a hero from one of Emily's stories, no doubt about that. Though she doubted he wore a gun, especially on the Lord's Day. She didn't have time to comment, however. Maggie flew into gear, feeding everyone, then encouraging them to get ready to leave.

"We're having supper on the grounds after service," Maggie explained. "So I need to gather up the food I'll be taking and get it loaded."

"Supper on the grounds?" Anne had never heard this term before and didn't know what to make of it.

"It means everyone in the congregation gathers together on the church lawn after service to eat lunch together and visit," Jake explained. "Some folks play horseshoes, and there's usually some singing. I think you'll like it."

"Ah, I see." Sounded interesting, to be sure.

"Yes, and I have a lot of food to take," Maggie said. "So we need to hurry up."

"I'll help, Mama." Jake went to work, making an easy task of loading up the food.

Anne changed into a Sunday go-to-meeting dress and made sure her sisters did the same. Kate looked lovely in her soft pink dress, but Emily grumbled when Anne insisted that she wear her yellow taffeta.

"It's itchy, Annie. I hate it. Besides, I look stuck-up. None of the girls here wear dresses like this."

"Trust me, it will grow on you with time. Before long, you will love taffeta."

"I'll stick out like a big, yellow sore thumb." Emily unhooked the buttons. "I want to wear the green cotton dress. Please."

"All right. But don't come crying to me if you change your mind." Anne turned to the mirror, fussing with her hair. "Should I wear it up?"

She didn't have time to answer her own question. Maggie called out, "Let's go, girls," and off they went.

Before she knew it Anne found herself at the church, seated in a pew with Jake on one side and her sisters on the other. A couple of times she caught Jake glancing her way. She did her best to act as if she didn't notice.

Just before the service started, Cody approached.

Jake turned to her with a smile. "Anne, you met my best friend Cody yesterday."

"Of course." She extended her hand, and he took it with a smile. "Thank you again for giving us a ride to O'Farrell's Honor in your car. That was very nice."

A beautiful young woman with red hair swept into place beside Cody and looped her arm through his. "My Cody's a peach, isn't he? He's always rushing in to the rescue."

Cody planted a little kiss on her cheek then turned to Anne and her sisters. "Ladies, this is my fiancée, Virginia. We're getting married on Saturday night."

"Oh, that's wonderful news." Anne turned to the bride-to-be with a smile. "I'm so happy for you. I attended so many lovely weddings in Denver. And there's nothing prettier than a June bride."

"Thank you." Virginia's cheeks turned pink. "I'm awfully excited. My parents are coming all the way from New York. They're set to arrive in a few days and then our plans will be set. Will you be staying until Saturday night?"

"Oh, I don't know. Likely not." She glanced at Jake. "Will the track be repaired before then?"

He nodded. "Yes. In fact, we should be done by Wednesday or Thursday, from what I've heard."

This news caused a little sigh to rise up inside of Anne. So, they would be leaving sooner than she'd thought.

"We might have to leave on Wednesday?" Emily crossed her arms at her chest. "That doesn't give me enough time to write my story."

"I'm sure your story will be brilliant no matter how long we stay." Anne started to say more but found herself distracted by a beautiful young woman approaching behind Virginia. She wore one of the most ridiculous-looking dresses Anne had ever seen. Oh, the blue silk certainly brought out the color of her eyes, no doubt about that. And the beautiful ribbon at the midsection accentuated her tiny waistline. But the skirt appeared to be widest at the hip and frighteningly narrow at the ankle.

GROOM
1914
TX

Quite odd, indeed. How could she possibly walk with such poise and elegance in a gown with such a narrow ankle? Was this some sort of costume? Anne did her best not to stare.

The young woman gave Anne a curious look. "Well, who have we here?"

"I'm Anne Denning."

"Anne's from Denver," Virginia added. "She's visiting with the O'Farrells for a few days. Anne, this is my best friend, Amaryllis. She's come all the way from New York to be my maid of honor."

Anne nodded in the beautiful blond's direction, taking in her beautiful ivory skin, which had been dusted over with enough facial powder to hide any imperfections.

"It's a pleasure to meet you," Anne managed. She took note of Amaryllis's beautiful upswept hair, which had been pinned with a jeweled silver clip. Lovely. Still, Anne could hardly get past that interesting dress. How did one walk in such a thing?

Amaryllis fussed with one of her curls. "Gracious, I must look a mess with the wind blowing so hard outside. Well, never mind that. It's nice to meet you, Anne."

Thankfully the music began, and before long the church service was underway. Anne thought about Virginia as the service progressed. How wonderful would it be to get married in a lovely country church like this one? And to a sweet boy like Cody. She pushed those thoughts aside and focused on the reverend as he delivered a sermon about the Good Samaritan. Anne couldn't help but peek at Jake and Maggie as the words to the sermon took root. Hadn't they acted in much the same way as the Good Samaritan? They'd taken in Anne and her sisters when they needed a place to stay and had cared for their every need.

Thoughts of gratitude nearly overwhelmed her as the service came to a close. By the time the reverend led them in the final prayer, Emily was already whispering in her ear. "Anne, we're going to have a church social."

"Yes, that's what Maggie said."

"I've never been to a social before. Not on the lawn, anyway. What do we do?"

"Hmm." Good question. The large, fancy church they had attended in Denver rarely hosted social events. How did one eat lunch on the lawn?

The answer came sooner rather than later. Before she knew it, Anne was on the lawn helping Maggie spread two beautiful quilts and lay out the food in preparation for their picnic.

"When did you cook all this, Maggie?" she asked, looking at the platters of sliced beef and the loaf of home-baked bread.

"Most of it was already done before you arrived yesterday," Maggie responded. "But I baked the bread this morning before you woke up."

"Heavens, do you ever sleep?"

"Of course." Maggie laughed. "But I love to cook. It's what I'm known for around these parts. You know what they say, honey. 'The way to a man's heart is through his stomach.'" She gave Anne a wink. "How are your cooking skills, honey?"

"Not very good, I'm afraid." Anne began to fan herself, suddenly very aware of the heat.

"We'll be ready to eat in a few minutes," Maggie said. "Better go find those sisters of yours."

"I'll do that." Anne looked around, trying to figure out where Emily and Kate had gotten off to. She found them visiting with

John's children on the church's front porch steps. Anne moved their way but didn't quite make it, because Virginia took hold of her arm.

"I do hope you can stay till Saturday night," the bride-to-be said. "There are so few girls our age here, and I'd love to have you at the wedding."

"That would be lovely, but..." Anne pursed her lips as she saw Emily arguing with John's oldest son, William. Emily doubled up her fist and looked as if she might take a swing at the unsuspecting boy. Anne wanted to holler, "What do you think you're doing, you little hooligan?"—but decided that would be inappropriate.

Amaryllis hobbled their way. Off in the distance, Jake crossed the lawn with two plates of food in hand.

"Looks like Jake is extra hungry today." Amaryllis smiled. "I do love a man who loves his food."

"If I know him, he's taking a plate to his mother," Virginia said. "He tends to her needs. Some around these parts call him a"— she lowered her voice—"a mama's boy."

"Mama's boy or not, I think he's about the handsomest thing I ever did see." Amaryllis frowned. "Though I do have to wonder if he will ever work up the courage to leave home, if he's tied to her apron strings. That might be problematic. I mean, I'm sure I'll love my mother-in-law, but to live with her? Out of the question."

"Silly girl. You've gone and gotten yourself married already?" Virginia laughed. "First you have to get him to look your way."

"Oh, I'll manage," Amaryllis said. "If I can get him to look away from his family obligations for a minute or two."

Anne found herself wanting to join the conversation. She

respected a son who cared for his mother's needs. If her mother had lived, Anne would have been just as dedicated.

Virginia quirked a brow. "Sometimes a baby birdie just needs a little nudge out of the nest." She giggled. "You're awfully good at nudging, Amaryllis. You've had years of practice."

The blond's cheeks turned pink. "Well, you can't blame a girl for trying, now, can you? And still I remain unattached." She laughed. "Certainly not for lack of trying on my part. Or my mama's. It's a crime, I tell you."

They all had a good laugh at that one.

"You're a beautiful girl," Virginia said, "with some magnificent features."

Amaryllis batted her eyelashes. "I do boast a rather small waistline, and Mama says my eyes are sapphire blue."

"Sapphire?" Anne took another look. Maybe sky blue, but definitely not sapphire blue. She'd seen blue sapphires once, and they were a different shade altogether from Amaryllis's eyes.

Anne silently scolded herself for thinking such things.

"Well, your eyes match that beautiful gown, to be sure. You must tell everyone about your dress," Virginia said, pointing to Amaryllis's gown. "It's the latest style, I hear."

"I must admit, I've never seen anything like it," Cody said as he approached. His grin let Anne know his take on the silly gown.

"Oh, it's the latest fashion." Amaryllis giggled. "They call it a hobble skirt. Want to guess why?" She tried to take a few steps forward but almost fell.

Cody extended his arm and she took it, her cheeks flaming pink.

Virginia laughed. "I love fashion too, Ami, but this one is just plain silly."

"Do you think so?" Amaryllis tried again to walk, this time holding Cody's arm. "I daresay I could catch a fellow's eye in this one, and isn't that the point?"

"You could catch his eye, all right," Cody said. "As he stooped to pick you up off the ground, once you tumbled in the dirt."

"Then I'll have to deliberately fall in one young man's direction." Amaryllis glanced over at Jake, who had settled onto the quilt next to his mother. For whatever reason, Anne found herself rankled by the young woman's words. Did girls from the East always come across this flirtatious and silly?

Laughter rang out again, and before long Virginia and Amaryllis were deep into a conversation about high fashion, talking about shoes and hats and other such nonsense, which prompted Cody to say that he needed to talk to Jake about the broken section of railroad track. Anne didn't blame him for leaving.

Watching the two young ladies—and listening to the way they chatted about things that really didn't have much to do with the real world—put Anne in mind of her days back in Denver. For a short season of her life, before Papa's drinking had gotten too bad, she'd spent some time in that world. Silly females, with little to do but fuss over their hair and clothes. How ridiculous it all seemed now.

Memories of a beautiful blue dress flooded over Anne. She'd worn it to the party following her graduation. What a special night that had been, and how one young man had hung onto her every word—silly as those words now seemed.

Off in the distance another young woman approached, this one the polar opposite of the others. Where Amaryllis was tiny in the waist, this girl was quite broad. Still, she had a pleasant smile and the loveliest cheekbones.

"You must be Anne." The girl extended her hand. "I'm Cassie Martin. I just had to come and meet you in person."

"O–oh?" Anne shook Cassie's hand.

"Yes." Cassie giggled. "You're the luckiest girl ever! You get to stay in the same home with Jake O'Farrell. I would die a thousand deaths to spend so much time that close to him."

Anne wondered why the local girls felt the need to go on about Jake. Oh well. Before long, he would be a distant memory.

She looked at him again, taking in his broad shoulders and boyish smile. A distant memory, yes…but a lovely one.

She snapped to attention, remembering why she'd headed this way in the first place. "Excuse me, ladies, but I need to fetch my sisters. It's time to eat." She nodded her head in acknowledgment then took a few steps in Emily's direction, arriving just in time to stop another quarrel between Emily and William.

"I daresay you will never marry if you're this mean to boys," Anne said, taking Emily by the arm.

"I don't want to marry them. I just want to write about them." Emily turned around and stuck out her tongue at William, who responded by lifting his fist. "Though, I can assure you, the boys in my story are far more mature than dumb Willy over there. He's nothing but a nuisance."

"Funny. I was just going to say the same thing about you." Anne led her away from the group and nodded for Kate to follow them.

* * * * *

Jake puzzled over the thoughts that had flitted through his head as he'd watched the interaction between Anne and Amaryllis moments before. They were different in nearly every respect—Anne with her dark hair and ivory skin, Amaryllis with her blond hair and sun-kissed face. Both came from money—one could ascertain as much from their clothing—but only one acted like it. The other, well, she charmed him with both her modesty and her devotion to her sisters. Dedication to family—especially when one's family had been through crisis—was so important.

And now, watching Anne approach with her younger sisters in tow, he realized just how wonderful she could be. Maybe when she got a bit closer, he would ask her to sit next to him. If he could work up the courage. Yes, that's exactly what he would do.

"Jake, would you be so kind as to refill my lemonade?"

"Excuse me?" He startled to attention. Amaryllis now stood at his side. How long had she been there?

"It's deplorably hot out today, and I'm melting in this dress. Would you refill my lemonade glass for me, please? I'm afraid I'll be the laughingstock of the congregation if I go hobble up to that table one more time. I'll probably trip all over myself, and then what would happen?" She paused to bat her eyelashes. "Someone would have to sweep in and rescue me."

"I'm happy to refill your drink." Jake rose and brushed the crumbs from his pants. "But don't worry about what people will think. Folks around here won't make fun of you." He reached to take her glass, and her fingers lingered on top of his for a moment as an uncomfortable silence rose up between them.

His older brother Joseph approached on Jake's right and slapped him on the back. "What do you mean, telling this pretty little lady that we don't make fun of each other? I thrive on making fun of you, little brother."

"As do I," John said, giving him another slap on the back.

"What's happening here?" Jeremiah asked, approaching from behind.

"Jake was just telling Amaryllis that folks in Groom don't make fun of others."

"Now that's a keen one!" Jedediah doubled over with laughter. "We live to make fun of Jake here. And he makes it so easy. I'm surprised he hasn't noticed. Looks like we're falling down on the job."

Jake drew in a breath and silently counted to ten. He wouldn't let the others see his temper flare, no matter what. Not in front of the ladies, anyway. However, he might just take his brothers down a notch or two once they got back home.

"I was explaining to Amaryllis that we would not poke fun at her for being thirsty," Jake said. "That's it." He strode to the table and reached for the ladle inside the bowl filled with lemonade. Moments later he returned to find Amaryllis standing alone. She appeared to be struggling to sit in that ridiculous dress of hers. After a few moments, she gave up altogether.

"I guess it's too hot to sit anyway." She giggled.

"I'm so sorry they subjected you to that," he said. "My brothers are..." For whatever reason, no words would come. At least no words he could say in front of a lady.

"I have brothers," Amaryllis said with a smile.

"Ah. Then you do understand." He handed her the glass of lemonade.

She released another playful giggle and fussed with the tendrils of hair at the nape of her neck. "I do wish I had a fan. Is it always this warm in Texas?"

He laughed. "You haven't seen anything yet. Just wait until August. That's the hottest month of the year."

"Our summers in New York are milder. Or perhaps I just stay indoors more. We don't have these lovely wide-open spaces like you do here." Her sigh caught him off guard for a moment. "I do love it here. Truly."

"I do too."

Out of the corner of his eye, Jake caught a glimpse of Anne seated next to his mother, with her younger sisters nearby. He'd missed out on the opportunity to sit next to her, thanks to Amaryllis and that cup of lemonade.

A peal of laughter rang out. His mother must've said something funny, because Anne was all giggles. He found himself captivated by her broad smile. With the exception of those few minutes under the setting sun, he hadn't yet seen her this carefree. Oh, what he would give to see that smile more often. And those gorgeous brown eyes of hers were sparkling as she laughed.

Stop it, Jake. She's leaving in a couple of days. Guard your heart.

He watched as she rose and headed to the punch table. Perfect opportunity to make a move.

"Jake?" Amaryllis reached out and touched his arm. "I don't believe you've heard a word I've said, have you?"

"Oh, I..." He tugged at his collar. "I do find the heat to be bothersome. Maybe I need a bit of lemonade myself." He turned on his heels and headed straight to Anne.

As he approached, she looked his way and her smile broadened. He loved having that effect on her. If drawing closer brought such a lovely smile, he'd have to go away and come back over and over again.

Emily's voice resonated from the porch steps, distracting him. Jake turned to see what all the fuss was about.

"You have to do what I say," Emily hollered at young William. "I'm the boss."

"Why are you the boss?" William put his hands on his hips and glared at her.

"Because I'm the oldest!" Emily yelled in response.

Jake sighed. How many times had he heard that logic from his older brothers? He'd been bossed around hundreds—no, thousands—of times. And he'd taken it without a fight.

Still, today, as he watched Emily slide into the position of natural-born leader, he couldn't help but smile at her ability to whip young Willy into shape. That youngster needed to be whipped into shape. He was too much like his father already, with his bullying ways.

Yes, perhaps a thrashing from a girl in a green cotton dress would be just the ticket to take him down a notch or two. And while that was happening, Jake would distract himself by offering a certain beautiful lady a cup of cold punch. Hopefully she wouldn't turn him down.

Chapter Nine

....

*We've all heard the adage that one rotten apple can spoil
the whole bunch. The same is true with people. One sour old
codger can ruin a perfectly good family function. But here
in the Texas Panhandle, we work hard to turn sour apples
into tasty pies or hot apple cider. In other words, we do our
best to live with even those who are as stubborn as mules.
Perhaps our years in working the land have taught us to be
more patient. Or maybe we're just friendlier because of our
peaceful surroundings. Sure, there will always be folks with
bitter dispositions. Maybe you've had a neighbor or two like
that. But here in Texas, we're quick to turn the other cheek.
A-course, if that doesn't work, we give those sour old souls
a swift kick in the backside and send 'em packing.* —"Tex"
Morgan, reporting for the *Panhandle Primer*

When the church social came to an end, Emily and Kate laughed
and talked all the way back to O'Farrell's Honor. Anne wanted to
join in the fun but found herself completely exhausted. She couldn't
stop yawning. Must have something to do with her lack of sleep last
night. Well, that and the scrumptious food Maggie had served up
for lunch. Nothing like a full belly to cause one to long for her pillow.

"Looks like someone needs a nap when we get home," Maggie

said. "Sounds good." She covered her mouth as she echoed Anne's yawn. "I could use a little catnap myself. Let's all make a pact that we won't get out of bed until we've slept a couple of hours. Agreed?"

"But I don't want to sleep. I want to see the ranch." Kate pouted.

"Me too," Emily said. "I need to go exploring."

"I'll tell you what...." Jake leaned forward, looking back and forth between the girls. "Let's let the other ladies sleep and I'll give you a tour of the property. How does that sound?"

"Wonderful!" Emily clasped her hands together. "Can I bring my writing tablet?"

"Of course."

"Are you sure you can handle these two alone?" Anne asked.

"I think so." He gave her a playful wink, which caused her heart to flutter. Hmm. Suddenly she didn't feel like taking a nap at all. Maybe she could explore the ranch with her younger sisters and Jake.

No, the more she thought about it, the more she realized she needed her beauty sleep. When they arrived at the house, Anne made her way to her bedroom, changed into her nightgown, and collapsed into bed. When she awoke, shimmers of red and orange danced through the window. Had she really slept that long? She rose and listened at the door to see if she could hear any noise from beyond it. Yes. Kate's giggles, coming from the parlor, along with Jake's happy-go-lucky voice, singing some sort of song.

And the smells! Mmm. What was that? Smelled like roasted chicken. Anne quickly changed into a dress, paused to glance at her reflection in the mirror, then pulled her hair up. She tried to fuss with it a bit longer than usual to get it to look more sophisticated—like Amaryllis's—but in the end, she let the long black locks flow freely. Maybe tomorrow she could take care of it.

She entered the parlor, and Jake looked her way. Anne couldn't help but notice his smile as he took her in. "Well, hello, sleepyhead!"

"Annie, you're up!" Kate rose and rushed her way. "Jake's been entertaining me with songs while Emily writes her story."

"Did you nap at all?" Anne asked, running her fingers through Kate's messy hair.

"No, but I saw the goats...and some pigs and lots and lots and lots of cows. Oh, they were big, Annie. Great big cows with..." She looked at Jake. "Antlers?"

"Horns. They're called horns."

"Horns." Kate beamed. "And some of the cows mooed at me. Really loud." Her eyes grew wide and she shivered. "I ran across the pasture and stepped in something stinky, so Jake made me wash my feet before coming in the house."

"Is that what I smell?" Anne laughed and glanced down at her sister's bare feet. "I thought for a minute there I was imagining something."

"No, it's not your imagination." Jake chuckled. "But that reminds me—we left her shoes to air out on the fence. I'll go see if they're dry."

"Gracious. Have I really been sleeping long enough for her shoes to dry?" Anne shook her head.

"You have." His beautiful eyes locked onto hers. "We were starting to think you were going to sleep clean through the night. Glad you didn't." He gave her a little wink and her heart fluttered again.

"Me—me too."

Jake flashed one last glance her way before heading to the door. Anne settled on the sofa next to Kate. "So, you had a good afternoon?"

"Mm-hmm. It's so fun here, Annie. I ran and ran and ran. And Emily got a thousand ideas for her story. You should have heard her talking about it. She's so funny."

"No doubt." Anne leaned back against the sofa. "Tell me all about it."

Kate proceeded to do just that, but in the middle of her humorous tale a knock sounded at the door.

"Would someone get that, please?" Maggie's voice sounded from the kitchen. "I'm up to my eyeballs chopping onions and can't touch anything."

"I will," Anne quickly responded, rising and making her way to the door. As she pulled it open, her gaze fell on an unfamiliar couple around Maggie's age. The woman stood a bit taller than the man, though not in a stately way. She did have an air of superiority about her, though. The sour expression on the woman's face made Anne wonder if perhaps she'd been eating pickles. The man gave her a curt nod, introduced himself as Leo, and eased his way past her into the house, muttering something about needing a cup of coffee.

"So you're the interloper, then." The woman stared at Anne for a moment and then sighed. "I told Maggie that taking in vagabonds was a risk, but would she listen to me? No. Then again, she never listens to me."

Anne did her best not to respond to the woman's brusque words. Instead, she plastered on a smile and said, "Ah. You must be Maggie's sister. Nice to meet you."

"Humph. Wish I could say the same. I'll let you know right off the bat that I don't believe you should be here, and I plan to tell Maggie so, just as soon as I can grab her by the ear."

"Oh, well, I…" How did one go about responding to something

so awful? Anne felt the sting of tears in her eyes but willed herself not to let this awful woman see that she'd been hurt by her words.

"That sister of mine rarely takes my advice. But then again, she was always this way, even as a child." Bets pursed her lips.

Maggie entered the room, wiping her hands on her apron. "I was always *what* way, Betsy Ann? Happy-go-lucky and carefree?"

"You know what I mean." The woman crossed her arms at her chest. "Stubborn and headstrong. And you've never changed. Not one iota."

"What's the point in changing when you're so near to perfect as you already are?" Maggie popped the woman on the bottom, causing her to gasp.

"Maggie, how dare you…"

"Stop being such a sour old thing, Bets." Maggie laughed, and then her expression grew more serious. "It doesn't sit well on you."

Thankfully Jake entered the room then, distracting them all. Even more distracting was the smell of the shoes in his hand.

"What is that offensive odor?" Bets pinched her nose and began to fan herself with her hand. She glanced at the shoes and clucked her tongue. "Honestly. This is the price you pay for having youngsters around. They're dirty."

"No, it's the cow's fault!" Kate walked straight up to Bets with an angry look on her face. "I'm not dirty."

"You're a child. That's all I have to say about it." Bets's icy look drove Kate to hide behind Anne's skirts and sent a shiver across the room. Anne could almost feel it.

"We missed you at church this morning, Aunt Bets," Jake said. He leaned over and gave her a kiss on the cheek, dangling the shoes a bit too close to her face for her liking. She slapped them away.

"Humph." She dropped down onto the sofa. "I woke up with a

headache. Likely because your uncle Leo snored all night long. He's going to be the death of me yet."

Leo rolled his eyes. "Got any coffee in that kitchen of yours, Maggie?"

"You know I do. Go on in and fetch yourself a cup."

He disappeared into the kitchen, muttering all the way.

"Please put those disgusting shoes out in the yard," Bets instructed. "Likely they will have to be buried."

"You're going to bury my shoes?"

"You can put them next to Kate's dolls," Emily said, entering the parlor from the hallway. "I buried two of them in the yard this afternoon."

"You buried your dolls?" Bets began to fan herself again then looked Maggie's way. "What sort of evil child is this?"

"The sort who delights in mischief." Maggie giggled. "In other words, she's my kind of girl."

"Whyever would she bury her sister's dolls in the yard?" Bets asked.

"Kate said I could," Emily explained. She dove into a nonsensical explanation of why she'd buried the dolls, but Bets wouldn't have it. She waved her hands in the air.

"Enough. This is all wearing on my nerves." She rested against the arm of the sofa and continued fanning herself. "Thank goodness I never had to deal with any children of my own. The good Lord knew I couldn't take it."

"I see." Emily sat on the sofa next to her—a little too close, apparently.

Bets turned and stared down her nose at her. "Well?"

"Well, what?"

"What are you staring at?"

"Oh." Emily shrugged. "I'm memorizing your features so I can use you as a character in my book. I've been looking for someone just like you to add to my story. This is going to be perfect. Just the ticket."

"Well, for once I hear something sensible come out of your mouth. I should very much like to be used as a heroine in a story."

"Oh, I'm not needing a heroine. I'm thinking of turning you into a villainous bank robber. With that tight gray bun and all those wrinkles, no one would ever suspect you. You could rob banks all over the country and never go to prison for it."

"Merciful heavens." Bets paled.

"It's going to be great," Emily said. She moved closer to Bets, her gaze narrowing. "Do you pack a gun, by chance?"

Everyone in the room erupted in laughter.

"Well, I like that," Bets said when the laughter ended. "Now I'm the brunt of a joke. You are a vicious little thing."

"You think?" Emily looked at the older woman with a delighted smile. "Thank you very much."

Anne sighed.

Maggie turned her attention to her sister. "We were concerned when we didn't see you in church this morning. The reverend and his wife asked about you, of course. They wanted me to let you know they're praying for you."

"The reverend would be better served asking his wife to tone down the loud piano playing in church. Her banging on the keys must hurt the Lord's ears. Just one more reason why I couldn't stomach going this morning. So much racket. Affects my nerves."

Maggie gave her a sympathetic look. "I really wish you had a telephone so I could check on you in situations like that. Things would be so much easier."

Bets ran her hands across her lap, smoothing out her skirt. "If I've told you once, I've told you a thousand times—I'm not going to have that noisy contraption in my home. I like my peace and quiet."

Anne caught a glimpse of Leo as he entered the room with a cup of coffee. He released a sigh as he settled into the wooden rocker.

"I just don't understand the logic of having a telephone in the first place." Bets began to fan herself once more. "What's so urgent that you have to find out about it right away? Honestly, you must feel you're better than your neighbors. Putting on airs."

If anyone appeared to be putting on airs, it certainly wasn't Maggie, though Anne would never say so.

Maggie paused, counting to ten in a soft whisper. "Bets, make yourself at home," she said at last. "Have a cup of coffee while Anne and I finish making supper."

"I'm glad to see you've put that girl to work." Bets glared at Anne. "The little wayfarer needs to earn her keep. I can't imagine what made you think it would be all right to bring total strangers into your home. For all you know, she could rob you blind while you're sleeping. Have you hidden the good silver?"

"Aunt Bets!" This time it was Jake who came to the defense.

Anne bit her lip to keep from spouting off the words that wanted to come out. How dare that awful woman say such a thing! Anne turned on her heel and stormed into the kitchen.

Jake followed behind her. "Anne, I'm so sorry. You can't listen to anything she says. She's just a sour old woman who…" He shrugged. "Who knows how to ruin what started out to be a great day."

Maggie arrived in the kitchen shortly thereafter. She patted her unruly hair. "Anne, don't pay any mind to Bets. Her bark is worse than her bite."

"Well, her bark is certainly something to behold." Anne paused and put her hands on the counter. Leaning forward, she drew in a deep breath and tried to regain her composure. "I feel like I've been assaulted. Maybe Emily was right. There do seem to be ruffians and renegades in this part of the country."

Maggie erupted in laughter at this. "That's a good one, Anne. You're right. My sister is a real pill. Don't know why she's always got her knickers in a knot. But I do know that somewhere, underneath that crusty exterior, lays a woman I love." She reached for her apron and lifted it to wipe the mist from her eyes. "Not saying she's easy. I'm just saying I've got to love her. The Bible says I have to." At this, Maggie started laughing again.

Before long, they were all chuckling. After a couple minutes, however, Bets's voice rang out from the parlor. "I wish you would hold it down in there. A body can only take so much racket."

Maggie put a finger to her lips, still giggling in silence. Anne couldn't help but join in. Oh, what a fun way to deal with such an unlovely person.

Maggie finally got herself under control and fixed a tray of cookies.

"Jakey, do me a favor and take this tray of snickerdoodles out to your aunt and uncle. We'll be out shortly."

"She won't eat them," he said. "She never eats sweets before a meal."

"I know she'll fuss about it, but Leo will eat them. And from the looks of that man, he hasn't had a decent meal in months. The least I can do is feed him so he has the strength to fight her off."

Jake chuckled as he took the tray then squared his shoulders and headed back into the parlor.

"That's my boy. Always willing to go the extra mile for people." Maggie gave Anne a knowing look. "A gentleman all the way."

Anne's gaze shifted to the ground so that Maggie wouldn't see the unavoidable smile. "Well, Bets's husband seems like a fine man."

"I've never really understood their relationship. And it's true she wears the pants in that family." Maggie eased her ample frame into a chair at the table. "It wasn't always that way, honey. They were young once. In fact, there was a time they made a really handsome couple. Bets was always a pretty girl."

"Really?"

"Yes, before the bitterness took hold. Lots of fellas were drawn to her back in the day. Why, she was as pretty as you are."

Anne felt her cheeks turn warm. "I've never considered myself pretty. Not even close."

"Oh, but you are. And I'm sure lots of fellas have given you a second glance. And a third. And a fourth."

Anne's heart twisted as the words were spoken. They brought back memories that she didn't care to relive.

"Oh, I've struck a chord with those words, haven't I?" Maggie rose and placed her hand on Anne's arm. "Have I said something I shouldn't?"

Anne paused for a moment, unsure of how much to share. She finally managed the words, "I almost had a beau once."

"Almost?" Maggie sighed. "Was it unrequited love?"

"No, he genuinely cared for me." The twisting sensation in her chest escalated, making it difficult to breathe.

"What happened...if you don't mind my asking?"

"He had aspirations of moving up in his father's business, and he..." Anne realized she'd started a story that she simply couldn't finish. Not without betraying her father's problems. How could she go about sharing that the man she thought she'd one day marry had left because he'd found out her father was a gambler? That his parents didn't see her as a fit bride-to-be because of her father's shame?

"Honey, are you all right?" Maggie gave her a curious look.

"Oh, yes. I...well, let's just say that it didn't work out."

"Well then, all I can say is that the Lord must've prevented you from a life of misery. I've always said it's better to remain unmarried than to marry the wrong person."

"Like Aunt Bets and Uncle Leo?" Anne asked. "Is that what made her so bitter? She married the wrong man?"

"Oh, honey, I don't think so. Not really. Like I said, there was a time—years ago—when they went together like bread and jam." Maggie rose and attended to her cooking once more. "Only problem is, they're both stubborn old fools. Neither wants to admit the other is right, no matter the situation. It's just pure selfishness."

"But they're still a match made in heaven?"

"More likely made somewhere else," Emily's voice chimed in. Anne turned to see both of her sisters now standing in the kitchen.

"I'm not sure that's the case, either," Maggie said.

"But Maggie!" Emily spoke in an exaggerated tone. "Your sister is really mean."

"I know, honey."

The incredulous look on Emily's face shared her thoughts on the matter. "She's a textbook villain. Beady eyes and everything. And have you ever seen such a long nose? I do have to wonder if she and Uncle Bertrand might be twins. Perhaps they were separated at birth and raised in different states. Or maybe…" She snapped her fingers. "Maybe they were raised in a carnival, and when they got old, they parted ways so that no one would figure out their secret."

Anne grabbed Emily's arm and shushed her. "Honestly, how you do go on. You shouldn't talk about people like that."

"How can I help it? Right after you left the room, she called me an orphan train child." Emily's face grew tight, and the wrinkles between her eyes deepened. "I wanted to double up my fist and take her down, but figured I'd leave it to her husband. He looked pretty mad at her too."

"Good gracious." Anne fanned herself. "See what you've done?"

Maggie stroked Emily's hair. "Honey, I apologize for Bets. She's a real pill, one I have to swallow regularly. But she's my sister, and there's only so long you can avoid your own family." Maggie shrugged. "Anyway, let's finish cooking this meal. Hopefully it will serve as a lovely distraction." At that proclamation, all the girls went to work preparing a tasty meal. Likely it would be the only easy thing to swallow tonight.

＊ ＊ ＊ ＊ ＊

Jake entered the kitchen, still shaken from the awful words his aunt had spoken to Anne a few minutes earlier.

"Everyone all right in here?"

Emily looked his way. "As all right as one can be after being brutally attacked with words." She pouted. "But don't worry. I'm plotting my revenge. This story will have a proper ending."

"Proper in whose eyes?" Anne leaned down to look her sister

in the eye. "Honey, I know you're angry. I am too. But we need to extend God's grace to her. That's the only way to win her over."

That's right." Jake drew near. "I've learned that the only way to deal with Bets when she's like this is to get her talking about something else—to distract her. And along the way, God gives me plenty of opportunities to extend grace."

"You go right ahead and offer grace. I'll be in my bedroom, looking for another doll to name after her. Then I'm going to bury it in the backyard." Emily marched out of the room and let the door slam behind her.

Jake couldn't help but notice the sad expression on Anne's face. "Are you all right?"

"I will be."

He rested his hand on her arm to offer comfort. "If it makes you feel any better, she's like that to everyone, not just you."

"Though she did go out of her way to make you feel unwelcome," Maggie said, "and I'm awfully sorry about that."

"And *I'm* sorry about Emily. Sometimes I think she's almost as hard-hearted as...well, as someone like Bets."

"Don't be too quick to fret over your little sister. Children are resilient. Besides, I love her just like she is. Emily is a keen and honest observer of the world around her. Now that she's discovered O'Farrell's Honor, she's in a place where there are discoveries to be made every day—good and bad." Maggie smiled. "Besides, she reminds me of myself as a youngster. I like a sweet girl same as everyone else, but give her a little sass. She has an adventurous spirit."

"She does at that." Jake paused to think about that. "I think we all have a lot to learn from her. I know I do, anyway. She's able to speak her mind better than most."

"You can say that again." Anne sighed.

Jake leaned her way and smiled. "She's able to speak her mind better than most."

Anne turned, eyes wide, and he found himself face-to-face with her. What a fabulous predicament. For a moment he thought she might lean back. Instead, the edges of those beautiful lips turned up in a delicious grin.

"What do you say we get back in there and pour a little sugar and cream into Bets's tea?" His mother's voice interrupted the moment.

Jake startled to attention. "But she doesn't take sugar and cream in her tea."

"Exactly. I wasn't referring to the real thing. Just a touch of grace, my child. Just a touch of grace."

He wanted to respond but found himself captivated by Anne's beautiful smile. He didn't have to go into the parlor to find a touch of grace. Why, he was staring it in the face right now.

GROOM
1914
TX

Chapter Ten

....

There's an old saying about the moon—that when it soars clear and bright, completely free of shadows or clouds, it's known as a lover's moon. Just one large ball of yellow-white, cradled by a perfect night sky. Here in the Texas Panhandle, we see some of the prettiest lover's moons imaginable. They glow like heavenly orbs, lighting up the night skies and offering a well-lit path into the arms of the one you love. Truly, there's no better place to get moony-eyed than under a lover's moon. So if you're gazing at one tonight, why not grab your lady and let the moonlight lead the way? —"Tex" Morgan, reporting for the *Panhandle Primer*

The night wore on, with Aunt Bets in rare fashion. Jake could only stand so much of her chronic complaining before he finally had to take his leave. He used the animals as his excuse but decided—after feeding them—that an evening walk would be just the thing to clear his head. The night skies shone clear and bright and the moon hovered overhead, a large white ball casting plenty of light across the property.

He headed out to the barn to check on Frances, giving her one last brushing and a gentle talking-to. Then he headed out across the field, following the fence line. He paused on several occasions to gaze heavenward and, as he often did, usher up a few heartfelt prayers. Tonight he had one thing on his mind in particular. His aunt's behavior had really upset him, and the feelings he harbored inside needed to be dealt with.

"Lord, I know You created her in Your image, but…" He sighed, unsure of what to say next. "Just show us how to deal with her." An unsettled feeling came over him as he realized how those words must sound. "No, show us how to love her like You love her." The words to a familiar hymn flitted through his mind, and Jake found himself humming as he headed back to the house.

When he arrived at the steps leading up to the front porch, he noticed Anne seated on the porch swing with Kate sleeping in her lap. He spoke a quiet "hello," and Anne let out a little gasp.

"Oh, Jake! You scared me."

"I'm sorry. Sure didn't mean to do that." He climbed the steps and leaned against the post, observing her face under the glow of the full moon. She'd been pretty enough in the daylight, of course. But something about the glow of the moon gave her an ethereal quality.

She laughed. "Mama always called me skittish. Guess it's true."

He gestured to the empty spot next to her. "Do you mind?"

"Of course not. I would move over a bit, but…" She gestured to Kate, who continued to sleep soundly.

"No need." Truth be told, he liked the fact that the spot next to her wasn't very big. Jake eased his way down onto the swing then shifted his gaze to the skies. "Didn't mean to interrupt your moonlight reverie."

"Moonlight reverie." She chuckled. "Have you been taking notes from Emily? That sounds like something she would say."

"No." He paused for a moment, his gaze still heavenward. "I suppose there's a bit of a writer in me too. I used to love to listen to my father's poems as he read them aloud. There's something so majestic about the written word. Just…" He turned to her and shrugged. "Sorry. You probably didn't take me for the bookish sort."

"I daresay I don't know you well enough to assume what sort of things you might enjoy."

No, she didn't know him at all, did she? But he would surely like to remedy that.

"I can't believe how big and bright that moon is tonight." She lifted her thumb and closed one eye, as if trying to block it out.

"That's funny."

"What?"

"I used to do that too." He settled back against the swing. "I've always figured that if you could block something as big as the moon with just a finger, then getting over life's problems shouldn't be much of a hurdle."

"Interesting way of looking at it. I'll have to remember that."

They sat in delicious silence for a moment. Jake relaxed, enjoying the glow of moonlight because it afforded him the opportunity to sneak a peek at Anne every now and again.

"So, are Bets and Leo still inside?" he asked at last.

Anne nodded. "Yes." She sighed. "Last I heard, she was telling him how the cow ate the cabbage. Poor dear soul. He just sat there, taking it from her. But your mama gave her a bit of correction. Not sure Bets took it well, but it did end the argument."

"God bless my mama. She knows just how to deal with the tough ones."

"I admire her for that. Despite my Christian upbringing, I feel my hand begin to twitch every time someone like Bets enters the room. I just want to…" She chuckled. "This is going to sound awful, but I just want to knock some sense into them."

Jake laughed. "Good thing you resisted the urge. I have a feeling Aunt Bets could take you down. There's a lot of strength behind those ugly words she uses."

"Oh, I don't know. I tend to think she's driven by weakness, not strength."

The front door flew open and Emily rushed past them.

"Emily, it's late," Anne called out. "I thought you were nearly ready to go to bed."

"I was, but I forgot something," Emily hollered. "I took my writing tablet out under the tree this afternoon while I was burying the dolls, and I left it there. I'll just die if I lose it." She ran like a banshee across the lawn then returned a few moments later, gasping for breath.

"So you found it, then?" Jake pointed to the tablet in her hand.

"Yes. Oh, I don't know what I would've done if I'd lost it. I'd have to reconstruct my story, and that would have been tragic. Now that Aunt Bets is here, I have a great new character to add. You're not going to believe what twists and turns my story is about to take."

"I can only imagine." Jake chuckled and tried to picture the look on his aunt's face should she read about herself in a book. Then again, she probably wouldn't recognize herself as being evil. Most folks in her position didn't.

"Well, I'm glad you found it." Anne gave Emily a stern look. "Now head inside and get dressed for bed. I'll bring Kate in momentarily."

"Sure you will." Emily looked back and forth between Jake and Anne then laughed. "You'll be out here all night long…swooning."

"Emily Denning!" The shock in Anne's voice was evident.

Jake did his best to hide the laughter that threatened to erupt.

Emily disappeared into the house, the door slamming behind her.

"Jake, I'm so sorry." Anne sighed. "I honestly don't know what to do with her. She's always making more out of things than she should."

"She's an observer of life," Jake said. "Adding a little color and shine to the dull parts." Not that sitting here with Anne was a dull part.

"I will say, she notices everything."

"Oh?"

"Yes. Even as a little bitty thing, she always seemed to know when Mama was upset about something. And when she got sick—Mama, I mean—Emily seemed to know it. Mind you, she was quite young at the time."

"I see. And now that she's older, she takes what she sees and turns it into stories?"

"Well, let's just say she takes what she sees, embellishes it, and writes it into stories." Anne laughed. "So you'd better beware if she happens to tell you that you're going to be the hero in her next tale."

"Oops." He laughed. "Too late."

"No doubt she'll either turn you into a pirate or a renegade of some sort. She's got quite the imagination."

"An imagination is a good thing." His smile quickly faded.

"What's wrong?"

She placed her hand on his arm, and his heart skipped a beat. Still, how much could he tell her without giving away too much of his personal story? He didn't want her to know that more often than not, he served as the brunt of everyone's joke.

Jake shook his head. "I was that boy who always got accused of being a dreamer. My brothers never thought I'd amount to much. Said I had an overactive imagination." He paused, deep in thought. "That imagination got me through some rough times, though. No doubt it's the same for Emily."

"She's been through some rough times all right. More than any ten-year-old should ever have to go through."

"I feel her pain. But she's handling it pretty well, I guess."

"It comes out in those stories of hers."

Jake thought about his words before voicing them. "Some people act out their pain—like Aunt Bets. Other people transfer it to the written page. I'm not sure which is the better answer."

"I suppose the better answer is to let God have it." Anne sighed. "It's just hard. Really hard."

"I understand. More than you know."

He understood something else too. That when you stared at a girl in the moonlight—even a girl you'd only just gotten to know—it did something to your heart, something he'd never before experienced.

Oh, if only this lover's moon could last forever.

* * * * *

Anne rested against the back of the swing, content and peaceful. How she enjoyed these quiet conversations with Jake. He seemed to understand her in a way that others did not. How could such a thing be possible with someone she'd only known for a couple of days? The moon cast a heavenly glow and she stared up at it, for once completely at peace.

Until the front door opened and Aunt Bets bolted out of the house.

"Just see if I ever set foot in your house again, Maggie O'Farrell," Bets called out. "I will not be spoken to in such a way by my own sister." She turned and glared at Anne. "It would seem she treats total strangers better than she does her own family."

Anne sat in shocked silence, unable to think of a response. Jake reached for her hand and squeezed it, letting her know his take on the matter.

"Aunt Bets, Mama is likely exhausted after a long day," he said after a moment. "Come back tomorrow and everything will be better."

"I will not come back tomorrow," she said, placing her hands on her hips. "Or the day after that, or the day after that. I will not come back until she offers the necessary apology."

Jake sighed.

So did Uncle Leo, who stood in the doorway. "Bets, we're going home." His voice spoke of weariness. "I've had enough."

"Humph." Bets grabbed her skirt with both fists and shuffled down the porch steps. Then she and Leo disappeared into the darkness.

Anne wanted to speak but only found tears. How dare that spiteful woman lash out at her? Why, they hardly knew each other. What about offering the benefit of the doubt?

The tears came with abandon. She cried—not just because of the harsh words that had been spoken, but because of the situation she now found herself in. Oh, how she longed for life to go back to normal, for peace to reign.

After a few moments, the tears dried up. Only then did Anne realize that Jake was still holding her hand. Embarrassment swept over her. "Oh, I–I'm so sorry."

"Don't be." He laced his fingers through hers. "If anyone deserves a good cry, you do. And trust me, I needed the time to pray."

"To pray?" She looked his way, brushing aside the tears on her cheeks.

"Yes. To pray that God would restrain me from taking off after her and giving her a piece of my mind."

"You would do that for me?"

"Of course." Jake gazed so deeply into her eyes that she almost felt he could read her thoughts. "You're one of the sweetest girls I've ever met."

"Th–thank you." She couldn't help but smile at those words. They served as an ointment, soothing her troubled soul. Yes, he certainly knew just what to say to make a girl feel better about life.

The front door opened and Maggie stepped outside. Anne felt Jake's hand pull away from hers, and he stood.

"Is Bets gone, then?" Maggie crossed her arms at her chest.

"Yes, and she says she's never coming back."

"I'm not that lucky." Maggie sighed as she took a few steps across the porch. "I'm sorry. That was uncalled for. But she certainly challenges me at every turn. I honestly don't know what to do sometimes."

"Let's not let it ruin our night." Anne smiled at Maggie, her heart quite full. "In spite of the unpleasant outbursts, this has still been one of the loveliest days of my life. Being here in Groom…" A lump filled her throat, and she could not continue.

Kate stirred, and Anne eased her into a sitting position. She'd just started to stand and sweep her sister into her arms when Jake took care of that for her. As he carried Kate across the porch and into the house, Anne was struck with a mixture of pain and joy. How often had she seen Papa lift Kate and carry her to bed—before the drinking got so bad?

Don't think about the sadness, Anne. Only look at what's in front of you tonight.

What she saw tonight in the glow of the moonlight suddenly made the pain of her yesterdays drift far, far away.

Chapter Eleven

....

Want to view the latest fashions from the runways of Paris or nibble the tastiest hors d'oeuvres from the best French chefs? Looking for the most exquisite silver service or the finest cut-crystal for that next soiree? Look no further than the Texas Panhandle, where money—and good taste—abound! Rub elbows with silver barons at the opera, discuss the price of beef with millionaire cattlemen at glorious galas, or dine with well-to-do business owners at the finest restaurants. There's never a shortage of societal events here. Milliners from Manhattan, couture dressmakers from Paris, entertainers from around the globe...they're all headed to the Texas Panhandle. Why? They're following the scent of money, of course! —"Tex" Morgan, reporting for the *Panhandle Primer*

The next morning Jake left for work early. Anne busied herself around the house, trying to be useful. She made up the beds and tidied her sister's mess on the rolltop desk. Then she headed to the kitchen to help Maggie.

"So I see you met Virginia and her best friend yesterday," Maggie said. "Tell me what you think of them."

"Virginia reminds me a lot of myself."

"I was going to say the same thing. She's our schoolteacher, you know."

"Oh, is she? I wondered why she lived here alone."

"Yes, she lives in the house the school board provides. Though, of course, that will change once she and Cody get married. His parents left him a large spread on the west end of town."

"I see. Will she go on teaching?"

"Yes. I can't imagine anyone doing a finer job, and I know Cody won't mind if she continues working. She's a wonder with the children."

"I think it's admirable that she's given her life to that. She seems very levelheaded, and I enjoyed getting to know her."

"Now that Amaryllis is something to behold, isn't she?" Maggie began to chuckle. "In all my life I've never seen a dress like the one she wore yesterday. I'd fall flat on my face."

"So would I. If that's high fashion, I'll suppose I'll stick to what I'm already wearing."

"Oh, honey, I just love pretty things. They're wonderful to look at. But I made up my mind years ago that the loveliest things a woman could own were her words. They show off much nicer than a new dress." She winked. "Though I love a pretty dress too."

"Me too." *But those days are behind me.*

Knocking sounded at the door—a constant rapping that spoke of urgency.

"Gracious." Maggie fussed with her hair. "I look a mess. Hope it isn't the reverend or his wife, come to call unannounced."

Anne followed her into the parlor and on to the front door, where they found Milly, Pauline, Ruth, and Cora. The women offered a warm welcome as they entered the house.

"Well, hello, girls." Maggie gave each of them a hug. "What brings you out so early?"

"We need to talk to Anne." Milly drew near and slipped her arm over Anne's shoulders, making her wonder what they had up their sleeves. "It's very important."

"Yes, it couldn't wait," Cora said.

"Hmm. Well, don't you girls go and get her riled up about something, you hear?" Maggie disappeared into the kitchen, muttering something about female nonsense.

Anne looked at Milly. "What's happened? Something about the train? Has the track been repaired?"

"Gracious, no," Milly said. "At this rate, we're hoping the track won't be fixed anytime soon."

"And why is that?"

"Because..." Pauline began to chew the fingernail on her index finger. "We, um...we're worried about Jake."

"Worried about Jake. Why?"

"Well, see..." Ruth fidgeted with her necklace. "We might as well confess...we've been trying to match him up with Cassie Martin for the past several months. She's a dear girl, though a bit overbearing at times."

"Not that I blame her," Cora said. "She's inwardly insecure because she's a bit larger than most girls her age."

"She has a lovely face," Ruth said.

"Oh, yes, she does," Pauline added. "And very pretty eyes."

"But, see, here's the problem." Milly gazed directly into Anne's eyes. "She's got her heart set on marrying Jake."

Anne eased her way onto the sofa, completely perplexed. "And this is a problem because..."

Milly took her by the hand. "You don't know?"

"I don't. Why should I care who marries Jake?" Anne asked, feeling her heart begin to flutter.

"Come now." Milly laughed. "I know a girl who's smitten when I see one. And it's clear that Jake is equally as smitten with you."

"We've just come to admit the error in our ways," Cora said. "And to ask for your forgiveness. Of course, we can't really be held to blame because we'd never met you until Saturday night, but even so…"

"Ladies, let me put your minds at ease. My thoughts are on my sisters, nothing else."

Pauline coughed. "I see."

"And though your brother-in-law is handsome…" Her words drifted off as his beautiful eyes came to mind.

"He is handsome, isn't he?" Ruth said. "I've always told John that Jake shouldn't have any trouble finding a bride because he's really quite dashing. Not quite the physical size that John is, to be sure, but a fine man."

"With a fine character," Milly added. She giggled. "Joseph could take a few lessons in manners from him."

"And Jedediah could stand to act more gentlemanly. If he'd just follow Jake's example…," Pauline said.

Anne's thoughts tumbled in her mind. How could she possibly respond to all of this? Did these girls really think she'd set her mark on Jake O'Farrell as a potential mate? If so, she would put their minds at ease right away.

Well, right after pausing to think about those broad shoulders once more. And that boyish smile…and those dimples. Hmm. Maybe she would have to wait until tomorrow to plead her case.

Thankfully, another knock sounded at the door, bringing the perfect distraction.

"I'll get that," Maggie called out from the kitchen. Moments later, Virginia and Amaryllis appeared.

Virginia looked a mess—her face soaked with tears and her hair disheveled. Maggie ushered them into the parlor, clucking her tongue the whole way.

At once the ladies flew into action, consoling her. Of course, with everyone talking on top of one another, any true consolation went right out the window.

"What's happened, child?" Maggie slipped an arm over Virginia's shoulder. "Tell us."

"It's the worst possible news. I hope you don't mind that I came here first, but I really didn't know where else to turn." She looked around the room. "Oh, I'm so glad you're all here. I need friends at a time like this."

"What's the matter?" Ruth asked. "Did that Cody up and change his mind about getting married?"

"Heavens, no." Virginia looked stunned at this comment.

"Go ahead, child," Maggie said. "Tell us."

Virginia dried her eyes. "My parents were set to arrive today, but with the track out, their plans have been delayed. Now everything is ruined. I can't possibly get married without my mother and father here. I depend on Mama for everything."

"They can still take the train as far as Oklahoma City and then come by car the rest of the way," Pauline said.

Maggie brushed her hands through Virginia's hair. "See?"

"Yes, they've thought of that, but the soonest they can get to Oklahoma City is Wednesday, and it will take another day to drive here. If they're able to get a car. It's so…complicated." She dissolved into a puddle of tears, going on about how much she needed her mother now of all times.

Maggie shook her head. "This is such a pity. My James would have known just what to do. Why, he would've taken the company truck and gone to Oklahoma City himself."

"Without my mother here, you ladies are truly the only ones I can turn to." Virginia clasped Maggie's hands in her own. Virginia plopped down on the sofa next to Anne, her eyes filling with tears. "I'm at a complete loss."

"You have me," Amaryllis said with a forced smile.

Apparently those words brought Virginia little comfort. She simply shook her head and turned back to Maggie, who fanned herself with her hand.

"I still plan to bake the cake, of course," Maggie said. "It's going to be so tasty."

"And I'll help with anything you like," Pauline said.

"I'm putting the finishing touches on your veil this afternoon," Milly said.

"You know I'm ready to help with whatever you need," Cora said.

"Me too," Ruth echoed. "Though I'm not very good with a needle and thread, as most of you are aware."

"I'm grateful to all of you, and the things you're doing are wonderful," Virginia said. "But my real concern is the planning and decorating of it all. Mama is so good at putting together big soirees. She could pull off a wedding in her sleep. I know that each of you ladies can help with the different elements, and I'm so grateful, but Mama is the one who has the gift of pulling it all together into one exquisite event."

Anne reached to take Virginia's hand. "Could I be of any help?"

"How do you mean?" Virginia looked her way.

"Back in Denver, I was quite active with several major charities. We hosted many large social events. And I often helped my father put together dinner parties to entertain his clients. Ever since my mother died..." She swallowed the lump in her throat and kept on. "I've been the one folks have looked to, to host events. There's no modest way to say this, but I've been told I excel at playing the role of coordinator."

"You do?"

"Yes." She nodded. "And as you've been sharing about the wedding plans, a thousand ideas have come to me. I don't want to push them on you, but if you're willing to hear them, I'd be happy to share what I'm thinking."

Virginia squeezed her hand. "Oh, Anne, I can't believe it. You're such an answer to prayer."

Off in the distance, Amaryllis rolled her eyes. The other ladies, however, seemed to find great joy in it.

Milly reached for pen and paper. "Tell us what you're thinking."

"Yes, don't leave out a thing," Virginia echoed.

Anne proceeded to do just that. She shared her thought about a garden-party extravaganza. "As you were speaking, in my mind's eye I saw a beautiful springtime gala built around flowers," she explained. "The little finger sandwiches were cut into flower shapes—even the vegetables were cut to look like flowers. The whole thing was exquisite."

"Oh, it sounds even prettier than my wedding," Milly said.

"And I can see the inside of the church now," Anne said. "We can make long garlands using local flowers. Those will be useful to us in a number of places inside the church and out. I'm assuming you'll be hosting a reception outdoors after the ceremony?"

"Yes, that's right," Virginia said. "And I adore your ideas. They're perfect." The now-happy bride-to-be rose and practically floated across the room. "Oh, Anne, I feel as if a weight has been lifted from my shoulders. You're a miracle worker. Truly."

Amaryllis cleared her throat, and Virginia reached to take her hand. "Oh, I haven't forgotten you, my dear friend. You'll be front and center in all this, dressed in a gown that's sure to catch a certain young man's eye."

At this, Milly, Pauline, Cora, and Ruth grew silent. Their gazes shifted back and forth between Amaryllis and Anne.

"Hmm." Milly rose. "Well, I suppose we'd better stay focused on the wedding."

"Yes, it's going to be spectacular," Maggie added.

Anne released a slow breath, hating to disappoint. "There's only one small catch."

Virginia's smile faded. "What's that?"

"If the railroad gets that track fixed, I won't actually be here on the afternoon of your wedding. That might be problematic." She paused to think. "Oh, but I can write everything down and delegate. Each of these wonderful ladies can take something from the list and carry it out. What do you think?"

"I suppose that might work in a pinch." Virginia paced the room and finally turned and snapped her fingers. "But I have a much better solution. It's so simple, really."

"What's that?"

"Even when the track is fixed, you don't have to board the train. You and your sisters can stay on through the weekend and attend the wedding as my guests. There will always be time to catch another train to Dallas."

"But Maggie—"

"I would be thrilled to let you stay a bit longer." Maggie's voice sounded from behind Anne. "Oh, honey, it's the perfect solution. I'd get a few extra days with you, and you would be such a blessing to Virginia. I know how much she's needing your help right now. I can bake a cake and prepare food, but I know very little about decorating and such. You've got the experience, honey, and that's what we need right now—experience."

"And remember, Mama will be here a day or two before the wedding." Virginia reached for her mother's letter. "So all is not lost. Papa can give me away as planned. Mama can help with my hair and final details. But if you could stay and implement those wonderful plans—oh, Anne! I'd be so grateful."

The ladies began to talk at once, their voices overlapping.

Anne drew in a deep breath before answering. What would Uncle Bertrand have to say? He expected his nieces to arrive in Dallas as soon as the repairs took place. "There are a few details to iron out," she said. "But I will do my best. In the meantime, we have to talk about your bridal bouquet. What flowers have you chosen?"

"Of course I'd hoped to use roses," Virginia said. "But they're hard to come by in this area, so perhaps I'll have to rethink that. I do love this garden-party idea so much. Maybe you have an idea for something really colorful?"

"I do. And I went to a particularly beautiful wedding in Denver where the chef created colorful flowers out of gum paste to put on the cake. They looked so real, you could practically smell them."

"I've only ever seen a white wedding cake," Amaryllis said. "Solid white, I mean."

"Me too," Virginia said. "But I know Maggie could pull it off." She turned to face her. "Can't you, Maggie?"

"I'll do my best, child. I can't say that I know what gum paste is, but if I can find some, I'll do my best to shape it into something that looks like flowers."

"Oh, and here's an idea," Anne continued. "If you do more than one level of cake, each one can be a different flavor. Maybe one can be white. Maybe another could be lemon with raspberry jam for filling. Another could be chocolate."

"Oh, stop!" Virginia rubbed her stomach. "You're making me hungry."

"Well, no one ever goes hungry in my house, honey," Maggie said. "Follow me to the kitchen and I'll whip up something to fill that stomach for you." She led the way to the kitchen and the girls followed, teeming with ideas. Anne lagged behind, whispering up a little prayer. Now that she'd laid out these ideas, she only hoped they could be pulled off.

* * * * *

Jake paused to wipe the sweat out of his eyes. In the hours since arriving at the section of broken track, he'd worked until his back ached. The job foreman hollered out additional instructions and Jake complied, though he felt himself torn. The sooner they got this job completed, the sooner Anne would board that train to Dallas. For whatever reason, a strange twisting sensation grabbed hold of his heart when he thought about her leaving.

"You all right over there, Jake?" Cody looked his way, eyes narrowed. "Seem awfully deep in thought."

"Guess so." He pulled on his gloves and reached down to help Cody lift a piece of broken track. Together they began to haul it toward the company wagon. "Just got a lot on my mind."

"I only know one thing that'd make a fella look so pensive."

Cody paused to shift his weight. "You've set your sights on a pretty woman."

Jake wanted to deny it but couldn't. He sucked in some air then started walking once more.

"Can't say I blame you. She's a right pretty girl."

"She is, for sure."

"Even if she has a strange way of talking."

"Wait—who are we talking about here?" As Jake reached the wagon, he swung his end of the track over the edge and released it.

"Well, Amaryllis, of course." Cody let go of his end of the track, and it fell to the pile of rubble below. "Isn't that who you..." He crossed his arms at his chest and stared at Jake. "Oh, I see how it is. My fiancée brings you a beautiful distraction from the East, but you've been waylaid by a pretty distraction from the West. That how it goes?"

Jake didn't want to admit it, but how could he deny it now? So he muttered a quiet "yeah" and hoped his best friend would drop the matter altogether.

No such luck. Cody brushed the dust from his gloves and gave him a crooked grin. He slapped Jake on the back. "Can't say I blame you. But let's don't tell Virginia just yet, shall we? We want to keep her—and Amaryllis—happy for a few more days."

"If I were you, I'd start thinking of ways to keep Virginia happy for a few more years, not days." Jake gulped, realizing how his words might be taken. "I mean...well, you know..."

"Yes, I do, and I plan to make her the happiest bride in Carson County for years to come. But let's go back to talking about Anne. She's caught your eye, eh?"

Off in the distance several other men took a break to eat lunch.

Jake and Cody joined them, but Jake couldn't seem to stop the thoughts from tumbling around as he bit into his sandwich.

"Doesn't make a lick of sense to let my mind go there," he said after a couple of minutes. "She's leaving in a few days—as soon as we get this track fixed. Then what would happen? We'd both be miserable. If she were to like me back, I mean."

"Hmm." Cody grinned and waggled his brows. "What say we come back to the track in the wee hours of the night and undo all the work we do today?"

Jake chuckled. "I don't want to manipulate God's plan. If this is God's plan, I mean. Could be she's just a lovely distraction from the West, as you said. And we know she's only stopping through on her way to someplace else. But I can't help but wonder…"

"If that train landed her on your doorstep for a reason?" Cody gave him a pensive look.

"Yes. I don't really believe in coincidence, but this is pretty unusual. Of all the places she could land…"

"She tumbles into the one place in Carson County with the only single fella in town. Is that what you were going to say?" Cody slapped his knee and started laughing. Several of the other men followed suit, and before long, Jake was again the brunt of several jokes.

Wonderful. Just what he needed.

Still, as the laughter rang out around him, Jake's thoughts gravitated to the one thing—er, person—who could make all of the teasing worthwhile.

Hmm. Maybe he *should* come back tonight and pull the track to pieces. Then, perhaps, she could stay on until his heart and mind came into alignment. In the meantime, he'd just go on daydreaming about the possibilities. Even if it meant being ribbed by the fellas.

GROOM 1914 TX

Chapter Twelve

....

The Texas Panhandle was once the place for shoot-outs and cattle rustling. These days, Panhandle residents tend to be kinder and more even-keeled. Likely this is due to the influx of so many local churches and the message they offer. We are known as the Wild West no more. Folks now tip their hats at one another and offer a gracious "God bless you" when you pass by. "Turn the other cheek" is the motto of the day. If your neighbor gets you riled up, forgive him. If your brother knocks you upside the head, turn and let him smack you on the other side. I must confess, this is a new idea to me, but I'm workin' on it. My wife tells me I should. —"Tex" Morgan, reporting for the *Panhandle Primer*

Anne walked out onto the front porch and smiled when she saw Maggie seated on the swing, snapping beans.

"Need some help?"

"Of course. Come and sit by me, honey."

Anne took a spot on the swing and grabbed a handful of the string beans. As she snapped, she pushed back a memory of helping her mother with this very chore as a little girl.

"I've noticed your cross, Anne," Maggie said. "It's so pretty."

"Ah." She paused and took hold of it. "It was my mother's. She wore it every day."

"Well, it's a lovely piece," Maggie said. "And I'm sure you're thrilled to have it."

Anne wanted to tell her how hard it had been to hide it from the debt collectors when they showed up at the house to confiscate her father's belongings, but she didn't mention it. Instead, she rubbed it between her fingers, as always. Almost immediately, her heart rate returned to normal.

"I've never been the sort to wear a lot of jewelry," Maggie said. "Mainly because I'm always working in the kitchen. It's hard to knead bread dough when your hands are covered with diamonds." She chuckled. "Though I might like to try it someday, just to make sure."

Anne laughed. "I don't really aspire to have fine things. I've tasted of that life and have to believe that there's more to our existence than finery."

"You are a wise girl, and a beautiful one too. And your dedication to your little sisters is so admirable." Maggie gave her a wink before going back to work.

"Speaking of Emily and Kate, I do hope Milly is able to handle them. It was awfully nice of her to invite them over to play with her children."

"Oh, she's great with children. You have nothing to worry about."

"I think you have wonderful grandchildren, Maggie." Anne snapped the end off one of the beans. "They're adorable."

"Kate seems to fit right in with the little ones, doesn't she?" Maggie smiled and reached inside the bowl for another handful.

"I'm sure she and Emily are having the time of their lives here." Anne wanted to add, "I honestly don't know how I'm going to pull them away," but didn't. There would be so many issues to deal with when it was time to leave. But she couldn't focus on that right now. It would spoil the moment.

"Kate is the sweetest little thing." Maggie wrinkled her nose. "Oh, it does my heart good to have such a precious little girl around. After all those years of raising boys..." She chuckled. "There's a world of difference between raising boys and caring for girls."

Anne rested against the back of the swing. "Emily might as well be a boy, the way she acts. I don't mind admitting, I'm so worried about her."

"Ah. You heard about the fight she and Willy had yesterday at the church social?"

"Yes. She can be quite a little hooligan. I'm so sorry."

Maggie laughed. "I've been saying this almost from the day William came into the world: he's got entirely too much spunk. Someone needs to knock it out of him."

"Even if it's a girl?"

Maggie laughed. "Well, I don't usually abide fighting, and the Bible does say to turn the other cheek."

"Yes, I hear he did that and she whacked him on the other side." Anne paused and chuckled. "What do I do with her, Maggie? She knows nothing about manners or etiquette or decorum. And without a mother..."

Maggie released her hold on the beans and reached to touch Anne's arm. "You've done a fine job with her, honey. Don't be so hard on yourself."

"How did you know it was really myself I was beating up?"

"I can tell. You take on a lot of responsibility where those sisters of yours are concerned."

"Of course I do. I have no choice. But even if the situation were different, I'd still be just as dedicated."

"Of course. That's what love does. It devotes itself to great causes. And your sisters are the best cause in the world." Maggie paused and reached inside the bowl again. "Now, let's get busy snapping the ends off these beans. And while we're at it, tell me a little more about this wedding we're planning. Sounds like you've been coming up with more ideas."

"Oh, I have." Anne smiled as the ideas flooded over her once more. "I was up till one in the morning coming up with plans. Once the ideas start, they just flow like a river."

"Well, that's quite a gift you've got, my dear. Creativity isn't as easy for most folks. I, for one, would never lose sleep due to my creative thoughts."

Anne laughed. "Sometimes it does feel like a curse, especially when it keeps me up till all hours of the night."

"Fill me in," Maggie said. "I want to hear absolutely everything. Don't leave out a word."

* * * * *

Jake arrived home from a long day of heavy lifting and lugging, ready to put the cares of the world behind him. As always, he headed to the barn to feed Frances. Though others might find it odd, he took comfort in visiting with her every evening before heading to the house. No one seemed to understand his troubles like Frances did.

Jake had no sooner entered the barn than someone lunged at him from the shadows, grabbed him, and covered his head with a feed sack. He fought to free himself but could not. Seconds later, several familiar voices surrounded him with laughter. His brothers.

"What in the world are you—?" He never had a chance to finish the sentence before one of them—sounded like Joseph, based on the voice—picked him up and slung him over his shoulder.

Anger coursed through him, and he began to fight against Joseph's hold. "What do you think you're doing?"

"We're gonna take you to the reverend's house and get you hitched so you won't bring shame on the family." This time it was John's voice.

"W–what?" He wrestled to get free, but to no avail.

"Sure. If you beat Cody to the altar, the joke will be on him. Then he'll be the last single fella in town, not you."

"I don't really mind that I'm—"

"We've got a couple of real purty options." This time it was Jedediah's voice. "That Amaryllis is something special."

"And this new gal from Denver is mighty nice too," Jeremiah threw in.

"'Course, we could just round up Cassie Martin and have her meet you at the reverend's house. She's probably already got her wedding gown sewn and the cake baked." John's booming voice echoed across the barn. "How would you feel about that?"

Jake squirmed, and Joseph apparently lost his grip. Jake went tumbling to the ground, landing with a hard thump—but his pride was really more wounded than his backside.

His brothers all had a good laugh at his expense. He fussed and fumed until they untied the feed sack and pulled it over his head. Jake wiped bits of grain out of his hair and off his face. He even picked a couple out of his ear. He mumbled a scripture about patience a couple of times before standing aright to face them head-on. Finally he felt ready.

"Look, fellas, enough is enough."

"What do you mean?" John leaned against the barn wall and stuck a piece of straw in his mouth.

"I've been the brunt of your jokes for years now, and it's got to stop."

Joseph's face fell. "Why?"

"Why?" Jake paced the barn and kicked some straw. "Because it's wearing on me. I'm tired of it. You need to pick on someone else for a change."

Jeremiah shook his head, as if he couldn't comprehend the idea. "But...we like pickin' on you. It's what we've always done."

"Besides, we can't pick on the ladies. They're...ladies." Jedediah shrugged. "So who else is there?"

"Here's a novel idea." Jake turned to face them. "How about... no one."

"No one?" They spoke in unison.

"How does that work?" John asked. "Never heard of it."

"It works like this. You just treat everyone the way you would want to be treated."

The wrinkle between John's brows grew more pronounced. "Hmm."

"But I enjoy kidding around. And I don't mind when people make fun of me," Jedediah said.

"You don't?" Joseph slapped him on the back. "Well, then. It looks like we have a volunteer."

"Really?" Jedediah put up his fists, as if ready to box. "You're ready to mess with me like we always mess with Jake?"

"You've got it, little brother." Joseph took a few swings at Jedediah, and before long they were on the ground in a playful fistfight. Well, playful until Jedediah socked Joseph upside the head. Then things turned ugly.

Jake peered down at them. "I guess you fellas just don't get it. The idea here was to keep you from making fun of anyone. Doesn't look like that's gonna happen."

"Just don't understand why it's necessary," Jeremiah said with a shrug. "But as long as you're happy, we're happy."

"Yeah, we're happy." Joseph rose, rubbing the side of his head.

Jedediah flexed his fingers. "Happy as a lark. 'Cept I think maybe I broke my hand against Joseph's hard head."

"Wait." Jake paused and looked at his four older brothers. "Are you saying that you guys thought your jesting was making me happy?"

"Well, sure." John gave him a quizzical look. "Figured you wanted to be part of the group and it was the only way to include a little runt like you who had no interest in cattle ranching." He put his hand over his mouth. "Oops. There I go again, makin' you feel loved."

"So you're saying that the teasing was a way to show your love?" Jake tried to swallow this idea.

"Sure." Jeremiah chuckled. "Ya didn't think I was gonna hug and kiss ya, did ya?" He slapped his knee, and a ripple of laughter echoed across the barn.

"So if I want to feel loved, I should accept the teasing."

"Nah." Jedediah slung his arm across Jake's shoulders. "I'll let 'em take out their teasin' on me for the next six months or so. After that we'll switch to Jeremiah. Then Joseph, then John. We'll work our way up the ladder." He turned to the others. "How does that sound, fellas?"

"Mighty fine to me." Joseph shrugged. "Just hope I can keep up with whose turn it is at bat."

"Hey, speaking of bats, did you see that we had a couple of bats in the barn the other night?" John's expression shifted, and suddenly he was all business.

This, of course, led into a rather lengthy discussion about the ranch. Jake used the opportunity to slip out of the barn and across the front yard. As he walked away from his brothers, he pondered the conversation that had just taken place. The more he thought about it, the funnier it seemed. He approached the porch steps chuckling.

"Someone's in a good mood."

He looked up to see Anne seated on the swing next to his mother, snapping beans.

"Looks like you've got your dancing shoes on today, son." His mama gave him a wink. "What's got you so happy?"

"Not sure it would make much sense if I told you. Just take my word for it that progress has been made today."

"Yes, it has." She nudged Anne. "You want to tell him, or should I?"

"Tell me what?"

"Virginia's got her talked into staying through the weekend for the wedding."

"Really?" At this revelation, his heart quickened. The idea of spending a few extra days with Anne seemed almost too good to be true. Why, a fella could take a heap o' ribbing from his older brothers if it meant more time with a pretty girl like Anne. "I'm—I'm glad you're going to stay," he managed, before offering a shy smile.

"She'd probably be a lot happier about it if you went in the house and cleaned up, Jakey." His mother clucked her tongue. "I don't know what got ahold of you, but every hair on your head is sticking straight up, and you're covered in some sort of…" She narrowed her gaze. "What is that? Grain?"

"Feed." He sighed. "And please don't ask. I'll be cleaned up in time for supper."

"Oh, take your time." His mother chuckled. "I got so caught up in visiting with our guests today that I'm behind on supper. It'll be a little late."

Jake hardly knew what to say in response. From the time he was a boy, Mama had placed supper on the table promptly at six. Looked like she'd found Anne and her sisters to be quite a distraction.

As the beautiful maiden on the porch swing glanced his way with eyes sparkling, Jake decided this was one distraction that he wouldn't mind sitting across the supper table from for a long, long time. With new determination, he sprinted into the house, headed for the bath.

* * * * *

Anne tried not to let the smile overtake her as Jake looked her way. Still, there was something about that messy-headed boy, even covered in feed. She couldn't shake him. Every time she tried, her thoughts kept drifting back to the two conversations they'd shared under the night skies.

"You all right over there, hon?" Maggie glanced her way with a half smile.

"Oh, fine. Been thinking about something rather ironic."

"What's that?"

Anne chose her words with great care. "The other night on the train, I was so disappointed to learn we were being detained. I just wanted to go on—make it to Dallas. Now I'm the happiest girl in the world. Don't you find it strange?"

"Not so strange, really," Maggie said. "Happens to me all the time. I'll think I'm on the right track—pun intended—only to find out that the Lord wants to take me on a detour. That's how I met my James, you know."

"Oh?"

"I had my mind made up. I was going to college. I hope it's not bragging to say that I was one of the smartest girls in my class." She giggled. "I suppose it's not bragging if it's true. It's just a fact. Anyway, I'd worked for months to prepare myself. At the last minute, someone else in my class got the scholarship. I was devastated."

"I would be too. I can't imagine how wonderful going to college might've been. I was hoping to get that opportunity myself."

"Yes, I did regret not getting to go. Instead, I found myself working at a restaurant, serving up hot food to hungry townsmen. And not three weeks into that job, I dropped a large silver tray and the handsomest man God ever created knelt down to pick it up for me. The rest, as they say, is history."

"That's the sweetest story ever," Anne said.

"You call that sweet?" Emily appeared on the porch steps, her skirt torn and dirt caking its hem. "There were no Indians, no blood and guts, not even a scalping scene. Just a plain, boring love story."

"Oh, honey, a love story's the best kind of story there is." Maggie leaned forward and placed the bowl of snapped beans on the little table next to the swing. "If you don't believe me, read the Bible."

"The Bible?" Emily looked perplexed.

"Well, sure. It's the greatest love story ever written. And it's loaded with action and adventure too. There's blood and strife and envy and killing and all sorts of high drama. And there's a fair amount of romance also. Oh, and if you like adventure, there are stories of seas being parted by mighty winds, folks walking on water, and even people being raised from the dead."

"Wait a minute…" Emily's brow wrinkled as she plopped down on the top step. "I went to church, and I didn't hear any of that."

"At our church, the minister mostly gave us a list of do's and don'ts," Anne explained.

"Ah." Maggie shook her head. "Well, that's a shame, because the stories are what captivate you. You've got to read them and then dig a little deeper. Look for the story inside the story." Her face lit into a smile and she gestured for Emily to squeeze into the spot between them.

"Honey, you're a writer."

"Yes, I am." Emily nodded with a serious expression on her face.

"The Bible can be your best textbook. There are hidden stories buried deep within. Don't get me wrong. All those stories in the Good Book are true. But if you read between the lines, you'll find some exciting stories buried inside that you might not have noticed."

Emily's expression softened. "Tell me, Maggie. I want to know what you're talking about. There's really action and adventure in there?"

"Sure. If you want action, you need to read the story of David when he faces the mighty giant, Goliath. Or the story of Samson, as he takes down the Philistines."

Emily's eyes widened. "Sounds like a story I read once in *Wild*

West Adventures, only the man who took down the bad guys was a cowboy." She shrugged. "But that was a made-up story."

"That's why I prefer the ones in the Bible," Maggie said. "They're not made-up. And you know who the author is, don't you?"

Emily shook her head.

"The Lord Himself."

"W–what? How did God write a book? Must be a mighty big ink pen."

"No, it didn't happen like that. He spoke the words to men, and they wrote them down."

"But...they were God's words all along? Not someone else's?"

"Right." Maggie nodded. "The Bible has everything a writer like you could ever want. Why, there's the romance between Hosea and his unfaithful wife...there's the miracle of creation in Genesis...and best of all, there's the story of Christ, who carried His cross all the way up the hill to Calvary to die for our sins."

"And every story is really two stories in one?" Emily asked.

"Sure. Take the story of Peter walking on water. It's about a man actually walking on water, but it's also a lesson for us—to teach us to keep our eyes on Jesus when things around us are shaking and out of our control."

Emily's eyes widened.

"Of course, there's also the story of Shadrach, Meshach, and Abednego in the fiery furnace. It's a real story about three men who were tossed into a real, blazing-hot furnace." Maggie's voice deepened, growing more intense. "They should have burned to death."

"Now, *this* is the kind of story I like." Emily grinned. "Did they all die?"

"No." Maggie shook her head. "A fourth man appeared in the fire with them. Would you like to know who that was?"

"An angel?"

"Actually, it was the Lord Himself. And do you know the story buried inside that story?"

Emily squinted. "Wait, let me think." She rose and paced the front porch then turned to face Maggie. "The men were in trouble and thought they weren't going to make it, but God showed up and helped them."

"That's right." Maggie clapped her hands together. "You're getting it. Those three men in the furnace weren't alone, and neither are you girls, even when you feel like you've been tossed into a fiery furnace."

Emily dropped onto the porch steps. "I'd rather be tossed into a fiery furnace than go to Uncle Bertrand's house."

"Emily, you don't mean that." Anne shook her head.

"That puts me in mind of another story." Maggie grinned.

"Is there a cowboy in this one?"

"Not exactly a cowboy. But it is the most exciting story of all." Maggie leaned forward in the swing, her eyes widening. "John 3:16 says that God loved this world so much that He sent his only Son to save us."

Emily shrugged. "Never thought of that as a love story before."

"Oh, it is." Maggie's eyes twinkled. "But there's more to it than that. Jesus didn't just come to save us, He came so that we could learn to love others...even the most unlovable people."

"So that's why you love your sister." Emily nodded.

"Yes. I love her—not just because she's my sister, but because she's one of God's children. And if you ask the Lord, He can show you how to love your uncle too."

Emily wrinkled her nose. "I suppose. But I'd rather bury him in the back yard."

Anne sighed. "Sometimes I think my sister is a hopeless case."

"Oh no. There are no hopeless cases. If you don't believe that, read the story of Jonah. God chased after him until He caught him in the belly of a whale."

"Now that sounds like an exciting one." Emily sighed. "All right, Maggie. I'll read the stories you're telling me about if you think it will improve my writing abilities."

"I don't just think it, I know it. You're such a talented young lady, and I know you're going to be published one day."

"You think?" Emily's eyes sparkled.

"I do."

"Oh, Maggie...I love you!" Emily's voice was laced with joy. "You're going to make me a better writer."

Anne quirked a brow at Maggie as Emily disappeared inside the house, then whispered, "And a better person too, I daresay."

Chapter Thirteen

....

Whether you're looking for the big-city nightlife, the simplicity of ranch-style living, or that small-town homey feel, you'll find it in the Texas Panhandle. Head over to Amarillo to the theater or out to Palo Duro Canyon for nature at its finest. Visit the ranches in Carson County if you're interested in branding cattle, or mosey on over to the high plains to gaze upon open fields of wheat and corn. If you're looking for a small town to settle in, we have them in abundance. While you're there, why not visit local businesses and marvel at the new growth taking place in the region? Best of all, get to know the people. Once you meet them, you'll never want to leave. —"Tex" Morgan, reporting for the Panhandle Primer

After helping Maggie clean up the supper dishes, Anne retreated to the parlor. She found Jake seated on the sofa, reading the newspaper. Emily had taken the spot next to him and was scribbling away on her writing tablet. Across the room, Kate sat on the floor, playing with Ginger.

"Anything exciting happening in the world?" Anne asked.

"Actually, yes. Just getting caught up on the skirmishes going on in Europe."

"Do you think Americans will get involved?" she asked, fear suddenly gripping her heart.

"I can't imagine it. It's their battle, not ours."

"I read the newspaper today too," Emily announced. "Did you know that Texans are up in arms over the new governor?"

"Who's that?" Anne asked.

"His name is Pa Ferguson. Maggie told me this morning that Texas will be a safer place to live now that Pa's in office." Emily went back to writing on her tablet.

"Pa Ferguson?" Anne shook her head, confused.

"His real name's Jim," Jake explained, "but everyone calls him Pa. And they call his wife Ma."

"I can't imagine calling the governor Pa." Anne chuckled. "What's he like? And why is Texas a safer place to live now?"

"He's a strong man with even stronger ideas," Jake said. "He wants government to work for the common man."

"Maggie says he's moral and upright," Emily added, looking up from her tablet once again. "Texas is going to be a far more civilized place now that he's in office. And I, for one, am glad."

"Oh?" Anne tried not to chuckle. "You have a vested interest in the governorship of Texas?"

"For my story. See, Maggie says he's a prohi…prohi…"

"Prohibitionist?" Jake asked.

"Yes. Prohibitionist. That means he doesn't believe in drinking." Kate sighed, and Anne looked her way.

"What's wrong, Kate?"

"I wish Papa had been a prohibitionist, don't you?"

A wave of shame washed over Anne. She hadn't planned to air their family's dirty laundry in front of Jake or anyone else. "Well, honey," she managed, "I think it's safe to say that we all need to guard ourselves against excess of any kind."

Jake looked her way, his brow wrinkled. Likely this conversation had him intrigued. No doubt.

"That's why I'm putting Pa Ferguson in my story," Emily said. "He's going to be committed to law and order for the state and will make it a crime for any man or woman to drink whiskey."

Jake put the paper down and shook his head. "I hope you don't take this the wrong way, but I'm not used to women talking so much about politics and such. Most of the girls around here spend senseless hours gabbing about their hair and dresses. You ladies are... different."

"Oh, we're different all right." Emily closed her tablet. "Papa used to say that I was unique."

"I think I am too," Jake said. "I'm worlds apart from my brothers."

"And I'm worlds apart from my sisters." Emily flashed a smile. "There's only one of me."

"Thank goodness," Anne was quick to add. She turned back to Jake. "I think it's nice to be unique. We're like snowflakes. No two are quite alike."

"Snowflakes?" Maggie chucked as she entered the room. "We haven't seen snow around here for so long that I've almost forgotten what it looks like."

"Oh, Maggie, it's the most beautiful thing you've ever seen, especially in the Rocky Mountains." Anne paused to choose her words. "From my bedroom window, I could see the Rockies. And in the wintertime, you can't believe how pristine and clean everything looked. I've never seen such a brilliant white. Sometimes it seemed as if God took a paintbrush and ran it across everything in sight, adding all sorts of sparkle and shine along the way. The ice crystals from my windowpane were perfect. And the snowmen…"

"I used to love to make snowmen." Emily sighed then looked at Anne. "Does it snow in Dallas? Can we make snowmen there?"

Anne looked at Jake, who shook his head.

"It snows every now and again in the Dallas area," he said. "But not as a rule. In central Texas, the winters are more moderate."

"I'm going to miss our white winters." Anne fought the temptation to release a sigh.

"All this talk of cold is making me want ice cream." Maggie's lips turned up in a grin. "Anyone around here like peaches and cream?"

"Peaches and cream!" Emily sprang from the couch, dropping her tablet. "It's my very favorite. How did you know?"

Maggie turned to her, eyes sparkling. "I didn't. It's my favorite too. What do you say? Should we make some ice cream?"

"Oh, let's." Emily fell into line behind her.

Anne watched as her two younger sisters disappeared into the kitchen with Maggie. Minutes later, Maggie popped her head back out.

"Jakey, if I'm going to make ice cream, I'll need rock salt. Would you be willing to take the truck into town?"

"Sure." He rose and stretched. "I'd be glad to."

"Would it be possible for me to ride with you?" Anne asked. "I need to stop at the hotel."

"I wouldn't mind a bit," Jake said…but the wrinkled brow spoke of his confusion. Likely he wondered what sort of business she had in town.

"A very kind woman on the train acted as our guardian angel," Anne explained. "And I'd like to thank her. If she's still at the hotel,

GROOM
1914
TX

that is." She had been longing to speak with Mrs. Witherspoon for days and was grateful to finally have the opportunity.

And it didn't hurt that she would get to ride alongside Jake on the way.

* * * * *

Jake started the engine on the family's truck; then he went around to the passenger door and opened it for Anne. She turned to him with a smile so sweet it almost stopped him in his tracks.

"Thank you so much," she whispered. "It's been a long time since anyone opened a door for me."

"My pleasure." A thousand emotions rushed over him as she gave him one last look before climbing inside the cab.

Moments later he was seated in the driver's seat and pulling away from O'Farrell's Honor. Ginger ran along behind the truck for quite a ways, chasing them all the way to the road.

"You'll have to forgive Ginger. She's accustomed to climbing up in the back of the truck and riding with me. But I figured you wouldn't want her tagging along today, so I gave her a little talking-to."

Anne shrugged. "Maybe not. Especially not if I'm headed into the hotel. Is it fancy?"

"Fancy?" He snorted. "Hardly. It's just a small one, enough to house a couple dozen people. Groom has never been terribly big, though we've worked hard to build interest in our fair town by adding a variety of shops to meet the needs of the locals. That way we don't have to go to Amarillo for everything."

"Sounds like you need to get Tex Morgan to focus more on this area," she said. "Perhaps he could draw in tourists. Bring in some money for those shop owners."

"Great idea."

"I've found this whole area to be quite beautiful."

"Yes, well, don't be terribly disappointed when you see that our only hotel is little more than a large house. It's nothing to write home about." He clapped a hand over his mouth. "I'm sorry, Anne. I keep saying the dumbest things."

"It's all right." She chuckled and glanced his way. "Not that you've been saying dumb things. I think you've been awfully sweet about all this."

His heart nearly sang with those words. She thought he was sweet? What a promising revelation.

Her gaze lingered on him a bit longer than would be expected, and Jake felt his cheeks grow warm.

"Emily told me she's added a new character to her story."

"Oh?"

"Yes. She's based the character on Aunt Bets." He chuckled. "Can you imagine how that's going to play out?"

"Heavens. I can only wonder." Anne paused and then glanced his way. "I'm so worried about my sisters. It's going to tear them up when we have to leave here."

"I know what that feels like."

"Oh?"

"Yes. It's going to tear me up too."

Had he really just spoken those words aloud? Yes, from the look of surprise on her face, he had. Well, why not? Might as well let the girl know he was interested in her, even if the whole thing felt like an impossibility.

He turned onto the main road leading to town. When they reached the hotel, he pulled up to the front and stopped the truck. Then he turned and looked Anne in the eyes. "You know how you said you're going to miss the beautiful winters in Denver?"

"Y–yes."

"I'm going to miss you—all of you—even more than that. Every time I think about you going…" He paused.

"Oh, Jake." A fine mist covered her eyelashes, and then a lone tear trickled down her cheek. He reached out with his finger to brush it away, leaving his hand resting against her cheek for a moment. Not that she seemed to mind. No, she continued to gaze at him with eyes that ripped his heart into pieces.

Until someone rapped on his window. Jake looked out, surprised to see Jedediah standing there. He pulled his hand away from Anne's cheek and climbed out of the truck.

"Say there, little brother." Jedediah's mustache twitched. "Looks like I interrupted a private moment. Sorry about that."

Jake half-expected some sort of joke to follow, but thankfully Jedediah remained silent. For a moment. "Just had to come into town to fetch a few things for the little wife. You know how women are, always needing something from us menfolk."

This startled Jake to attention. He went around the side of the truck and opened the door for Anne, who climbed out, gave him a quick nod, then scurried toward the hotel.

So much for a romantic ending to his little speech. Oh well. It would have to wait till another day.

* * * * *

Anne rushed into the lobby of the hotel, her heart beating so fast that she thought she might just faint. Had Jake really just told her that she would be missed when she left? Oh, and the feelings that had coursed through her when he reached to wipe away her tears. There was such gentleness in that move. Such caring.

Stop it, Anne. You can't let your imagination run away with you. You will be moving on in a few days.

She snapped to attention as the hotel clerk offered a cheerful hello.

Anne took a couple of steps toward the desk. "Yes, hello. I'm looking for a woman by the name of Mrs. Witherspoon. Is she staying here?"

"I believe she's still with us. Let me check the register." He ran his finger down a long sheet of paper then looked up with a smile. "She's in room nine, just down the hall." He gestured to his right. "Should I announce you?"

"I believe I would like to surprise her, if you don't mind."

"Of course not. Have a nice visit."

She smoothed the wrinkles from her skirt, fluffed her hair, and then took a few steps down the hall toward room nine, still thinking about Jake's words.

Anne arrived at the door to Mrs. Witherspoon's room and gave a tentative knock. The door swung open, revealing the woman in a beautiful green dress. Her hair was unpinned and flowing to her shoulders.

Anne had no sooner tried to say a quick hello when Mrs. Witherspoon gathered her into her arms and planted a kiss on her cheek. "Oh, my dear! I've been so concerned about you and your sisters. Thank you so much for coming to see me. It puts my mind at ease."

"I'm sorry to come so late in the day," Anne said.

"It's never too late for a visit with a friend." Mrs. Witherspoon ushered her into the room. "Though I hope you don't mind that I've just unpinned my hair. Keeping it up is such a challenge. It never wants to stay in place." She gestured for Anne to sit in the chair by the desk.

"I struggle with that same problem," Anne said as she took a seat.

"With hair as thick as yours?" Mrs. Witherspoon ran her fingers through Anne's hair and smiled. "I would think it would stay in place with little effort."

"You are so kind, Mrs. Witherspoon."

"Call me Cornelia, darling. All my friends do."

"I don't want to keep you...Cornelia. I just couldn't let another day go by without stopping to thank you for arranging our meal on the train. And that sleeping car...what a treat!"

"Dear, my heart went out to you, traveling with two little ones—and such a long way. Did I hear you say that you'd come all the way from Denver?"

"Yes. My father..." Anne paused and released a little breath. "My father passed away six weeks ago. But we have a relative in Dallas, so that's where we were headed."

"I live in Dallas myself," Cornelia said. "I'd gone to Amarillo to visit my husband, who is there on business for the next couple of months."

"I see." Anne smiled.

"Well, if you're coming to Dallas, you really must look me up. I am on several committees and always out and about. Here, let me give you my number so you can ring me when you arrive."

"That would be wonderful." Suddenly Anne felt her tensions

about moving to Dallas lift a bit. If this wonderful woman lived there, perhaps they really could be friends.

She took the slip of paper Cornelia gave her and pressed it into her pocket. "I must be honest and say that I haven't been looking forward to living in Dallas. I'm going to miss Colorado so much."

"Oh, Colorado is a magnificent place. I've visited there on a couple of occasions. But I think you'll find that Dallas is teeming with every good thing—theater, restaurants, even the opera. Why, we have access to some of the best stores in the country."

Anne flinched at her words. They reminded her too much of her former life. "I'm not sure I'll be seeing many of those things. My situation has changed a great deal over the past few months, and luxuries…well, they're a thing of the past."

"Oh, I'm sorry, Anne. Still, you will love Dallas. We have the prettiest parks and several lakes. And folks in Dallas are well-connected. We have the best railroad station in the South, if I do say so myself." She paused and gazed into Anne's eyes. "Tell me why you're not looking forward to your stay in Dallas. Does it have something to do with this relative of yours?"

Anne realized she had laid her secret bare. She nodded. "He's a prominent businessman. He runs a department store, I believe."

This seemed to get Cornelia's attention. She sat on the edge of the bed. "Oh? And what might his name be?"

"Bertrand Denning."

At this news, Cornelia very nearly toppled from the bed. As she clutched the quilt, her hand began to tremble. "Bert Denning is your uncle?"

"Yes." *But I've never heard anyone refer to him as Bert before.*

"Well, if that doesn't beat all." Cornelia rose and paced the room. She finally paused long enough to say something. "I've known Bert for years. Simply years. Our paths have crossed at many social functions."

Anne could hardly believe her good fortune. "I can't believe it! Well, maybe you can tell me more about him. I know nothing about his home or anything. And we've all found it strange that he's never married." Anne shrugged. "We've always wondered about that. Though he does have a bit of a nasty disposition, so I can see how a woman would be put off by him."

"Is it getting warm in here?" Cornelia rose and paced the room. "Feels like it. I should open these windows."

"It's not too bad." Anne shrugged. "Anyway, I think it's wonderful that you know him. Maybe you can advise me on how to deal with him."

"Deal with him?" Cornelia turned back to her. "He needs dealing with?"

"Well, he's such a sour old grump, and I'm going to be living with him."

"Oh, I see." The edges of Cornelia's lips turned up. "So that's the plan. You and your sisters were on your way to live with the sour old grump when life sent you on a little detour."

"Yes, that's it. Not that we want to be going to Uncle Bertrand's house, I assure you, but we have no choice. But now that I know you'll be nearby, maybe it won't be so awful. Especially if you know him. Maybe you could come over and—"

"I won't be coming over, honey." Cornelia sat and took Anne's hand. "That won't happen. But I will be nearby, if you need a female to talk to. You can always come to me."

Anne stopped cold at that last revelation. Clearly something had transpired between Uncle Bertrand and Cornelia Witherspoon. But what?

One thing she could no longer deny—there was more to her uncle than she'd known till now. Hmm. Better not let Emily find out. She'd turn his story into a book—likely one he wouldn't much care to read.

GROOM
1914
TX

Chapter Fourteen

....

*Tired of living in the frigid North or humid South? The Texas
Panhandle, with its temperate climate, is the perfect compro-
mise. Sure, we have our share of moderate winter snows, but
they are beautifully balanced by warm, lazy summer days
with low humidity. Springtime is beautiful here, with light
showers watering the foliage. And our autumns can't be beat.
Best of all, sunny skies prevail year-round. If you love the
sunlight—and bright, cheerful smiles from your neighbors—
the Panhandle is the place for you. —"Tex" Morgan, reporting for the Panhandle Primer*

On Tuesday morning, Anne and Maggie met Virginia at the
church.

"I just love it in here," Anne said as she made her way up the
center aisle. "It's so quaint."

"Yes, small-town churches are likely quite different from the one
you attended in Denver." Maggie paused to run her hand over the
back of a pew. "Oh, but I do love it here. The Lord has spoken to my
heart on many occasions in this place, so I will always cherish it."

"There's no comparison between the buildings," Anne said.
"But I do think I like this best. I certainly prefer the message I heard
on Sunday."

"I've been hoping and praying the town would grow so that I could see an influx of children for our Sunday school program," Virginia said. "It would be wonderful to think of a way to bring in more tourists." She offered Anne a smile. "You're the creative one. Maybe you could come up with some ideas."

"Yes, that's a wonderful idea," Maggie said.

"If only I had the time. I'll be leaving soon, you know."

"True." Virginia's expression shifted to one of sadness. "I keep forgetting that. It seems like we've known each other for years and that we'll go on being friends for a lifetime."

I would love that.

Anne startled to attention. "Well, let's get busy talking about your wedding."

A concerned look crossed Virginia's face. "I don't know what's keeping Amaryllis. She was supposed to join us but wanted to stop off in town at the store first."

"She can add her thoughts when she arrives." Anne took a seat on the front pew and reached for her writing tablet. "Virginia, tell me about your dream wedding. What have you always longed for?"

"Oh, everything you've already suggested."

"But what else? What's missing?"

"Hmm." Virginia paused. "Up in New York, of course, there would have been a lovely dance afterward. The bride and groom would have a special dance together—and the father of the bride would have a dance with the bride as well."

"I've seen this done in Denver. It's quite touching. But how do folks in these parts feel about dancing? Is it allowed?"

"I've danced a jig or two in my day." Maggie kicked up her heels, and the girls laughed. "Why, when I was a young filly, my papa used to play the fiddle and we'd dance all over the place. My oh my, but these feet could move!"

"Do you suppose the reverend would allow a dance to take place at the church?" Virginia looked plenty unsure.

"If it's on the lawn, I can't see that he would mind." Maggie gave her a little wink. "You just leave that part to me. Bets will have a fit, of course. She doesn't believe in dancing." Maggie began to chuckle. "I daresay a little dancing might just set her free. Loosen up her joints. Get her back to living once again."

"Get who back to living once again?"

Anne turned, stunned to see Bets standing behind them at the back of the sanctuary.

"Um, well, I..." Maggie ran her fingers through her always-messy hair. "Life is for the living, Bets. That's all I've got to say about it."

"Humph." Bets marched up the aisle toward them, her mission clear.

Maggie squared her shoulders and stared her sister down. "The girls are putting together plans for the wedding and they're talking about hosting a little dance on the church lawn afterward. Doesn't that sound lovely?"

"Lovely?" Bets began to fan herself. "Dancing is sinful, just like that loud piano playing we have to tolerate every Sunday, which is exactly why I've come to speak to the reverend. Figured it's about time I gave him a piece of my mind."

"Don't give him too much of it," Maggie said. "Or there might not be enough left for levelheaded thinking."

Anne bit back the laugh that threatened to erupt.

"Maggie!" Bets's face turned red. "Apologize at once."

"I don't see the point in apologizing for speaking the truth. And as for your comments about the music, I daresay the Bible has a lot to say about offering up musical praises to the Lord."

"Perhaps, though a bit quieter would be better."

Maggie placed her hands on her hips. "I suppose someone forgot to tell King David that dancing is sinful. I recall reading a biblical passage just yesterday about how he danced and praised the Lord when the ark was returned to Jerusalem. He found it cause for celebration. And we find Virginia and Cody's marriage cause for celebration too, which is why we plan to ask for permission for a dance after the ceremony."

Bets shook her head. "There will be no dancing on the church grounds. The reverend won't allow it. And if he dares to defy me on this..."

"You'll what?" Maggie took a step closer. "You'll ruin a perfectly lovely wedding? Why can't you just relax and enjoy life, Bets? Why do you always have to be so cranky?"

"I'm not cranky. I'm just practical. Someone has to be. There are rules to be followed, you know. Not that you've ever followed one, but good folks do."

"Cranky folks press their ridiculous rules on others and weigh them down." Maggie shook her head. "I understand rules. But I also understand that there's a time to celebrate. And a wedding is the perfect opportunity to kick up your heels, make merry. How are we ever going to know how to celebrate in heaven if we don't practice here?" She began to dance a little jig, and within seconds Bets was fanning herself again.

"Merciful heavens, Maggie. How you do go on. You've always been such a free-spirited thing. If Mama had lived to see one of her daughters kicking up her heels in the house of God..."

"She would have joined in the dance." Maggie stopped and stared her sister down. "And you'll be better off if you just relax those rules you've created in your head and join in the dance as well."

"I'll go to my grave with holy feet." Bets crossed her arms at her chest. "They will walk undefiled into heaven."

"Not mine." Maggie started to dance once more. "Mine are going to dance their way past those pearly gates, even if it means I have to baptize 'em on the way in. And I feel certain Saint Peter will join me in the dance. In fact, he's probably up there with his toes tapping right now."

"Heathen words." Bets shook her finger in Maggie's face. "You will not have your way on this, Maggie. And these girls..." She turned to Anne, squaring off, face-to-face. "They might be young, but they're not going to bring in these kinds of changes. Groom is a respectable place, and respectable people don't dance."

Maggie did a little jig in the aisle.

Anne drew in a deep breath, knowing she now had to face Bets on her own.

"Listen here, young lady." Bets stood so close, Anne could feel the woman's breath on her cheek. "You might do things differently in the big city, but we're a bit more dignified here. So you can take your ideas and you can..."

"Betsy Ann, you bite that tongue. Don't say another word to that wonderful young lady. She's done nothing but help." Anne and Bets both turned as Leo's voice sounded from the back of the sanctuary. He took long strides up the aisle toward them. "And another thing." He narrowed his gaze. "I say it wouldn't kill us to change a few things around here. Just because we've always done things a certain way doesn't mean it's the right way."

"But…"

He paused and gazed into her eyes. "Besides, I remember a time not so many years ago when you would run into my arms for a waltz around the room. What happened to that girl? Where is she now?"

Bets's eyes filled with tears. She shook her head, and her gaze shifted to the ground. "That was a lifetime ago, Leo. Things are different now. I'm different now."

"Well, it's a pity. And I said our lives could stand a bit of shaking." He pointed at Anne, who felt a little shiver run down her spine. "If having this young woman in Groom has caused you to quiver a little, all the better. I say more power to her."

Anne tried not to let the edges of her lips turn up, but inside her heart was singing. Looked like Uncle Leo had waited awhile to speak his mind, but now that he'd opened this can of worms, Aunt Bets seemed determined to avoid them. She hiked her skirt, turned on her heel, and stormed down the aisle, muttering something about men.

"Don't fret over her, ladies," Leo said with a curt nod. "You just leave her to me. Things are going to be different around here from now on. *I'm* going to be different."

Maggie let out a raucous "Praise God" and kept on dancing.

Virginia gave him a hug. "Oh, thank you so much. I've been so worried about what she would think and the influence she might have on others."

"Well, worry no more. You just enjoy your big day. It only comes around once." He sighed and mumbled, "Then you have to live with that person for the rest of your mortal life," as he headed down the aisle.

"She reminds me so much of my uncle Bertrand." Anne plopped onto the front pew and wiped away the beads of sweat on her forehead. "Always in such a bad mood. I've never understood it. Why do some people feel like they've got to bring everyone else down? It's so unkind."

"It makes no sense to me, either," Virginia said. "I've been so blessed to live with kindhearted parents."

Maggie took the spot beside Anne. "Honey, would you like to know what makes some older people a little sour?"

"I suppose."

"Sometimes we older folks are a little disappointed that our lives haven't turned out quite like we expected." She hesitated. "I'm not talking about myself here, just so you know. I've had the most glorious life a woman could ask for. Married the best man in the world and raised the best boys in the world."

Anne took her hand and gave it a squeeze.

"But I've watched my sister, Bets, face life with the opposite spirit. Things in her life haven't gone as she would have liked. As a young woman, she longed to have a houseful of children. Unfortunately, she never saw that dream fulfilled and it's soured her, as you can tell." Maggie fanned herself. "I do hope I haven't gone to gossiping by mentioning her circumstances."

"I don't think so," Virginia said. "You are speaking out of your personal experience with her."

Anne nodded her head. "I do understand what you're saying, though."

"Yes. I'm just wondering if perhaps your uncle Bertrand has had an unhappy life. Maybe that's why he's an old codger."

"Could be." Anne paced the room, deep in thought.

"Did he ever marry?" Maggie asked.

"No." Anne continued to pace. "I can't imagine any woman

abiding him." But even as she spoke the word, images of Cornelia Witherspoon filled her head.

"More likely he fell in love as a young man and had his heart broken," Maggie said.

"Yes, he sounds more like someone who's been jilted in love," Virginia added.

Anne paused to think about that idea. "It's so funny you should say that. I've just been thinking the same thing. I suppose I'll never know. He's not the sort to open up and share his heart. When he's around me, he's just cold and angry most of the time."

"I've seen that sort of bitterness firsthand with my sister, as you've now witnessed. And I can't say I understand it. I just know that people like that need to be set free from the bitterness that binds them. Otherwise, they'll destroy many lives, not just their own." She paused and fussed with her apron. "Anyway, enough about other people. Let's you and I agree that if life doesn't turn out as we like, we won't sour like lemons."

Anne chuckled. "Maggie, you're the least sour person I know. And I realize you've already been through many things in your life that have been painful."

"I've been heartsick over losing James," Maggie said. "But I refuse to get angry about it. I do my best to live for today and trust God with tomorrow."

"That's all any of us can do." Virginia leaned over and gave Maggie a kiss on the cheek.

"And what would be the point to stepping out of the dance just because we've faced a grief or two?" Maggie's face lit into a smile. "No, I daresay this is the very time the Lord wants us to get back to living. Otherwise, why would He have left us here when those we love have already gone on?" She looked at Virginia. "Now you get back to work on that wedding, doll. We've only got a few days left, you know."

"I know. Just four more days until the big day."

Anne's heart twisted as Virginia spoke those fateful words. Only four days left to enjoy the people she'd grown to love. And then she would leave heaven and board a train for a life that would likely turn out to be the very opposite.

* * * * *

Jake looked out over the stretch of track as he paused for a drink of water. Just another day or so and they'd have everything up and running again. He swiped the moisture from the back of his neck and took another swig of water.

Strange... Though he'd always loved working for the railroad, he suddenly despised it. The words he'd spoken to Anne last night in the truck washed over him afresh. Had he really shared his heart... told her how much he was going to miss her when she left?

"Jake, you all right over there?" The job foreman slapped him on the back. "You seem lost."

"Just thinking."

"Me too." The foreman sighed. "Thinking about how happy I'm going to be to get this track fixed and for life to return to normal around here."

"Normal." There it was, that word he hated. If "normal" was the definition of his life before meeting Anne, then he never wanted to go back there again. But what could he do about it?

With a grunt, he reached for his work gloves, shoved them on, and got back to work.

Chapter Fifteen
....

You've probably heard the expression "Backdoor guests are best." Here in the Panhandle, we're not bound to formality. C'mon in the back door and stay awhile. Share in a hot cup of coffee and talk about the price of feed or, if you're a lady, the latest fabrics at the general store. In other words, feel welcome! You'll never find a better place to visit. Unless you've come to stir up trouble, of course. If so, we'll just tip our hats and bid you a fond farewell. —"Tex" Morgan, reporting for the Panhandle Primer

On Wednesday morning Anne and her sisters helped Maggie tidy up the parlor. Her thoughts drifted back to that conversation she'd had with Jake in the truck on the way into town. They'd been talking about the weather—nothing too startling—but he'd managed to sneak in a line or two that made her think he could care for her.

What could she do about that? She wanted to fight it but found herself giving in. Her heart seemed to come alive every time he walked into the room.

A knock sounded at the door.

"Would one of you get that?" Maggie raked her fingers through her wild hair. "I look a fright."

"Let me!" Emily took off running with Kate on her heels.

"Might be Jake. He comes home for lunch once in a while. He's probably got his arms loaded with things from the store." Maggie gave her a little wink. "He seems to be spending a lot of time around the house lately, for some reason. Can't quite figure it out."

Anne pulled off her apron and ran her hands across her hair.

Seconds later, someone else entirely walked into the parlor. Anne gasped as she saw Uncle Bertrand. He looked as stiff and formal as ever, and judging from his stern expression, he was not in a pleasant mood. It felt as if Anne's stomach had gravitated to her throat.

"Anne." He crossed his arms at his chest.

"U–uncle." Just one word, but it was truly all she could manage.

Off in the distance, Emily made a terrible face and Kate looked as if she might be sick.

"Well, who have we here?" Maggie brushed her hands on her apron and took a few steps in Bertrand's direction. "Don't tell me this is the most-loved uncle I've heard so much about."

Most-loved? Anne coughed to keep from saying anything she shouldn't.

"Well, I, um…" The flustered look on Bertrand's face spoke volumes. "I am their uncle, to be sure. And I've come from Dallas to fetch them." He stood so stiff and straight, he reminded Anne of a fire poker. She hoped his being here wouldn't cause as much damage. "Though at this point, I hardly see the logic. I was told in town that the track will be repaired later today and passengers will reboard the train to Dallas. As I see it, this drive has been rather pointless."

"How could coming to Groom ever be pointless?" Maggie stared him down.

"Well, you get my point. The girls could have reboarded the train this very day and saved me the trip. But anyway, I'm here now and ready to head back."

"Oh, Uncle Bertrand." Anne took a hesitant step in his direction. "I'm afraid we can't leave for at least three more days. Didn't you get my message? I telephoned your store."

"My secretary told me that you called and wanted to stay here until week's end," he said, "but it inconveniences me for you to arrive over the weekend. So I've come to fetch you now. We must hurry. I have a lot of work waiting for me."

"Oh, but we can't. We simply can't." She felt the sting of tears but willed herself not to cry in front of him.

"And why is that?" He pulled out his pocket watch and glanced at it. "I've brought my car. There's no reason why we can't leave right away."

"Oh, there's one very good reason," she said. "I'm helping plan a wedding for Saturday night."

"A wedding?" He shook his head. "As long as you're not the bride in this wedding, I don't see why you would be missed."

"Why she would be missed?" Maggie's eyes flashed with anger. "Let me tell you something, you old coot. She will be missed no matter when she leaves."

Bertrand turned slowly—very slowly—to face Maggie.

Anne pursed her lips to keep from saying something she would regret. Still, this was bound to turn into a catfight. And she had a pretty good feeling she knew who would come out on top. Maggie might be genteel in many ways, but when it came to getting what she wanted, she was a woman on a mission. Hadn't Anne witnessed as much in the exchanges between her and Bets?

The grandfather clock gonged and Anne glanced at it. Ten o'clock. As the second hand moved in steady pace, she felt the ticking down of her time with Maggie and Jake. It suddenly felt like an ultimatum. Despite her best internal objections, the clock ticked on.

"Let me get you a cup of coffee and we'll talk more sensibly." Maggie nodded and pointed to the sofa. "Have a seat. I'll be right back. And don't you dare go off with these girls while I'm in the kitchen. I have five grown sons, all in better shape than you, and they'll find you in a hurry."

His eyes widened, though for a moment Anne almost thought she saw a hint of a smile. He sat down on the sofa, looking more perplexed than anything. Seconds later, Ginger leaped up into the spot beside him.

"What the devil is this?" Uncle Bertrand's lips tightened and he pushed the dog away. Ginger nuzzled up against him, licking him on the arm. He yanked it away, mumbling something about how animals were meant to stay in the yard or the barn.

"Oh, Ginger doesn't like the barn, Uncle Bertrand," Kate said. "She's scared of the goats."

"Scared of the goats? What good is a dog that's afraid of animals? I would think a farm dog would be trained to—" He never got to finish his sentence. Ginger weaseled her way across his lap and plopped down, closing her eyes.

"She likes you!" Maggie said as she reentered the room with a cup of coffee in hand. "Well, that's a good sign. Dogs have a good sense about them. If Ginger likes you, you must be a good fella. Perhaps I was too quick to jump to conclusions."

Emily turned, but not before rolling her eyes. Anne flashed her a warning look. No point in getting their uncle more riled up than he already was.

He took a slow sip of the coffee then set the cup on the end table. After a few moments of awkward silence, he finally spoke. "Perhaps I could stay a day or two until I can figure out how best to handle this."

"Really, Uncle Bertrand?" Anne drew near but fought the temptation to give him a hug.

"Perhaps, but if I'm going to stay, I'd better head over to the hotel to see about getting a room. And I'll need to call the store to let them know." He paused and gazed down at his suit. "I do wish I'd brought a change of clothes."

"We've men's clothes aplenty around here," Maggie said. "So don't you worry about that. We'll keep you well dressed." She winked. "How do you look in overalls?"

"Overalls?" He grunted. "Haven't worn them since I was a boy." He gave her a curt nod. "I'll just head over to the hotel now, and we can speak more about your plans later today."

"Oh, that reminds me. There's a woman staying there who knows you." Anne joined him on the sofa. "Her name is Cornelia Witherspoon. Does that sound familiar?"

"Cornelia?" His eyes widened. "I...why, yes, it does. Cornelia and I were good friends at one time, but then things changed. I haven't spoken to her in nearly a year." He reached for his cup, which now trembled in his hand.

"I see." Maggie narrowed her gaze. "Well, I've been told that my matchmaking skills are sharper than an arrow. Found brides for nearly all my boys. Would you like me to—"

Bertrand rose, splashing coffee onto his pants leg. "No." He placed his cup on the end table and began to pace the room. "That will not be necessary. I won't be in need of a matchmaker, I can assure you—and Cornelia Witherspoon is the last person I would…" He paused to look out the window. "What the devil is that?" He pointed to a spot beneath the trees where Emily had placed several little crosses.

"That's where I buried Kate's dolls," she explained.

"Is this the kind of child I'm taking into my home? One who performs burials in the yard?"

Emily nodded, her face lighting with a smile.

He turned back to face Maggie. "And to go back to what you were saying earlier, your matchmaking services will not be required. Cornelia Witherspoon is a married woman." At that revelation, he turned back to the window, said something about the heat, and tugged at his collar.

A hint of a smile turned up the corners of Maggie's lips. She walked over to Bertrand and placed her hand on his shoulder. "Let me ask you a question." The twinkle in her eyes let Anne know right away that she was up to tricks.

"And what might that be?" He turned to face her.

"I realize you have work waiting for you back in Dallas, but is it truly urgent?"

He turned from the window. "Just the usual running of the store." He tugged at his shirt collar again. "Why do you ask?"

"When was the last time you took a Sabbath rest?"

"A Sabbath rest?" He pulled his shoulders back and stood aright. "I'm a good Christian man. I observe the Sabbath. But this is only Wednesday, a workday."

"You're misunderstanding my question. I'm not making an

accusation. Just wondering if or when you've had a season of rest and reflection. There's truly no lovelier place in the world than the Texas Panhandle." She put her finger on his chest. "I would like you to consider the possibility that the Lord has brought you to Groom for a sabbatical from your labors. A holiday."

"Holiday?" He snorted. "I don't take holidays."

"Well, then, it's about time you did. I can tell from the wrinkles on that brow that you've not relaxed in a month of Sundays. Stay awhile. Rest. Soak in your surroundings. Spend time with the girls." She paused and looked him over. "I don't mean to be rude, but you're as skinny as a rail. Someone needs to fatten you up."

"I beg your pardon?"

"You just leave that part to me. Stay on through the weekend and I'll serve up some meals like nothing you've ever tasted. I'll send you back to Dallas on Monday fat and sassy. Then you'll have plenty of energy to do all the work you need."

"Monday?" He shook his head.

"Well, of course. You'll stay for the wedding Saturday night so that Anne can work her magic for the bride and groom. You wouldn't travel home on Sunday, of course. You did just tell me you're a good Christian man, did you not?"

"Well, I suppose I could..." His words drifted off and he appeared to be thinking about the idea. Then, just as quickly, his expression shifted and he was back to the old Uncle Bertrand once again. "How the devil did you manage this, woman?"

"Manage what?" She batted her eyelashes.

"How did you manage to convince me to stay through the weekend? I had no intention of staying more than a night or two. Not that I had actually planned to stay at all. I'd come to fetch the girls and take them to my place straightaway. And now you've got me completely discombobulated."

"I've been told I have that effect on men. Er, people." She giggled. "But why fight it? Just stay and rest. Looks like it's going to take at least a day or two to iron out those wrinkles on your forehead. I'll be right back with my ironing board. You stay put."

Anne did her best not to laugh, though everything inside of her wanted to do so. Emily looked her way, eyes wide. So did Kate, who whispered, "Is she really going to iron his forehead?"

Anne shook her head and continued to bite her lip. Until Uncle Bertrand looked her way.

"I will thank you to never mention Cornelia Witherspoon's name in my presence again. Do we have an understanding?"

"W–what?" She felt the color drain out of her face. "I–I'm sorry, Uncle Bertrand. How was I to know...?"

"You don't know, and you will never know. But you will never mention her name to me again. Understood?"

Behind Uncle Bertrand's back, Emily mouthed the words "Cornelia Witherspoon! Cornelia Witherspoon!" Anne glared at her.

"I promise, Uncle Bertrand. You will never hear her name from me again," Anne managed. She wanted to ask questions but knew better. For now, silence was the best response.

* * * * *

After a long day of final repairs on the track, Jake stopped at the store to purchase some supplies and a little gift for Emily, who'd dropped more than a few hints about a certain item she needed. While there, he also decided that a new shirt was in order. A fella could never have too many shirts. When he brought his purchases to the counter to pay for them, he couldn't help but notice several vases filled with the prettiest yellow roses he'd ever seen.

"These are really nice."

"They're just in from Tyler," the clerk explained. "I've never seen any quite like them. They're larger than most and should go on blooming for days."

"I think I'll take some home. A dozen, please."

"Your mother will like those, Jake." The clerk smiled as she pulled them out of the vase and wrapped the stems in paper. "And they smell wonderful."

He didn't want to tell her that the roses weren't meant for Mama. No, he planned to give them to someone else entirely. Someone whose hand he wanted to hold at least one more time before she left for Dallas. He might have to explain the symbolism of the yellow rose of Texas, but once she heard the story, it would forever link them.

As he left the store, Jake started humming the familiar tune. By the time he reached the road, he added the lyrics.

"There's a yellow rose in Texas, that I am going to see;
Nobody else could miss her, not half as much as me.
She cried so when I left her, it like to broke my heart,
And if I ever find her, we nevermore will part.
She's the sweetest little rosebud that Texas ever knew;
Her eyes are bright as diamonds; they sparkle like the dew;
You may talk about your Clementine and sing of Rosalee,
But the yellow rose of Texas is the only girl for me."

As he continued down the road toward home, the lyrics of that song rushed over him. Jake did his best to brush aside the pain that gripped his heart when he thought about Anne leaving. Though he could not say what the future held, he did, with all assurance, have faith in the One who held it. And for now, that faith would have to see him through.

Chapter Sixteen

....

Looking for the perfect place to fall in love? Whether you're searching for a crab apple tree to carve your initials or an open field of flowers for a romantic picnic, you'll find the perfect backdrop in the Texas Panhandle. Fellas, if you're lookin' to gather up some wildflowers to give that fair lady as a special gift, you'll find them aplenty in the Panhandle. Rose of Sharon, leadplant, fern bush, Texas red yucca, and Russian sage grow in abundance, as well as a host of other exotic flowers. Yes, this is certainly the place to woo that pretty lady. And if her heart doesn't come alive in the Texas Panhandle, then send her packin'. It simply wasn't meant to be. —"Tex" Morgan, reporting for the *Panhandle Primer*

Jake drew a deep breath as he reached the porch and tried to come up with a workable story about the roses. Unfortunately, he didn't have much of a chance. At the very moment he climbed the steps, Cora, Milly, Pauline, and Ruth all came rushing out of the house.

"See you tomorrow, Anne," Ruth called out.

"Thank you for letting us help with the wedding plans." Pauline giggled.

Cora reached Jake first, her mouth falling open as she laid eyes on the yellow roses. "Oh, Jake."

"You shouldn't have!" Milly pulled them out of his arms and danced around in a circle.

Jake wanted to slap himself in the head, but that would require dropping the rest of his packages.

"What's all the noise out here?" His mother appeared at the door. She took one look at the flowers in Milly's hands and gasped. "Oh, Jakey, they're lovely. I'm tickled pink." She laughed. "Or should I say tickled yellow?"

He'd just opened his mouth to explain the significance of the flowers when Anne and her sisters appeared in the doorway.

"What have you got there, Milly?" Anne asked. She took a few steps in Milly's direction, and her eyes widened as she took in the roses. "Oh. Oh my."

"Do you like them?" Jake asked.

"Like them? They're perfect!"

All the ladies grew silent, and Jake shifted his gaze between them. Now what? He'd have to give them to their intended recipient, but he hadn't planned to make a production out of it.

"Whatever possessed you, honey?" his mother asked.

"Yes, who are they for?" Milly asked, passing them back to him. "Really?"

"Tell us, please!" Cora said.

"Can't a fella buy roses without standing before the firing squad?" He pulled the roses to himself, trying to work up the courage to turn Anne's way. He finally managed the task, reveling in the beauty of her smile as he pressed them into her arms. "I just thought our visitor might like to have a little taste of Texas. Sort of a welcome to the state. Texas is known for its yellow roses."

"So I've heard." Anne's cheeks flamed pink, almost matching the blouse she wore.

"Oh, Jake, you're the sweetest boy ever!" Pauline said.

"You need to give our husbands some lessons," Ruth added.

Milly placed her hands on her hips. "Yes, I daresay they have a thing or two to learn from their little brother."

"Like how to woo a woman." Cora giggled. "That's what you're really doing, right, Jakey?"

He groaned.

Thankfully, Anne's sweet expression kept him grounded. Otherwise he would've already bolted into the house. A saner man would've at least headed to the barn, claiming he had to feed the goats.

Anne gazed at the flowers as if they were the loveliest ones she'd ever seen. "Where did you get these?" She looked over at him, her eyelashes fluttering. Did she mean to stir his heart with that move? Likely not, but it was stirred one way or the other.

"At the general store."

"Do you think you could get more? Lots more?"

"Well, sure. They have them in abundance. Just got a shipment from Tyler. Why?"

"Do they have them in different colors?"

He nodded. "I saw pink. And red."

"Oh, that's perfect." She reached up and threw her arms around his neck. Jake felt his cheeks grow warm at the unexpected embrace. "We're gathering fresh flowers for the wedding on Saturday. I'd planned to use wildflowers and a mixture of flowers from your mother's garden...but I hadn't yet found any roses, and I know that's what Virginia's longing for most of all."

Anne pulled them close to her face. "Oh, they smell wonderful. I can't wait to get these into some water. Maggie, will you help me?"

"Of course."

His mother followed Anne into the house, leaving Jake alone on the porch with his four sisters-in-law and Anne's two little sisters.

"Nice work," Emily said with a sly grin. "A true hero always brings a lady flowers. I couldn't have written that any better myself."

"I do know a thing or two," he said and then winked.

"It's perfect, Jake." Cora sighed. "Perfect."

"You're smitten with her, then?" Ruth asked.

He shifted his position, growing uncomfortable inside and out. "I really don't think we need to be talking about—"

"Oh, c'mon, Jakey." Pauline laughed. "You know you're not going to get away with keeping this a secret anyway. You like her, don't you?"

He leaned against the porch railing, feeling a bit on display. "What's not to like?" he said after a moment's pause.

"I knew it!" Emily clasped her hands together.

Kate let out a squeal. "Oh, it's wonderful."

"So what happens next?" Ruth asked. "How can we help?"

"You can help by not helping." He put his hand up. "I don't want to insult anyone, but this is one thing I need to do on my own. Everyone needs to trust me. And I would be grateful if the six of you could keep this to yourselves, please. The folks in Groom have already been talking about me behind my back for weeks, and I don't like the way it feels. If I stand half a chance with Anne, this has got to be done right."

Milly drew near and gave him a gentle hug. "You have my word, little brother."

"I won't tell a soul," Pauline said as she gave his hand a squeeze.

"Neither will I," Ruth added.

"You know me, Jake." Cora sighed. "I'm not very good at keeping secrets...but I promise to do my best. Will that do?"

"For now." Jake turned his gaze to Emily and Kate. "Okay, now... what about the two of you?"

Emily nodded. "As long as I can write about it in my book afterward."

"Will you change the names of the characters?"

She grinned. "Of course. I always do."

"Fine." He looked at Kate. "You won't tell anyone, will you?"

"Tell them what?" she asked and then winked.

"Perfect."

As he took those first few steps across the porch toward the front door, Jake couldn't help but hum "The Yellow Rose of Texas" once more.

* * * * *

As Anne climbed into bed Wednesday night, her mind reeled. First the beautiful yellow roses from Jake. Then the cryptic hints from her little sisters. She'd gotten the message, of course.

He cares about me.

And I care about him too.

She pulled the covers up and rested her head against the pillow. The more she thought about Jake, the more conflicted she felt. How could she possibly give her heart—even a piece of it—to someone she would likely never see again?

Anne tried to sleep. Ironically, the sound of a train off in the distance roused her from a near slumber. A train?

Oh yes. The track. Workers had finished the repairs on it. Not that she planned to board a train tonight, but the very idea that she could leave now if she chose to sent a thousand thoughts running through her mind. Just a few short days ago she had considered turning around and going back to Colorado. But now...

She sat up in bed, her thoughts shifting to the one person who had caused both her heart and her mind to shift gears—Jake.

Jake, with those captivating dimples. Jake, with his boy-next-door charm. Jake, the one who always seemed to put others first. Jake, the one who'd given her the yellow roses that now sat in the vase on her bedside table.

How could she leave Groom now, knowing he cared about her?

Anne tossed and turned, yanking on the covers until they came loose at the foot of the bed. About a half hour later, she'd come up with a plan. Dallas and Groom weren't that far apart, were they? Of course not. If the Lord had somehow arranged all of this, then surely He could arrange a plan for them to see each other, at least on occasion.

Anne finally drifted off into a fitful sleep. She awoke some time later to a loud cry. Sitting up in bed, Anne attempted to get her bearings. Through the shadows she made out the room. Everything seemed fine.

Only, someone wasn't fine. Beyond the closed door, she heard her younger sister's cries.

"Emily."

Anne leaped from the bed and reached for her housecoat. She opened the door and stepped into the dark hallway. To her right, she still heard Emily's wails. Anne felt her way along, keeping one hand on the wall until she reached the door to Emily's room. She'd just started to open it when Maggie's soothing voice spoke.

"There, there, honey. It's going to be fine now. Did you have a nightmare?"

"I dreamed that Mama was still alive." Emily's voice trembled as she responded. Gone was the rough and tough rapscallion who told stories of Indian scalpings and bank robberies.

At these words, Anne stepped into the room. Unable to make out anything in the darkness, she took a tentative step forward and bumped into the rolltop desk.

Emily and Maggie gasped in unison.

"It's just me. Annie."

"Annie!" Emily's voice took on a tearful tone. "Oh, Annie, I dreamed about Mama. She was wearing a white dress and looked so beautiful, almost like an angel. But when I tried to reach out and touch her, she wasn't there. She disappeared like a vapor."

"Oh, honey." Anne made her way to the bed and sat at Emily's feet. She reached for her sister's hand.

"I wanted to touch her so badly, Annie. And I thought I could... but she wasn't really there. Why would I dream that? I barely remember Mama."

"I have to wonder if these nightmares are a result of those stories you write. Or maybe they were triggered because you buried your dolls."

"I have yet to figure out why you've done that," Maggie said.

Emily shrugged. "Oh, I buried them for a reason. I plan to dig them up before we leave and then interview them. That's the whole purpose."

"Interview them?"

"Yes. I want to ask them what it's like to come back to life. If anyone would know, they would."

"Ah." Anne grew silent.

"We won't really know what life in heaven is like until we get there," Maggie said. "But from what I've read in the Bible, it's a wonderful place. I'm sure your parents are both very happy."

"And they would want us to be happy too," Anne said. "If I know Mama, she would want us to get back to the business of living."

Maggie gave Emily's hand a squeeze. "You're such a brave girl when it comes to the stories you write. I know that, if you pray, God will help you get through this difficult season."

"It's easy to be brave on paper." Emily sighed. "It helps me pretend I can be brave in real life too. Does that make sense?"

"Of course," Anne said. "But don't you think it's time to lay down the stories about massacres and blood and so forth? Maybe you could write something poetic or sweet."

Emily sighed. "That's just so boring, Annie. If I'm ever going to sell my stories, they have to grab people by the throat."

"Then write adventurous tales but leave out some of the blood and guts. I'm afraid it's affecting your sleep."

Emily yawned and leaned against her pillows.

"Think you can sleep now?" Maggie asked, running her hand over Emily's hair.

"Mm-hmm." Emily offered a hint of a nod, and her eyes fluttered closed.

Anne watched as Maggie rested her hand on Emily's arm and prayed aloud. "Father, watch over this precious girl while she's sleeping. Give her sweet dreams and peaceful rest."

GROOM
1914
TX

At once Anne's eyes filled with tears. She turned away, unable to watch the gentle motions Maggie made as she tucked Emily in. Memories of her mother washed over her.

"I'll just...wait out here." Anne took a couple of steps into the hallway, hoping Maggie hadn't witnessed her tears.

Seconds later, the older woman appeared and took Anne's arm. "I'm wide awake. What about you?"

Anne nodded. It would probably take her hours to fall back asleep, in fact.

"Let's go into the living room and have a little chat, shall we?"

Though she wasn't sure she felt up to it, Anne followed Maggie down the dark hallway. Arriving in the living room, the older woman announced that she needed a glass of water. "I'll fetch it from the kitchen and come right back. Would you like one?"

"That would be nice."

As Maggie left for the kitchen, Anne took a couple of steps into the shadowy darkness of the living room and bumped into something. Or rather, someone.

"Didn't mean to startle you." Jake's breath felt warm against her cheek. His nearness brought comfort, and she leaned into him.

"Emily had a nightmare," she whispered.

Anne felt his arm slip across her shoulders.

"Ah. Is she going to be all right?" he asked.

"I think so." Anne welled up with tears again. "I'm so worried about her, Jake. She's hiding so much pain, but I don't know what to do for her."

He stroked Anne's hair. "You're doing it already, Anne. You're there for her, setting the perfect example."

Anne began to cry and he held her tight. When the tears finally gave way to silence, Anne sighed. "Some example I'm setting," she whispered.

"Oh, I don't know about that," he whispered in response. "I've learned a thing or two from you since you arrived."

He ran his fingers through her hair once again, and she resisted the urge to reach up and kiss him for saying such a sweet thing.

Just about that time, a light came on the room. Anne took a giant step backward, bumping into the end table and almost knocking over a picture frame. She grabbed it to keep it from falling.

Across the room, Maggie looked at the both of them with a half smile on her face. Thankfully, she didn't ask any questions. Instead, she handed Anne a glass of water and a handkerchief, rested a hand on her shoulder, and said, "Emily's a strong little girl inside and out. There's just something about the middle of the night that makes us more vulnerable."

"Indeed." Anne whispered the word and then realized how vulnerable she'd felt in Jake's arms. Not that he seemed disturbed by the idea. In fact, a boyish smile lit his face as he glanced her way.

"Well, don't let me disturb you ladies," he said with a nod. "I've got to be up early. Just wanted to check on you."

"Th–thank you." Anne offered a nod. As he turned back toward the hallway, she said, "Oh, Jake?"

"Yes?" He turned to face her.

"Thank you again for the roses. They mean so much to me."

He gave her a quick nod, a quiet, "You're so welcome," then disappeared into the shadows of the night.

Chapter Seventeen

·····················

One thing I've observed about folks in the Texas Panhandle—they have a resilient spirit. I've known many a person who turned their grief and heartache into something good. Perhaps I'm more keenly aware of this because we've recently faced a death in our family. My dear mother—God rest her soul—left us this past week. And though our hearts are heavy, I can think of no place I'd rather be than in Texas, with my friends gathered around me. Perhaps that's what makes us so strong. Here in the Panhandle, we bear one another's burdens. This week I'm so grateful for folks willing to stand alongside me with hands extended, ready to carry my load.
—"Tex" Morgan, reporting for the Panhandle Primer

After holding Anne in his arms, Jake returned to his room. He got into bed with the memory of that moment still fresh—not that he could sleep. Oh no. Every time he closed his eyes, he imagined Anne in his arms. He could feel her cries, sense her pain. He replayed the event at least a dozen times before finally growing weary. His sleep was light, and when he awoke at six o'clock to rise for work, images of Anne flittered through his mind again.

She had captivated him. No doubt about it.

Jake sat on the side of the bed knowing he should pray but feeling conflicted. The only words that wanted to cross his lips were,

"Lord, please don't take her away." After several minutes of wrestling through his emotions, he managed a different prayer, one he knew the Lord would answer.

"Father, not my will...but Yours be done."

Truly they were the hardest words Jake O'Farrell had ever spoken.

* * * * *

Anne awoke on Thursday morning with a headache. She'd been up half the night wrestling with the sheets. But with morning's light—headache or no headache—she had work to do. Virginia and Amaryllis would be by at nine to begin their flower picking for the garlands. There was no time to give in to her emotions. Not with so much work to be done.

Maggie prepared breakfast and gazed at Anne from time to time. Anne half-expected her to ask about what she'd witnessed last night but was relieved when she did not. Instead, Maggie offered up occasional tidbits about Jake, which Anne eventually found humorous.

"You know, that Jakey is quite a clean boy. He bathes every day whether he needs it or not."

"O–oh?"

"Yes. And you've never met anyone more polite. I daresay I did my finest work raising my youngest boy. Perhaps that's because the others were already out of the house by then."

"He is very polite." Anne offered a bright smile and tried to figure out how to put an end to this conversation.

"Who's polite?" Emily asked, entering the kitchen.

"Jake."

"Oh, I know. He bought me a new doll from the store last night so that I can bury it alongside the others."

"He did not." Anne couldn't fathom such a thing.

"Yes, he did." Kate chimed in as she entered the kitchen. "Emily's hiding her under the bed so you won't see her. She's a beautiful doll with blond hair and pink lips."

"Did you ask him to buy you a doll?"

"Yes, but I didn't tell him why." She wrinkled her nose. "I asked for a gray-headed one with a bun, but he couldn't find one like that, so I'm going to smear ashes in her hair to make it gray."

"Are you telling me he bought you a beautiful blond-haired doll as a gift but you plan to bury it? No doubt that's why you had a nightmare."

Emily shrugged. "Don't fret, Annie. I think the bad dream was because Uncle Bertrand showed up. Scared the daylights out of me." She giggled. "Or should I say the nightlights?"

Anne fought the temptation to roll her eyes. "Well, if you go over to Milly's this morning, I don't want you talking about dead dolls—do you understand me? You will scare the children with stories such as that."

"I don't talk about death in front of the children." Emily's expression grew more serious. "I know better than that." She grabbed a blueberry muffin from the tray on the table. "Is it all right with you if we leave early this morning? Willy wants to teach me how to fish. I already told him I'm going to catch more fish than him so he'd better watch out."

"I'm going too," Kate said. "But I don't want to touch the worms." She looked Emily. "Do I have to?"

"Nah. I'll do that part for you."

Anne watched the exchange between her sisters, realizing just how tied they'd gotten to Jake's family. "You two go ahead and get dressed, and then let me fix your hair."

Less than twenty minutes later, both girls were out the door. Anne went to her bedroom to fetch the vase of yellow roses so she could show them to Virginia when she arrived. She crossed paths with Maggie as she reentered the parlor with vase in hand.

"Those yellow roses are rather special," Maggie said. "Did you understand the significance?"

"I've heard of the song," Anne said, "but I don't really know much about the meaning. Never paid much attention. Just figured he wanted to welcome me to Texas, that's all."

"Hardly." Maggie chuckled. "You really don't know?"

"No." Anne did have to wonder what all the fuss was about, though.

"I'll give you a little hint," Maggie said. "It's a little song about a fella pining away for a girl. Life's circumstances have parted them, and it's breaking his heart."

"Oh." Anne hardly knew how to respond. So, Jake had been sending a larger message than she realized. How interesting.

She didn't have time to think about it, however, because a knock sounded at the door. Anne opened it to find Virginia and Amaryllis engaged in a heated argument about hair ribbons.

"Gracious. What's this about?"

Virginia tried to explain, but Amaryllis marched past her into the house, clearly agitated.

"Come now, girls. Let's talk about something of real importance." Maggie gazed at Virginia. "Any word from your parents?"

"Yes. They are in Oklahoma City today and will be here tomorrow. Mama's very excited about our plans and can't wait to help. She especially liked the idea about the fresh flowers. Mama's always been partial to flowers."

"Perfect." Maggie clasped her hands together. "Everything is working out just as it should. Oh, speaking of which—Anne, will you show the girls the yellow roses?"

Anne tried not to read too much into Maggie's phrasing. Instead, she reached for the vase of yellow roses and held them up. "These were purchased at the general store, and from what I understand, there are lots more."

"Will these flowers still look good the day after tomorrow?" Virginia asked. "If so, then we'll need to buy as many as we can."

Ann nodded. "They will if we keep them cool and in water."

"We'll put them in the cellar," Maggie said. "That should help."

"And I learned a little trick to keep them fresher longer," Anne said. "You drop a bit of aspirin powder in the water."

"Well, for heaven's sake." Maggie looked stunned. "I've never heard of that."

"You're full of wisdom, Anne," Virginia said. "Have I mentioned that I'm tickled you're here to help with all this?" She threw her arms around Anne's neck and gave her a tight squeeze.

When she released her hold Anne offered a smile. "I've enjoyed every minute so far, but we still have a lot of work to do. Did you bring baskets for gathering flowers?"

"Yes, they're on the front porch," Virginia said.

"I do hope my hair doesn't get mussed while we're picking flowers," Amaryllis said. "And I just filed my fingernails last night. I would hate to get them dirty." She shivered as she gave them a once-over. "That would be awful."

Anne resisted the urge to laugh.

"I know where we can get some beautiful calla lilies," Maggie said. "They would be perfect."

"Oh, I've always loved calla lilies!" Virginia's eyes sparkled.

"Where are they, Maggie?" Anne asked. "Far from here?"

"Just up the road...at my sister's place."

"Ah." Anne chose her next words with care. "Does she...I mean, did she give permission?"

"Permission?" Maggie paused. "Well, I figure they're partly mine. I gave her the cuttings for those callas several years ago when mine were in full bloom. Unfortunately, mine didn't last the winter, but hers sprang back with a vengeance. They were probably too scared not to. Despite her shortcomings, she's got a very green thumb. The woman keeps a beautiful garden. Besides..." She leaned forward and whispered the rest. "I asked Leo, and he gave me permission. She has so many, she won't notice if we take a few."

"Oh, Maggie, I don't know." Anne released a slow breath. "If she catches us..."

"I won't live to see my wedding day." Virginia shook her head. "I don't really have to have calla lilies in my garlands or my bouquet. Truly."

"Well, of course you do." Maggie pursed her lips and remained silent for a moment. "And our timing is perfect. Leo told me to come between nine and ten because she's at her quilting club. So let's get going before I chicken out."

The girls followed on Maggie's heels down the road to Bets and Leo's. Anne's heart quickened as they drew near.

"Wait here while I scope out the place." Maggie gestured for the girls to stand behind a tree while she tiptoed to the garden located a few feet away. She'd no sooner reached the calla lilies than the front door swung open. Fortunately, Leo stepped out.

"It's fine, Maggie," he said with a welcoming smile. "She'll be gone for at least another hour. You ladies take what you like, but don't take so many that it's obvious."

"Bless you, Leo." Maggie turned to face the girls. "C'mon and join me, ladies. Let's make quick work of this."

"If you're sure it's safe." Virginia shifted her empty basket to her other arm and scurried to the side of the house. Amaryllis followed behind her but refused to kneel in the flower beds in her new white dress.

"I'll stand here and hold the basket while you fill it up." She fussed with her ribbon sash. "My mother paid a lot of money for this dress. If I get back to New York with grass stains on the skirt, she'll have my head."

"Well, we couldn't have that." Maggie knelt in the flower bed alongside Virginia. "Look at these different colors of calla lilies. Aren't they the prettiest flowers you've ever seen in your life?"

"They are." Virginia clasped her hands together and sighed. "Oh, I can hardly wait to see my bouquet! Yellow roses and calla lilies? I'm so blessed. And those garlands are going to be divine. I can see them now!"

As they worked, the conversation continued. Before long, however, the tone shifted. Perhaps the late morning heat had something to do with it. Amaryllis eventually retreated to the porch swing, claiming that the heat was affecting her delicate skin. Not that Virginia seemed to mind. She and Anne continued to talk as if they were old friends.

"Can I ask you a question, Anne?" Virginia looked up from her basket of colorful flowers.

"Of course."

"I don't mean to pry. Heaven knows it's none of my business. But I'm curious about your mama. Why did she…? I mean, how did she…?"

"How did she pass?" Anne finished the sentence for her.

"Yes." Virginia dropped another flower in the basket then rose and brushed the dirt from her skirt. "How did it happen? Was she ill?"

"No." A lump rose in Anne's throat, making it hard to speak. "She was the most beautiful woman you ever saw. In fact, she was so beautiful that Papa paid a famous painter to have a portrait done just a year before she died. She'd never been sick a day in her life."

"What happened, honey?" Maggie asked.

"It happened when she was expecting Kate. She was perfectly fine until those last few days. Then she got terribly sick. The doctor called it…" She shook her head, trying to remember. "Eclampsia?"

"Eclampsia. Yes." Maggie nodded. "I had a touch of that with John. You should've seen my ankles. They were, well…" She paused and shook her head. "Go ahead."

"At first the doctor was hopeful. But Mama got so sick that he finally decided Mama would have to have surgery to deliver the baby."

Virginia's eyes widened. "I've read about that. Cesarean section."

"Yes." Anne rose and began to pace. "I remember seeing Kate for the first time that April morning. She was such a tiny little thing. The doctor said she was only five pounds, but she was a scrapper. He felt sure she would grow big and strong."

"And she has." Maggie's words rang out. "She's a wonderful, healthy girl."

"Yes." Anne could still remember how frantically she'd prayed for the tiny newborn. More than that, though, she remembered her fears for her mother. "I wanted to go in and see Mama, but they wouldn't let me." Anne shook her head, the tears now coming. "The next day the doctor told Papa that she had an infection. I was young and silly and didn't think much of it. I remember saying a prayer in passing, but I didn't really plead with God to save her." Anne shook her head. Her voice lowered to a whisper. "I always felt that if I'd prayed harder, God would have answered me. Sometimes I think it's my fault...."

"Oh, honey." Maggie rose and pulled Anne into an embrace. "Don't finish that sentence. I don't let anyone speak untruths in my presence, and to say that you were in any way responsible would be wholly untrue. Your mother's death had nothing to do with you. You were a child, distracted with your new baby sister and the usual things a child is distracted by. God doesn't hold you accountable."

"In church they said we have to pray without ceasing. And I know that my prayers weren't as strong as they should have been. I'm not sure why I've carried so much guilt over this, but I have."

"We don't serve a God who slaps our hands when we make mistakes. Sure, it would be ideal if we got it right all the time, but then why would we need His grace and mercy?" Maggie ran her fingers through Anne's hair, bringing a sense of comfort.

"Oh, Anne." Virginia looked her way with tears in her eyes. "I had no idea the depth of the struggles you've been through. If I ever lost my mama..." Her gaze shifted downward to her basket. "I'm sorry. I shouldn't have said that."

"No, it's fine." Anne offered a smile. "No reason you should have to walk on eggshells because of what I've been through. That's the point, really...to get on with life."

"You're such a strong, brave girl." Maggie tightened her hug. "I'm so proud of you."

"Thank you," Anne said. "But I must confess, it's been a lot harder to pray since the night my mother died."

Virginia rose with her basket in hand. "Oh, Anne."

"No, it's true. I keep trying, but it mostly just feels like my prayers are rising as high as my bedroom ceiling and then bouncing back down."

"They're going much further, trust me." Maggie gave a nod. "Even if it doesn't feel like it. So you keep praying, honey. Don't stop. Promise me?"

Anne nodded. She pulled out her tiny cross necklace, which she fingered as she spoke. "I've worn this little cross every day since my mother died. It was hers. And I've wanted to believe that God still cares. But somewhere between feeling guilty for not praying hard enough and being angry that the Lord took her away from me, I just…" Her words drifted off.

"Your faith just shriveled up." Maggie patted her on the arm. "Oh, Anne, don't you see? You're human. We all feel guilty for things we shouldn't, and we all go through seasons where we're angry at God."

"Really?" Anne could hardly believe it. "I never met anyone who ever said that before. I just tucked away what I was feeling and didn't tell anyone. I hid this little cross under my blouse and tried to forget what I used to believe. And besides, I felt like such a hypocrite."

Maggie gave her a compassionate look. "I think the greatest way you could honor your mother right now would be to take that little cross and start wearing it on the outside again. Don't be afraid to trust God, even with the things that make no sense."

Anne rose and joined Virginia. Together they helped Maggie to her feet. Just then, Leo stuck his head around the front door. "Would you ladies like some lemonade before you leave?"

"No thanks, Leo," Maggie said. "I think we'd better hurry. Bets could be along anytime now. Besides, if she saw our empty lemonade glasses, it would be a dead giveaway. She would give you fits over it."

"I know how to wash a glass." He winked.

"Still, it's too risky." Maggie shook her head. "But thank you for the offer anyway."

"How can I thank you enough?" Virginia climbed the steps to the porch and gave Leo a warm hug. He looked a bit taken aback but hugged her in return.

"Well, I'm happy to do it. I'll be there on Saturday night, ready to kick up my heels."

"So you plan to dance, then?" Maggie looked at him as if she couldn't quite believe it.

"Yes. And if Bets won't join me, I'd be honored to take a spin around the floor with any of you fine ladies." He gave them a nod then disappeared inside the house.

"Will wonders never cease." Maggie shook her head. Before long, they were all laughing.

Anne glanced up at the sun, wondering about the time. "Is it safe to walk down the road? What if Bets passes us on her way home?"

"There's a back way." Maggie's brows elevated. "Follow me." She grabbed her flower basket and led them behind the house and to the right, then beyond some trees to a clearing. "It's a little longer this way, but we'll make it just fine."

Amaryllis began to complain about the heat. She swatted at a couple of mosquitoes and proclaimed that they would be the death of her. Before long, she trailed behind the others. Anne and Virginia kept a steady pace just behind Maggie, who seemed determined to get them back to O'Farrell's Honor in short order.

"Anne, I have a special favor to ask." Virginia shifted the flower basket to her left arm and slipped her right one through Anne's as they walked.

"Oh? What's that?"

"I know we're new friends and all, but I would be honored if you would stand up with me at my wedding."

"W–what?" Anne could hardly believe it. "Really?"

"Well, sure. I've already told Amaryllis. She loved the idea."

"She did?" Anne glanced back at Amaryllis, who continued to fuss—this time about the unlevel path they were on.

"Well, mostly." Virginia's eyes twinkled. "You've become like a sister to me."

"Thank you," Anne whispered, too overcome with emotion to say anything more. She suddenly found herself grateful for the dresses in her trunk. The ones she hadn't sold off before leaving Denver, anyway. "I have the perfect dress," she said. "It's a soft blue sky color. Reminds me of the skies here in Groom."

"Sky-blue." Virginia reached to grab her hand. "Perfect."

"Yes, perfect." Anne gave her new friend's hand a squeeze, realizing just how well that word suited her mood today. Oh, if only it would last forever.

Chapter Eighteen

....

Looking for a trip back in time? The Texas Panhandle gives you the perfect location to do just that! The next time you're in Ochiltree County, venture over to the south bank of Wolf Creek. There you can witness "The Buried City"—stone ruins speculated to be a prehistoric town. I visited the area for the first time shortly after my mother's death. As I gazed at those stones—just a shell of what once was—I was struck by an intriguing thought: how often do we bury our pain and grief, hoping to somehow preserve ourselves? In the end, we are little but ruined cities. I shared these thoughts with my wife, who claimed I was getting emotional in my old age. Still, I haven't been able to shake the idea that the life I'm living now needs to be far more than a shell of what once was. Just a few thoughts to chew on, my friends. —"Tex" Morgan, reporting for the Panhandle Primer

When Anne and the other ladies returned to the house, Uncle Bertrand met them on the front porch.

"Well, hello." Maggie climbed the steps and placed her basket of flowers on the railing.

He nodded. "Hope you don't mind that I dropped by. I took a little drive through town today but decided to come out for a visit."

Anne hardly knew what to make of this. Could this possibly be the same man who'd treated them with such disdain during his last visit to Colorado?

Maggie brushed the soil from her skirt. "You've caught us coming in from a flower-picking expedition. Would you like to help me cut these calla lilies and put them in water?"

Every eye shifted to Uncle Bertrand. He rose from the swing, offered a nod, then opened the front door for Maggie. She stepped inside, all smiles.

"I do hope you're hungry," she said. "I made chicken salad. My boys say it's the best in the county."

"Sounds wonderful." He followed on her heels into the parlor. Anne walked behind them, still not quite understanding what was happening. Virginia and Amaryllis came too, though Amaryllis complained about the late hour and claimed she had a headache.

"You girls go on," Anne said. "It won't take long to clean the flowers and put them in water."

"Are you sure?" Virginia asked.

"Of course."

"When will we put the garlands together?" Virginia asked.

"The other ladies are coming by tomorrow morning to help with that. We'll make the garlands and the bouquet as well as the rest of the decorations then." Anne took Virginia's flower basket and shooed her out the front door. "From this point on, you just focus on getting the rest you need. You have a very big day coming up. Besides, your parents are arriving today. You need to spend time with them."

"Yes, I do." Virginia threw her arms around Anne's neck. "Oh, how can I ever thank you?"

"By having the best wedding day possible."

Once the girls left, Anne entered the kitchen with the two

baskets in hand. She found Maggie washing her hands at the kitchen sink and chatting with her uncle, who sat at the table staring at the other flower basket.

Maggie turned her way with a smile. "We could use some help in getting all these down to the cellar once they're rinsed. Why don't you go fetch those sisters of yours from Milly's place?" She gave Anne a knowing look. "Take your time. No rush. I'll get these flowers trimmed back and put them in water."

"Are you sure?" Anne asked, feeling more confused than ever.

"Yes, I'm sure." Maggie's gaze narrowed and suddenly Anne got the message. She wanted to be left alone with Uncle Bertrand. Well, good. Perhaps Maggie could talk to him about his parenting skills. If anyone could get through to him about what Emily and Kate needed, it would be Maggie.

Anne quickly washed up and pulled up her hair to get it off her shoulders. Then she headed out the front door on her way to Milly's to check on the girls. At the top of the porch steps, she bumped into Jake—literally.

"Well." He grinned. "Hello to you too."

She giggled. "Sorry about that. Wasn't watching where I was going."

"That's quite all right." His eyebrows elevated playfully. "Can't think of anyone I'd rather run into."

A wave of embarrassment washed over Anne, but she did her best not to let it show.

"Where were you headed in such a hurry?" Jake asked.

"I'm on my way to Milly's to fetch the girls."

"I'd better go with you."

"Oh?" She gave him a curious look.

"Yes, um…there are snakes in the field."

"Really?"

"Well…" His face lit up with a contented smile. "On occasion. So I'll go along to protect you."

"Ah." She smiled and took his arm when he offered it. As they approached the gate, she slowed her step. "Can I ask you a question?" she asked after a moment. "It's kind of a funny one."

"Sure."

"When you went to the store to fetch those yellow roses, did you also happen to buy a doll for Emily?"

He nodded. "Yes. Maybe I should have asked you first. Are you upset?"

"No, I was just wondering…did you know she buried it in the yard?" Anne stopped walking and gazed at him.

He groaned. "No. I had no idea. I can never tell what Emily might do from one moment to the next."

"Me either." Anne paused. "I must say, I've been so concerned about her. Ever since Papa died, she's had an unusual fixation with death. I can't seem to get her to shake it."

"Losing a father is so hard." Jake's gaze shifted to the field. "It's been three years since my father's death, but it seems like just yesterday." He turned to look at her, and she was stunned to see that his eyes were filled with tears. "I've never known a man I respected more."

Instinctively, she reached to take his hand. "How did it happen?"

"Doc Robbins said it was a heart attack. We never saw it coming. My father went out to the fields one morning to brand the cattle and never came back."

"Oh, Jake…" She couldn't think of anything to say, so she left her words hanging. Seconds later she started walking again, and he kept the pace with her.

"My father was always the hardest-working man in the county. He had the idea that O'Farrell's Honor would be the largest ranch within a hundred miles. And he very nearly accomplished that. Still, I'd trade all of this"—Jake pointed to the open fields—"for one more day with him."

"I understand, trust me."

Jake paused and appeared to be thinking. "You know that picture I painted? The one in Emily's bedroom?"

"Sure. It's really something else."

"Thanks, but I wasn't fishing for compliments. I just wanted to tell you why I painted it. My father worked the fields for hours a day, as I said. But you've never met a man more dedicated to family. He knew when to quit working and start playing. He was quite a card, my dad. Always laughing. I sometimes think that's why my brothers are such cut-ups."

"He sounds wonderful."

"He was. But after he died, my memories started fading quickly. It was the strangest thing I'd ever experienced. I tried and tried to remember things he'd said or places we'd gone together. The only image that ever came to my mind was the one of him lying on the bed, silent and still, just before the undertaker came. Isn't that awful?"

Anne could hardly believe it. "I had the hardest time with that too. I couldn't erase that picture from my mind."

"I struggled with that problem for months after my father's death." Jake sighed. "But I finally decided to do something about it. I went out to the field on the back side of our property where I'd seen him branding the cattle. Figured if I painted a picture of him with that brand in his palm, it would sear the image of what he'd looked like into my brain. And I also figured it would keep the memories fresh of what he did out on the property. How he worked so hard to make a home for his family."

"That's a wonderful story, and it makes the painting even more special," Anne said. Off in the distance she heard the sound of children's voices and realized how much ground they'd covered. Soon they would be at Milly's place. Oh, but she didn't want this conversation to end. With that in mind, Anne slowed her pace almost to a stop.

Jake halted and turned to face her. "It's the strangest thing. Since I painted that picture, other memories have come flooding back—not just bad things, but good ones too. It opened up a well deep inside of me. Sort of like a little spring that feeds a large river. Now I have all sorts of memories of my time with him. Like the time he took me fishing at the lake and I caught my first catfish. And the time we went on a camping trip at the canyon but ended up having to come back home after only one night because I got sick."

"I think it's wonderful that you're able to remember so much," Anne said. "I wish my memories of my father were better. To be honest…"

She couldn't finish the sentence. What was the point in remembering, anyway? It seemed every time she thought of her father, she pictured a bottle in front of him and a glass in his hand. No matter how hard she tried, she couldn't erase that image.

Anne swallowed the lump in her throat. "This is a horrible confession, but I'm not sure I've ever known a man I respected less than my father, at least in the last few years of his life. Is that terrible?"

"Oh?" Jake looked at her with concern registering in his eyes. "Why is that?"

"My father…" She bit back the sigh that threatened to erupt. "He had a lot of problems in his final years. If I'm going to be completely honest, I can't really blame all of them on him. He didn't handle my mother's death well. He...well, he turned to alcohol."

She waited to see if Jake would respond negatively, but he did not. Still, the conversation made her nervous. Anne took a couple of steps away and paused to clear her thoughts. She finally turned back to Jake.

"Papa's drinking had always been a bit of a problem, but he gave himself over to it in the end. I can't tell you how awful it was to witness such a thing firsthand. He became a completely different person when he was drinking."

Jake gave her a sympathetic look. "Grief does strange things to people, doesn't it?" He drew near.

"Yes, and many times I remind myself of that. Still, most of the time I realize that he chose to grieve with a bottle of whiskey in hand. Or bourbon. Or vodka. No one made him. And he had three daughters who needed him. If I were him..." She shook her head. "I would have made a wiser choice."

"That's because you're always thinking of others."

"I am?"

The sound of children's voices rang out again, and she glanced toward them to make sure they were still at a distance. Emily had Willy by the shirt and appeared to be giving him a piece of her mind.

Jake nodded. "Well, sure. I've never met anyone who's as dedicated to her family as you. I can't believe others haven't pointed it out to you. You're completely devoted to your sisters, and I find that admirable. They're blessed to have you."

Anne's heart swelled. Truly, no one had ever taken note of her devotion to her sisters before. It felt mighty good that someone had actually noticed.

"What about you?" Anne asked. "You've been there for your

mom every step of the way. If anyone understands that sort of dedication, I do."

A smile lit his face. "You don't think I'm a mama's boy?"

"A mama's boy?" Anne fought to keep her surprise from showing. "Is that what people say you are? Because you're there for your mother?"

"Yep." He nodded. "It's a running joke in my family and with people in town. They think I'm staying because she cooks and cleans. They just don't understand."

"No, they don't. You could no more leave her alone than I could leave Emily and Kate to fend for themselves. The very idea is ridiculous." She smiled as Jake reached over and laced his fingers through hers. "Just goes to show you that people don't understand the word 'dedication.' If they did, they would see that we're both acting out of love, not selfishness."

"Well, there's a little selfishness on my part." Jake offered a sheepish grin. "I do love my mother's cooking. The last time I tried to fry up some sliced potatoes, I nearly caught the house on fire. Not to mention the fact that I cut my finger slicing them."

She did her best not to laugh. "That's another thing. I've never learned to cook. Even when Mama was alive, we always had a cook." She paused as the memories swept over her.

He took a couple of steps toward her, and Anne reflected on how comfortable his nearness felt.

"These past few months have been the hardest of all. Papa drank away our money. At least that's what Uncle Bertrand claims. It must be true, because one day the butler wasn't there. Then the cook left. Sadie, our maid, stayed with us until the end. But I knew she wasn't getting paid. She stayed because she loved us so much."

"Was your father ill during this time?"

"Yes." She cringed as she remembered how thin he'd gotten, how sallow his face had become. "The last several months were terrible. He took to his bed more often than not. And we rarely saw him eat anything. He always managed to have a bottle on the bedside table, though."

"Anne, I'm so sorry." Jake drew so close that she could feel his breath in her hair. "You've been through so much."

"So have you. You lost your father too."

"Yes, but both parents? And with all you went through with your father... My heart goes out to you."

"Losing my father was terrible, but I must confess that losing my mother was even harder. There are times when I miss her so much that it hurts." Anne reached for the little cross she always wore, her heart rate steadying as she took hold of it. "It doesn't seem right that I shouldn't be able to remember her like I used to. It's almost like a photograph that fades over time. You can still see the outline of it, and you remember it in part...but it's not quite as clear as it once was."

"Maybe forgetting helps to ease the pain." Jake shrugged. "Or maybe it's just that we're so distracted by the here and now that yesterday's memories are crowded out."

"That could be, I suppose. I just know I feel guilty for forgetting. And yet I want to look ahead, not back, if that makes sense."

"It makes perfect sense. Your mother would want you to look ahead, Anne."

Anne gripped the tiny cross necklace and lifted it so that he could see. "This was hers. I wear it to remember who she was."

"I'm sure she would be thrilled to see you wearing her cross, but I don't think she wants you to actually carry that cross. Does that make sense?"

"Carry the cross?" Anne looked at him, perplexed.

"The cross of grief," he said. "It's far too heavy. I only know of One who can carry something of such magnitude."

Anne smiled as the reality of his words settled into her heart. "You're right, of course. I've been trying to carry the cross as if it were a huge burden. But it's not mine to carry."

"Precisely. Can you let it go?"

She fingered the cross around her neck. Suddenly a thought occurred to her. "Oh, Jake. Maybe that's why I've been given the gift of this little cross, to remind me that God wants to carry my burdens—that I can't do it alone."

"Could be."

He slipped his arm across her shoulders, and she leaned her head against his. In that blissful state, she finally found herself ready to let go of the pain of the past. Funny how a stranger from Groom, Texas, had prepared her heart to finally let go.

* * * * *

Jake enjoyed the quiet embrace with Anne, but on the inside he found himself feeling very conflicted. *You're such a hypocrite, giving advice so freely when there are so many things you're still holding onto.*

After a moment, Anne gazed into his eyes. "Is something wrong? You're very quiet."

"Just thinking." He paused and released a breath slowly. "I told you how much my father loved this ranch."

"Yes."

"My brothers..." He paused and gestured to the yard where Emily and the others played. "My brothers have carried on his legacy. They've kept the ranch running and have made a fine living for their families. And Mama will never have to worry about money."

"And you?"

He leaned back against the fence. "I'm a horse of a different color. That's what my father always called me, anyway. Never really cared for ranching. From the time I was a boy, I had a fascination with the railroad. I'd sketch pictures of the cars and even designed my own engines. So I guess it didn't surprise anyone when I decided to sign on with the railroad. And I've loved every minute of it."

"Do you travel?"

"I've been to Tulsa—and to Dallas."

Right away, her expression shifted. She whispered the word "Dallas" and his heart plummeted. She would be leaving for Dallas...soon.

"Anyway, I've been several places. Hope to one day get to Missouri. That's where my mother is from."

"So I've been told. I heard all about how she wished she could have gone back for the World's Fair several years ago. But she had a houseful of children to tend to."

"Oh, I hear that story quite a bit. And I'm sure St. Louis is a wonderful city. Like I said, I'd love to travel there. But I feel pretty sure nothing will ever compare to the Panhandle."

"Now you sound like Emily. She picked up a tourist paper about the Panhandle when the train stopped in Amarillo."

"The *Panhandle Primer*?" he asked.

"Yes, that's the one. Seems like that Tex Morgan fellow is enamored with this area. The article I read was a bit exaggerated."

"Oh, he sings the praises of the Panhandle, to be sure. But he's right on every count. There's no finer place in the country."

"Do tell."

"I will." He squared his shoulders. "We have some of the best lakes in the state. And the ruins over near Wolf Creek tell of our history. But if you're really wanting the breath knocked out of you, you'll have to go to the canyon."

"The canyon?"

"Palo Duro Canyon. There's not a prettier sight in the world."

She shook her head. "Never heard of it."

"Hmm." He thought about his response. "Well then, we'll have to remedy that. What are you doing this afternoon?"

She shrugged. "Most of our work for the day is done. Tomorrow morning we're working on garlands for the wedding. All your brothers' wives are coming over to help."

"Perfect." He could hardly believe his good fortune. "How would you like to go for a drive to the most scenic spot in the Panhandle?"

"Right now?"

"Sure, why not? It's early in the day. Not even ten thirty. And I know the most perfect spot in the world for a picnic. You've never seen anything like it." When she hesitated, he added, "You can bring your sisters if you'd like. They could serve as our chaperones."

"We need chaperones?" She quirked a brow and gave him the cutest smile he'd ever seen.

If you keep looking at me like that, yes.

"Wait a minute. This is Thursday. Don't you have to work?"

He shook his head. "Nope. We put in so many hours the past few days that we were told to take the rest of today off as well as tomorrow."

"Wonderful."

"I couldn't agree more. So, what do you say?"

She offered a shy smile. "I say yes, of course. Let's go!"

From a distance, Emily's voice rang out. "Are you two going to stand there all day mooning over each other?"

He shrugged and offered Anne his arm; then the two of them walked toward Milly and Joseph's place together.

Chapter Nineteen

....

Still not convinced that the Texas Panhandle is the place for you? Then you surely haven't witnessed the grandeur of Palo Duro Canyon, a sixty-mile-long canyon carved out of the majestic high plains of north Texas. Eight hundred feet deep, the canyon offers breathtaking cliffs ribboned with nature's finest colors: fiery red, sunny yellow, brilliant purple, and cotton-cloud white. In this inspiring place, you can enjoy Texas's flora and fauna at its finest: abundant patches of redberry juniper await you along with my personal favorite—the hardy mesquite tree. Majestic sunflowers line the slopes of the clay canyon with prickly pear cacti offering a colorful contrast. I've heard it said that the good Lord above carved out Palo Duro Canyon with His fingertip, leaving behind just the right splash of colors. What else could account for such a work of art? Just one more reason to see the Texas Panhandle in person. —"Tex" Morgan, reporting for the *Panhandle Primer*

Milly somehow convinced Emily and Kate to stay at the ranch and play with the other children, which left Anne and Jake free to travel to the canyon by themselves. When Maggie offered to go along as chaperone, Jake looked as if he might be ill. However, it turned out she was only teasing.

"You two go on and have a good time," she said. "And while you're there, see if you can pick some wildflowers. Those garlands may need a bit of filler." She filled a picnic basket with enough goodies for a wonderful lunch and then sent them on their way with a hint of mischief in her eyes. Uncle Bertrand seemed to be acting a little odd as well. He actually offered Anne a smile. A genuine one. Would wonders never cease?

By noon, Anne and Jake were on their way to Palo Duro Canyon in the family's truck. They enjoyed pleasant conversation, talking about the plans for the wedding and then shifting gears to talk about Jake's work with the railroad. The hour's drive passed quickly, though Anne's stomach did rumble a bit as she thought about the chicken salad sandwiches Maggie had packed. Of course, the motion in her stomach was nothing compared to the fluttering in her heart every time Jake looked her way.

"Are you sure these are canyon lands?" Anne asked when Jake announced that they were getting close. I don't see anything... Oh!" A glance to her right revealed a break in the terrain. Slowly but surely a ribbonlike canyon appeared. And as the truck began to travel down, down, down the road into the canyon, the wonder of nature appeared at every turn.

"Oh, Jake! I've never seen anything like it. Not ever."

He smiled but kept his eye on the road. "I thought you might like it."

"Like it? I love it!"

He continued the descent until they arrived at the lowest possible point. He pulled the car off next to the creek then climbed out and walked around to her side to open the door for her. Anne wasn't sure which impressed her more—the glimmer in his eye or the beautiful surroundings.

She allowed him to take her hand, and he led her down the narrow path toward the water's edge.

"This is Palo Duro Creek," he said. "It links arms with the Red River."

Anne looked out over the narrow strip of water, which was surrounded on both sides by red clay. "I think I can see where the Red River gets its name."

"Yes, there's a lot of color down here in the canyon. That's one reason I like to come in the afternoon and stay through sunset. You're not going to believe how pretty this is in just a few hours. I will say, though, that you don't want to be down here when it rains."

"Why is that?"

"This area is prone to flash floods. I once got trapped as the water from the creeks and rivers began to rise. Barely made it back up the road. It put the fear of God into me."

"No doubt." She paused and drew in a breath. "But on a day like today, when everything is sunny and bright, it's perfect."

"Glad you think so." He gave her hand a squeeze then reached up and brushed a loose hair out of her face. "There," he whispered. "Don't want anything to block those beautiful brown eyes."

She felt her face grow hot and quickly looked the other way. "Are—are you getting hungry? We could set up a picnic spot here by the creek. It's nice and quiet."

"I would love that."

They worked together to spread a blanket. Jake pulled the picnic basket from the back of the truck and Anne opened it. Her delight grew when she saw that Maggie had packed not only sandwiches but lemonade and homemade cookies as well.

"It's a feast fit for a king," Anne announced, settling onto the blanket.

"For a king and queen," Jake corrected.

Her heart seemed to come alive every time he looked her way, and she felt young and giddy. And a little nervous too. She almost dropped the bottle of lemonade. "Oops."

"Here, let me help with that." Jake reached for the glasses and poured them, his hand steady. Anne marveled at his composure. Either he was more confident, or he did a better job of hiding his nerves.

For nearly two hours they sat at the creek's edge, eating, talking, and laughing. In that glorious place, Anne felt herself transported. No longer was she the woman carrying the weight of the world on her shoulders. No, in this place she was free to be Anne—Anne, who happened to be crazy over a boy named Jake.

* * * * *

The afternoon hours at Palo Duro Canyon passed far too quickly for Jake's liking. He wanted this day to stretch out as long as the Red River itself. What would he do, just a few days from now, when Anne left? His heart twisted every time he thought about it.

And so he did his best not to think about it. Not today, when anything seemed possible.

By five o'clock he had driven to most of his favorite spots in the canyon and they'd picked enough wildflowers to finish off the garlands. That meant there was only one spot left to go—his favorite

GROOM
1914
TX

lookout point. He drove as far as the road would take them then took her by the hand and climbed the rest of the way to the bluff.

While they made the journey, Jake gripped her hand as if it might be the last time. Many times he found himself wishing he would never have to let go.

All too soon they reached the spot. "Turn to your right," he whispered.

As she turned to face the colorful mesa walls, Anne released a little gasp. "Oh, Jake! I—I hardly know what to say."

"It's something else, isn't it?" He slipped his arm around her waist, and they stood side by side.

"I've truly never seen anything of this magnitude in my life. Those colors. And that stone wall. It's unbelievable." She paused, and her eyes filled with tears. "Doesn't it just overwhelm you to think that people have stood on this very spot for hundreds of years, looking out at this magnificent view? And here we are, drinking it in. It's lovely."

"Yes, the canyon has a rich history," Jake said. "Lots of people have come through here. In fact, a very famous battle took place right here in the canyon back in '74."

"The sort Emily would want to write about?" She turned and gazed into his eyes, almost causing him to forget the story he'd been telling.

"Oh yes. Lots of Indians—Comanche, Cheyenne, and even Kiowa. They'd come to the canyon to seek refuge and had been stockpiling food and other supplies to get them through the winter. The 4th US Cavalry made their move up from the south, hoping to trap them in the canyon."

"Oh my."

"There was a Comanche chief named Red Warbonnet involved

in that battle." Jake smiled. "I was always fascinated by that name as a boy. So were my brothers. They would dress up like him and pretend they were on the attack."

Anne chuckled. "I'll have to tell Emily. She'll use his name for sure."

"He didn't survive the battle," Jake said. "When the cavalry reached the canyon, they gained the upper hand. The Indians fled to the plains, and the battle brought about an end to the Red River War."

"It's hard to believe all of that took place in this area. It seems so peaceful now." She snuggled a bit closer and his heart felt like bursting.

"That's how life is…after the fact," he said. "We go through battles and then we look back to where we've been and see no sign of death or destruction."

"I pray you're right." She released a little sigh. "I'm so tired of fighting, to be honest. I feel like it's been one battle after another ever since Mama died."

"You're a tough warrior, Anne." He gazed at her with great admiration.

"Not always as tough as you might think."

"For one so young? I'd say you're pretty tough. And you've taken on the huge task of caring for your sisters. You'd have to be tough to handle children."

"I'm nineteen." She took a little step away from him, breaking the spell that had held him captive for the past few minutes. "I know some people would say that's old enough to raise my sisters by myself without moving to my uncle's place. But…the truth is, I've never had to work. Not at a real job, anyway. Until Papa's drinking got really bad, he managed to earn a nice living. But it didn't take long after his death to see that any illusions of life going on as normal were over."

"Anne, I'm so sorry." He reached for her hand and laced his fingers through hers.

"At first I thought we would be able to stay in the house. I thought, perhaps, that I could get a job to sustain us in the home we'd always loved." Anne shook her head. "But apparently there were creditors who felt otherwise. Less than three weeks ago, they sold off the furnishings to pay his debts. The home is gone." She paused, and her eyes filled with tears. "We were blessed to be able to keep our personal belongings. We've got our clothing and a few small items, but that's about it."

"That's why you're going to stay with your uncle."

"Yes. I didn't know what else to do. We have no other relatives—not that we're close to Uncle Bertrand, as you've likely noticed. We've only seen him three or four times up until now. He's never been much for children, but he did come for a visit last year. Honestly, I think his last visit probably had something to do with Father's debt. I'm pretty sure Uncle Bertrand bailed him out of a predicament. He's as hard as a rock with the girls and so stern with me. But what other choice do I have? He's willing to let us come, and I've run out of options."

"You don't have to explain anything to me. I understand, and I sympathize." He pulled her close and they gazed out over the canyon together.

"If I'd known a place like this existed, I would have arranged for the train to stop here permanently," Anne whispered. "But you and I both know that life is hard and we don't always get what we want."

"That's true," Jake said, "but I also know that God doesn't want us to give up on our dreams. He would prefer we pick up the pieces and go on."

She began to tremble, and he held her tighter. "That first night at O'Farrell's Honor, when we stood underneath the stars, I thought that maybe I was dreaming," Anne said. "The whole thing seemed rather surreal. Now—getting to know you and your family—it's very real to me. Painfully real."

"What do you mean?"

"I mean, it's just too...perfect. It's like we were given a little taste of heaven on earth, but it's an unfair taste because it's only temporary."

Jake could not explain the protective feelings going on inside of him. He only knew that every time she mentioned leaving, his heart constricted. "Let's just enjoy this moment," he said at last.

"It is beautiful. I want to close my eyes and commit it to memory so that when I'm far from here, I'll be able to summon up this portrait in my mind."

And when she closed those beautiful eyes, Jake felt his courage take hold. Though he'd never considered himself terribly brave, he did the bravest thing he'd ever done in his life. Jake planted a half dozen tiny kisses in her hair. And with each kiss he offered a prayer to soothe her troubled soul and heal her broken heart.

* * * * *

Anne felt Jake's nearness and could almost sense his heart beating alongside hers. As her eyes drifted shut, she reveled in the fact that he cared enough about her to pull her into such a comfortable embrace. Then, when she felt that first tiny kiss in her hair, she found herself tempted to open her eyes. She fought the temptation and remained in a quiet, blissful state, allowing him to comfort her with his kisses. Afterward, she reached to take his hand and then opened her eyes, catching her first glimpse of the sunset over the canyon.

"Oh, Jake! It's heavenly."

"Yes, it is."

She looked his way, thinking he must be talking about the sunset. Instead, he gazed directly into her eyes and she caught his true meaning.

"I...well..." Embarrassment took hold and she turned back to look at the sky, the brilliant reds and oranges capturing her imagination. "Oh, I've never had a happier day."

"Neither have I."

Her heart began to sing a triumphant song, one filled with the wonder and majesty of God's creation and the sheer joy of sharing with someone who truly understood her heart's cry. He gave her hand a squeeze as they gazed into the sunset together. Maybe, if she stood here long enough, her feet would plant themselves to the ground and she would be forever rooted in this magnificent place. A girl could certainly dream, anyway.

All too soon, evening's shadows began to fall and Jake led the way back to the truck. He drove up the embankment and turned on the road toward home.

By the time they arrived at the ranch, Maggie and her sisters were finishing supper. Maggie insisted they join them at the table for fried chicken and corn on the cob. Though she'd eaten a lot at lunch, the walking—and the crying—had taken the strength out of her, so Anne readily agreed. She and Jake sat down and told the others about their day. Emily seemed most impressed with the story about Chief Warbonnet and the Indian battle.

"I'm glad you enjoyed the canyon, Anne," Maggie said. "There's something about it, isn't there? So majestic. When you see it with your own eyes, you realize we serve a very creative and powerful God."

"Indeed." She paused, realizing just how true those words were and how close to Him she'd felt standing on that bluff, overlooking the canyon. Oh, how good it felt to be able to put her trust in the Lord once more.

Still deep in thought, Anne almost missed Emily's words.

"Anne, you missed it!"

"What did I miss?" She turned to face her little sister.

"After you and Jake left, we went to town so Maggie could go to the store. Uncle Bertrand drove us in his big, fancy car."

"I'm sure that was quite a sight to see—his Cadillac rolling down the main street of Groom."

"Yes, but that's not the best part. It's what happened when we got to the store. You'll never believe who was there. Never in a million years."

"Who?"

"The person whose name we're never allowed to speak in Uncle Bertrand's presence."

"Cornelia Witherspoon?" Anne put her hand up to cover her open mouth. Still, she could hardly wait to hear the rest of the story.

"Yes." Emily giggled. "Oh, Annie, it was just like a scene from one of my books. When he saw her, he knocked a whole row of canning jars off the shelf. It was brilliant, I tell you."

"Gracious." Anne reached for her glass of water. "I can't imagine what provoked that."

Emily leaned forward and whispered, "They used to be in love."

"How do you know this?"

The youngster rolled her eyes. "I'm a writer, Annie. That's how I know it. The expression on his face told me everything I needed to know." She paused. "Well, that and the questions Maggie peppered him with all the way back to the house."

"I see." Anne glanced Maggie's way.

"From what I can gather, Mrs. Witherspoon was in Amarillo visiting her new husband," Maggie said.

Emily interrupted her. "The man she just married six months ago. He's there on business and she joined him for a holiday. That's why Uncle Bertrand was so put off. He's heartbroken."

"No." Anne could hardly believe it.

"I could tell the man was wounded, but he wouldn't speak of it." Maggie looked a bit sad. "I did my best to get him to share what he was feeling, but apparently he's not one to do that."

"That's putting it mildly," Emily muttered. "Do you have any idea how difficult it is to pattern a character after someone who refuses to share valuable information?"

"Emily, it sounds like Uncle Bertrand needs his privacy, not your nosing in."

"Oh, pooh." Emily rolled her eyes. "Anyway, when we arrived back at the house, he made Kate and I promise once more that we would never speak her name in his presence. And Maggie..." Emily giggled. "Oh, she's a hoot. She makes me laugh so much."

"What did she do?"

They all looked Maggie's way.

"Well, the man wouldn't talk to me about it, so I decided to do the only thing that made sense. I cooked him the biggest lunch you ever saw."

"And when she was serving it, she told him that he was better off without such a skinny woman. Told him that Cornelia Witherspoon was liable to be picked up with the next wind and floated across the county." Emily roared with laughter. "She called her by name too."

"Heavens." Anne fanned herself. "I'm glad I missed this."

"Oh, it was wonderful," Maggie said. "Someone needs to knock some sense into that man. Might as well be me."

"Today was almost as much fun as that time we went to the theater in Denver." Emily pushed back her plate and leaned her elbows on the table. "I felt like I was watching a scene unfold right in front of my eyes. And it's given me such glorious ideas to add to my book. I can't wait to get started." She scooted her chair away from the table. "May I be excused, Maggie? I want to add Chief Warbonnet to my story before I forget the details."

"You may."

"Me too?" Kate asked.

"You too." Maggie rose from the table, a hint of a smile gracing her lips. She took to whistling a happy tune while clearing the table. "I'm glad everyone had such a nice day, but I think we'd better turn in early tonight. We've got a big day ahead of us tomorrow, and I'm worn out."

She made quick work of filling the sink with water.

"Let us take care of the dishes tonight, Maggie." Anne took the dishrag away from her. "You've had a long day, and I feel like helping."

"Well, thank you, honey."

Anne began scrubbing the dishes. Jake stood beside her with a dish towel in his hand, chatting up a storm and drying the dishes she passed his way. Maggie stood off to the side, her eyes wide.

"Everything all right, Maggie?" Anne asked at last.

"In the twenty-two years that Jake O'Farrell has been alive on this earth, I've never seen him dry a dish." Maggie shook her head. "I'm not sure my heart can take it."

He raised the dish towel as if ready to hand it to her. Maggie put her hands up in the air. "No, sir. You're doing a fine job. Mighty fine. Just go on with you. I'll put myself to bed. I need my beauty sleep."

"Me too." Anne released a yawn as she washed the last plate.

Jake looked her way and chuckled. "Hardly."

Just one word, but it made her night.

GROOM
1914
TX

Chapter Twenty

....

I don't want to say that Texans are prone to exaggeration, but I've heard quite a few tall tales in my day. Sure, folks tell 'em like they're gospel truth, but that's because the stories have been around so long that they feel like they are. Likely you've heard the tales of Pecos Bill and his woolly ways. Then there's "Bigfoot" Wallace, the roughest, toughest Texas Ranger to ride west of the Pecos. Yep, we've become skilled in the art of exaggeration. A true Texan knows how to spin a good yarn and then wrap you in it until you're cozy enough to actually believe it's true. —"Tex" Morgan, reporting for the *Panhandle Primer*

On Friday morning all the O'Farrell ladies met to put together the flowers for the wedding. Jake joined them, looking a bit like a fish out of water in the presence of so many females. Anne led the way, giving instructions and thoroughly enjoying the process. The conversation in the room was energetic and loaded with fun. At one point, she realized this could be one of the last times she might be in this room with all these people. Just as quickly, she chided herself. *Enjoy the moment. Don't grieve tomorrow's unvisited woes.*

She found the internal prompting far more doable with Jake in the room. Every now and again she caught him looking her way. In those moments, she remembered the feel of his hand in hers…could almost hear the conversations they'd shared out on the open fields of the family's ranch. And then someone in the room would call out to her for assistance and she would rush their way.

By eleven o'clock the garlands were complete and on their way to the coolness of the cellar. After a light lunch, Anne spent some time finalizing the details for the wedding and then walked to the schoolhouse to meet Virginia's parents for the first time. She felt at ease with Virginia's mother right away.

After they had talked through the wedding plans, Mrs. Harrison changed the direction of the conversation. "Anne, did you work as a wedding coordinator in Denver?"

"Oh no. I just volunteered my time at several charities and such."

"Well, it certainly paid off. These plans you've laid out for my daughter's big day are wonderful. I daresay you could open your own wedding business when this is over."

Her heart quickened. What a glorious idea. "Do you really think so?"

"Why not?" Mrs. Harrison patted her on the arm. "Promise me you will pray about it."

"Oh, I will."

"In the meantime, please accept my most sincere thanks. You've worked so hard to make sure my daughter's wedding is special. I wish there was some way to bless you. I do wonder…" She paused. "I don't want to offend in any way, but I wonder if you might be willing to accept some compensation for your work."

"Compensation?" Anne could scarcely believe her ears. Someone was offering her money? "I—I don't know."

"Think about it, my dear." Mrs. Harrison reached over and

touched her hand. "Because my husband and I would like to bless you before you leave town."

When their meeting ended, Anne made the walk from the schoolhouse to O'Farrell's Honor, deep in thought about Mrs. Harrison's offer. Could she really accept compensation for her time and efforts? And could she really give thought to helping other brides prepare for their big day?

By the time she arrived at the house, Anne realized she'd actually spent an entire day not thinking about moving to Dallas. She'd had so many other wonderful things on her mind, after all.

She walked inside and was surprised to find the entire family present—all of Maggie's children and grandchildren as well as Uncle Bertrand and her sisters.

"We decided to have a special dinner to honor you, Anne," Maggie said. "You've given of yourself tirelessly all week, and we felt you deserved a special meal. Besides..." Maggie's eyes misted over. "You'll only be with us a few more days and we'll be so busy with the wedding. I just want to make sure we have some special time with you before you go." Maggie shot a glance at Uncle Bertrand, and he shifted his gaze to the table.

"Maggie, I hardly know what to say." Anne gave her a tight hug and soon found herself swallowed up by Maggie's ample bosom.

"Guess what I made," Maggie said, when she finally released her hold on Anne.

"Smells familiar." Anne paused to think then snapped her fingers. "Oh, my new favorite. Chicken-fried steak?"

"That's right. And guess who helped me?"

Emily and Kate raised their hands. Then, strangely, so did Uncle Bertrand. Heavens. Anne almost felt faint.

She washed up then took her place at the table in the spot across from Jake. Most of the smaller children were shooed to the children's table in the little room off the kitchen, but Emily remained with the grown-ups.

After they were seated, Maggie looked at Uncle Bertrand. "Bert, would you do us the honor of praying over the meal?"

Bert?

As he bowed his head and prayed, Anne had the strangest memory creep over her. Last Thanksgiving, Papa had bowed his head to pray over their meal. It was the last time she remembered seeing him in decent form. Uncle Bertrand's voice, though slightly deeper, suddenly reminded her of Papa's, and it startled her.

"Anne, are you all right? The prayer is over now."

Anne glanced at Emily, who gave her a perplexed look. "I'm fine. Just thinking."

"Thinking is good," Maggie said as she reached for the platter of steak. "I highly recommend it."

"I tried going without it once," Jake said. "The consequences were not good."

Everyone laughed.

The next few minutes were spent filling plates and eating. The clinking of silverware against plates filled the room along with laughter and joyous conversation. At one point, Anne closed her eyes just for a moment, to commit it all to memory. All too soon it would be gone. For now, however, she'd made up her mind to enjoy every last moment.

* * * * *

Jake was happy to be sitting across the table from Anne. Though he enjoyed being next to her—and holding her hand—there was something about watching the sparkle in her eyes when she told a story that held him spellbound.

She shared a great story about an opera production she'd seen as a child, and it had everyone in stitches.

As soon as she finished, Emily got everyone's attention. "I have a story too. Did you know that I used to sing and dance in a vaudeville show?"

For a half second, Jake almost believed it. Until he glanced across the table and saw the stunned look on Anne's face.

"You did?" Jake shook his head. "I can't believe Anne never mentioned it. Vaudeville, of all things."

Emily rolled her eyes. "Anne is so stuck-up. She doesn't want anyone to know."

"Well, for pity's sake." Across the table, Anne dropped her fork and stared at Emily like she'd lost her marbles.

"My stage name was Esmeralda and I did the best song-and-dance number you've ever seen."

"I suppose you're going to show us your song-and-dance number?" Jake said.

"If you like." Emily began to sing "Camptown Races" at the top of her lungs. Unfortunately, her singing voice left something to be desired. What she lacked in vocal quality, however, she more than made up for in enthusiasm. After a few minutes of singing, her toes got to tapping, and before long she was dancing a little jig across the kitchen. She finished the dance and dropped into her chair, clearly exhausted. Everyone gave her a round of applause. Well, everyone but Anne, who still looked upset.

"You're quite a performer," Jake said. "It's hard to believe you left your life on the stage for academic pursuits. Must have been a huge sacrifice on your part."

"Oh, it was...but I had to. I had no other choice. I am called to write, so I traded one art form for the other. No longer will I bring characters to life in front of an audience. From this point forth, they will forever live on the page, not the stage."

"Amazing." Milly took a bite of her mashed potatoes.

"I can hardly believe such a talent in one so young," Pauline threw in.

"Yes, you must tell us where you're performing next so we can come see the show," Cora added.

"I'm performing in Paris," Emily said. "I've already been there plenty of times and will be going back next spring to dance in the Follies."

"Gracious." Maggie used her napkin to dab her mouth. "You really are something, aren't you, child?"

"She's something all right." Anne stared at her little sister, shaking her head. "Emily Marie Denning. Why in the world are you telling these lies?"

"They're not lies; they're stories. There's a difference."

Anne now spoke to the others. "Honestly, folks, I don't know where she comes up with this. I really don't." She turned her attention back to her sister. "Emily, you've never been out of Colorado till now, let alone halfway across the world. How do you think up such nonsensical things to say?"

"You're just jealous because Papa took me and you didn't get to go." Emily shook her head, a defiant look registering on her once-innocent face. She plastered on a smile and turned to Jake.

"Our papa was in Paris on business and took me along so I could perform. He was a famous businessman, you know. He owned a newspaper in Denver and Paris. I used to write stories for him all the time."

"Well, I'm not altogether sure this is the best time to be talking about Paris," Uncle Bertrand said. "Not with so many rumors of war going on."

"Oh, but how can I not talk about it?" She released an exaggerated sigh. "It was there, at the top of the Eiffel Tower, that I discovered my love for writing."

"Oh?" Jake responded, still playing along.

"Yes, I wrote my first book overlooking the Seine River, while wearing a beret."

"Which story was that?" Ruth asked.

"Oh, I should let you read it sometime. It's about a Frenchman who is jilted in love, so he plots his revenge by sinking a ship that's carrying the woman who broke his heart."

"Good gracious." Maggie began to fan herself.

"She sounds a lot like Jake did as a boy, doesn't she, Mama?" John grinned. "Always ready with a big tale."

Oh no. Let's don't do this. Not with Anne at the table. Jake flashed John a warning look.

"Jake's such a dreamer," Joseph added. "You should've heard the things he came up with when we were boys."

"Like what?" Anne asked.

"Oh, once he told me that he was going to build an Indian village on the west end of the property. He constructed this crude setup and then dressed in war paint and feathers."

"And then there was the time he told us he was going to travel to Europe someday." Jeremiah laughed. "That would be something. Yep, sure was a dreamer."

"Jake's always been the one with the crazy ideas, that's for certain." Jedediah laughed.

Across the table, Anne cleared her throat. "What you're saying is, he's creative. He does things that other people don't think to do."

A hush fell over the room. "Well, when you put it like that..." John shrugged.

"I like creative thinkers," his mother added. "They keep us on our toes."

"Yes, they certainly do." Anne quirked a brow then went back to eating.

He would have to thank the beautiful woman seated across from him for creatively redirecting the conversation. For now, however, he would simply enjoy gazing upon that exquisite face.

* * * * *

As soon as the supper dishes were done, Anne summoned Emily to the porch.

"What's wrong, Annie?" Emily asked.

"Honey, I know you love a good story. We all do." Anne paused, thinking through her next words as she took a seat on the swing. "But somewhere along the way you crossed a line. Those fanciful stories are fine on paper, but lately you've been stretching the truth regarding your own story."

Emily's gaze shifted to the yard.

"You know what I'm talking about, don't you?"

"I like to pretend."

"Pretending is fun, but if you speak something as fact, it has to be true. That's where I believe you've run into trouble. Writing stories about made-up people is one thing. Taking the liberty of changing your own life story is something altogether different."

"But the stories I make up about my life are so much..."

"Better?" Anne asked.

Emily's eyes filled with tears. "Yes. Do you think I want to tell people the real story of my life? It stinks like rotten eggs." At this point she began to sniffle. "Don't you get it, Anne? Our life might be truth, but it's awful truth. So I'll trade it for a pretty lie if I want to. And you can't stop me. I like my stories. They make me feel better."

With that announcement, Emily rose and took off running across the field. Instead of calling out to her, Anne let her run. Maybe her little sister would shake off some of the pain as she ran. In the meantime, Anne sat in silence and prayed. Only when she felt someone take the spot next to her did she open her eyes.

"Jake." She whispered his name, and he wrapped his arm over her shoulders. "I'm so worried about Emily."

"I know."

He drew her close, and she leaned her head against his shoulder. She thought about engaging him in conversation about her sister but decided against it. For whatever reason, when Jake took her in his arms, the world was right again. And she wouldn't do anything to spoil this perfect moment. After all, they had so few of them left.

Chapter Twenty-One

....

It's June in the Panhandle, and you know what that means... weddings. I married off my youngest daughter last June. I'd never seen a more radiant bride. The Texas bride has a variety of local flowers to choose from for her bouquet, and our churches are among the finest in the state. If she's settled on a groom from the Panhandle region, likely he's already set up on a nice piece of property where they can start their new life together, ranching or farming. And because she's marrying in June, she can expect blue skies overhead. Yes, the Texas Panhandle is the perfect place to offer up your "I do's" and an even better place to grow old with the one you love. —"Tex" Morgan, reporting for the *Panhandle Primer*

Saturday dawned bright and sunny. Anne sprang from the bed, ready to get to work. She dressed in a simple everyday dress, knowing the risk was too great to be able to put on her blue formal one just yet.

"What time does this shindig begin?" her uncle asked when he joined them for breakfast. "And are you sure I would be welcomed?"

"Very sure."

Jake loaded up the garlands and tablecloths into the family truck along with several other items, leaving no room for the

241

cake. Maggie had to ride to the church with Uncle Bertrand, who offered to take the cake—and Anne's blue dress—in his Cadillac. She didn't look terribly disappointed by that proposition...until Emily and Kate announced that they wanted to ride with them.

Yes, things were certainly quite odd with Maggie these days. Anne had seen her happy and playful before, of course, but there was a new sparkle in her eyes. And the dress she'd chosen for the wedding was something to behold. The green satin made her green eyes and red hair look even more pronounced, more magnificent. Anne found herself distracted by the woman's simple beauty. Then again, Maggie was beautiful from the inside out. It was no wonder so many people were drawn to her.

Still deep in thought, Anne heard Jake's voice. "Hope you're riding with me."

"I would love that." In fact, she wanted to spend every available minute with him. He opened the passenger door to the truck and she climbed in, feeling as if a host of butterflies had been set free in her stomach. Part of the feeling, she knew, was nerves. She had experienced this feeling in the past just before a big event. But these butterflies were up to something more. They seemed to come every time Jake drew near.

Not that she had time to be thinking about romance today. Well, not her own, anyway. No, this day was all about the bride. And Anne could hardly wait to see her.

They arrived at the church in short order and Jake went right to work at setting up tables on the lawn. Within minutes his brothers and their wives arrived, and before long, the whole family was at work, setting up and decorating. The time passed too quickly for Anne. By ten fifteen, all the garlands had been hung and the tables were decorated in full, and the beautiful wedding cake had been given a place of honor.

She entered the church, double-checking the work Maggie had done inside with the garlands. They looked perfect. So colorful, adding just the right touch. And the candles and flower arrangements at the front of the sanctuary were perfect as well.

It was time to see about the bride.

Anne knocked on the door of the little Sunday school classroom where Virginia was getting ready.

"Who is it?" Amaryllis's voice rang out.

"It's me, Anne." She peeked her head inside the door and gasped when she saw Virginia in her wedding gown.

"Oh my goodness! You're the prettiest thing I ever saw. Truly, of all the weddings I've been to, this is going to be the finest."

"She is a sight to behold, isn't she?" Virginia's mother dabbed her eyes. "I've dreamed of this day for years, and now it's here. My baby girl is getting married."

"Thanks to Anne." Virginia reached over and squeezed her hands.

"Yes, how can we ever thank you?" Mrs. Harrison drew near and slipped her arm over Anne's shoulders. "With your help, it's all come together."

"Oh, posh. It's nothing. I just tossed out a few ideas and she jumped on them. Nothing more."

"Nothing more!" Virginia shook her head. "You orchestrated everything."

"Hardly everything." Anne chuckled. "I didn't orchestrate that break in the train track."

"No, but we know who did." Virginia chuckled. "And I will always thank Him for that, by the way. Because that broken track brought you to us."

As Anne changed into her beautiful blue gown a few moments later, she pondered Virginia's words. A broken track had very well led her to Groom, Texas, hadn't it? She couldn't help but consider the analogies. Her life—her sense of direction—had been completely broken that day on the train. Sure, she knew her destination— her physical destination, anyway. But as for a sense of spiritual and emotional direction, she'd been as lost as a goose. And now... now she felt as right as rain.

She checked her appearance in the mirror, tidying up her hair and pinching her cheeks to give them a rosy glow. Finally she could join the others dressed in her wedding-party attire.

She'd no sooner entered the sanctuary than she heard a familiar voice.

"How's the prettiest girl at the wedding?"

Anne turned to find Jake standing behind her. She felt her cheeks grow warm. "Oh, I just checked on Virginia. She's doing really well. Her parents made it just in time."

"I'm sure Virginia is lovely, but I was referring to someone else. Someone who looks like she dropped out of heaven in a blue dress."

Anne's heart fluttered and she felt her cheeks go hot as she whispered a grateful "Thank you."

"You're welcome. It's true, you know. You look radiant." He placed his hand on her arm. "How are you holding up, Annie?"

A rush of emotions swept over her as she thought about her mother, who had always called her by that name. These days, the only ones who called her Annie were Emily and Kate. Still, it felt right, coming from Jake. He could call her Annie. Heavens, he could call her anything he liked, as long as he kept looking at her with such tenderness pouring from those gorgeous eyes.

"I'm doing well," she finally managed. "Holding up just fine. The sanctuary is decorated, and the sandwiches are prepared and ready to be set up on the tables outside after the ceremony."

"Mama said to tell you that the punch bowl has arrived and your uncle is making coffee."

Anne shook her head. "I still can't quite believe the transformation in him."

"Yes, well, I have my suspicions about that." Jake waggled his brows. "Methinks he's been captivated by a woman."

"Methinks you're right." She giggled.

"Seems to be a lot of that going around." He paused to gaze into her eyes then reached for her hand. "You're a marvel. You do know that, don't you?"

"How do you mean?"

"You swept in here and saved the day. You somehow managed to calm a frenzied bride, decorate a church, corral a group of local women, talk your uncle into staying, and pull off the event of the season."

"Ah." She giggled. "Well, when you put it like that..."

"When I put it like that, I see what a talent you are. Denver is going to miss you. But it's their loss and our gain."

As he gripped her hand, that same gripping sensation took hold of her heart. "Only for two more days," she whispered. "We leave for Dallas on Monday."

He shook his head, his eyes growing misty. "Let's not talk about that, okay?"

She gave his fingers a little squeeze and then released her hold on Jake's hand as the reverend approached them.

He gave Anne a pat on the shoulder. "I've been pastoring this church for fourteen years, Anne, and I've never seen it look this wonderful. You've given my wife a hundred ideas for our homecoming service in the fall. I do wish you were going to be here to help her with that."

"Me too, Reverend." Anne did her best not to sigh aloud. She would love to do this and so much more, of course, but she knew this wasn't the time or place to think about it. Right now she had a wedding to coordinate.

She excused herself and walked outside to give everything a final look before the wedding began. She sighed as she took in the whole picture—the tables with their beautiful lace cloths. Those breathtaking garlands. Jake had done a magnificent job of hanging them. They made the entire area look festive and bright. That cake—oh, how pretty! And to think there was more to come! Yes, everything was as it should be.

The guests started arriving at twenty till eleven, and before long the moment arrived. The pastor's wife took her place at the piano and the wedding was underway. The whole thing felt like a blur to Anne. She remembered Virginia coming down the aisle on her father's arm, of course, and the look in Mr. Harrison's eye when he gave her away. She heard much of what the pastor was saying, but the rest was lost in the haze of emotions that gripped her.

When the reverend pronounced Cody and Virginia as man and wife, a cheer went up from the crowd. It intensified as he pulled her into his arms and planted a passionate kiss on her lips. Anne felt herself blushing. What would it feel like, she wondered, to be the bride? Would she ever know?

She didn't have time to think about it. When the ceremony drew to a close, it was time to fly into action. There were sandwiches to be placed on the tables, punch to be stirred, cake to be cut.... She would oversee it all.

As soon as she was free to do so, Anne raced to the church lawn with Maggie on her heels. They flew into action, getting ready for the guests to come out of the church for the reception.

First down the steps were the bride and groom. Virginia headed straight for the cake table, her mouth falling open as she took in her surroundings.

"Oh, Anne, that cake! You were right. Those sugar flowers are exquisite. It's almost as if you picked fresh flowers and laid them on the cake."

"Maggie did a fantastic job, and I think the colors turned out so nice."

"And the garlands are perfect. I'm so glad you wouldn't let me peek before the ceremony. The ones inside the sanctuary took my breath away, but these are even better." Her eyes filled with tears as she glanced at the next table. "And those darling flower-shaped sandwiches. How did you do that?"

"We created a cookie cutter in a floral shape and then used it to cut out the little sandwiches. Really, it was fairly simple. They're just sandwiches."

"No, they're far more than that. They are an act of love, and it shows in every detail." She threw her arms around Anne's neck. "Every single element is perfect. How can I ever thank you?"

"By living happily-ever-after with Cody."

"Oh, I plan to do that." She reached over and grabbed one of the little sandwiches and gave it a nibble. "Mmm. I still can't believe you came up with this recipe. Who would have dreamed you could put cream cheese in a sandwich?"

"Or in frosting on a cake." Maggie drew near and shook her head. "This is the first time I've made a cake with cream-cheese frosting, but I'm addicted. Don't see as I can ever turn back. My waistline just won't be the same after this." She put her hands on her broad hips and grinned. "Think anyone will notice an extra pound or two?"

"Maggie, on you, it will just look like love." Anne leaned over and gave the dear woman on a kiss on the cheek.

"Girl, you are almost as sweet as that cake." Maggie grinned. "Almost."

"Thank you, Maggie. I could say the same about you."

Before long, the music began and toes started tapping. Folks enjoyed a dance or two, along with sandwiches and punch. Finally the time arrived to cut the cake. Virginia and Cody enjoyed the first slice…after Virginia smeared it all over Cody's face. He returned the favor in short order and everyone had a good laugh.

As Anne sliced up pieces of Maggie's cake, she pondered the suggestion Mrs. Harrison had made just yesterday. Maybe once she got settled in Dallas, she could hire herself out as a wedding coordinator. But how did one go about advertising services such as that? And would she really be comfortable, offering her services in a place where she knew no one? Perhaps Mrs. Witherspoon could be of help. Yes, surely she had connections.

Anne didn't have time to give it much more thought. Folks rushed the table for that delicious cake. Cassie Martin came back later and asked for a second piece. "I've never had cake with raspberry jam between the layers. Whose idea was that?"

"Oh, well…" Anne shrugged.

"Yours?"

"Yes."

"You're making it harder and harder for me to dislike you."

"Dislike me?"

"Yes." Cassie sighed. "I see how Jake looks at you."

"O–oh?" Anne passed her another piece of cake, hoping to avoid the conversation.

"Anyway, the cake is great." Cassie plunged her fork into the second piece and shoveled a bite into her mouth. "Mmm. Almost makes the broken heart bearable." She shrugged and headed back to the other side of the church lawn, leaving Anne's thoughts whirling.

Oh well. Just one more thing she wouldn't have to worry about once she arrived in Dallas. Cassie Martin could rest easy, knowing that Jake wasn't distracted by a wayfaring stranger. Almost immediately, a lump rose in Anne's throat. She did her best to swallow it but couldn't quite manage it. Thankfully, Uncle Bert showed up for another slice of cake, which provided the perfect distraction. Today she could use all the distractions she could get.

* * * * *

The musicians played a rousing song, and wedding guests took to dancing. Well, all but Aunt Bets and Uncle Leo, who stood off to the side as always. Bets's arms were folded at her chest, and she had a sour expression on her face. Perhaps it had something to do with the fact that Leo had taken Maggie's hand and led her to the floor for a rousing folk dance.

Jake watched from the sidelines, wishing Anne would finish

serving up cake so he could ask her to dance. He observed John, taking Ruth by the hand and gliding her around the dance floor. Then came Joseph, who bowed and took Milly by the hand. She giggled and the pair began to dance. Same with Jeremiah and Cora...and Jedediah and Pauline. Looked like all the O'Farrell brothers had been caught up in the dance...minus one.

Then an idea occurred to Jake, one he couldn't squelch. He walked over to Aunt Bets and offered her his hand. For a moment, she looked as if she didn't know what to do. Then, with her face as tight as a drum, she took his hand and allowed him to lead her to the center of the floor. He swept her into his arms and led her in a waltz. Her ease of steps caught him by surprise. So much for thinking she didn't believe in dancing.

Seconds later, Jake deliberately bumped into his mother and Leo. "If you don't mind," he said to Leo, "I'd like to switch partners."

In that moment, it felt as if everything in the place shifted to slow motion. Jake released his hold on Bets and took his mother's hand instead. This, of course, left Leo and Bets standing in the middle of the dance floor, staring at one another. Leo, God bless him, grabbed his wife and managed to get her to dance. For a moment or two, anyway. When the song ended, she ran from the dance floor, up the steps of the church, and inside, away from the crowd.

* * * * *

"Anne, did you see what just happened?"

Anne glanced up from her cake slicing, noticing the excitement in Emily's eyes. "No, what's that?"

"Bets and Leo were dancing."

"No." She glanced at the dance floor. Through the crowd she made out Leo, but he was alone.

"Bets got upset and ran into the church. Maggie went after her."

"Oh, dear. Emily, stay here in case anyone needs more cake, all right?"

Emily's eyes widened and she nodded.

"I'll be right back." Anne hiked up her skirt and ran toward the church, almost tripping up the steps in her hurry. By the time she got inside, Bets was seated in the back pew with Maggie at her side. Anne had never seen a person weep with such intensity. She sobbed until Anne wondered if she might make herself sick.

When Bets finally came up for air, Maggie handed her a fresh handkerchief. "There, there, honey. I'm so sorry you're upset."

"He...he...danced with me."

"Well, of course he did. He's your husband. Who better to dance with you?"

"Oh, Maggie, I don't expect you to understand. You and James had the best relationship in the world." Bets looked over at her sister, her nose red and eyes still damp. "With Leo and me, it's different."

Anne couldn't help but ask the question that had left her puzzled for days. "Why did you marry him, Bets?"

"W-what?" She looked at Anne, eyes wide.

"I don't mean to pry, but it's clear you're unhappily matched. Please forgive me if I'm out of line in asking, but whyever would you marry someone you can't abide?"

Bets stared at her and her eyes filled with tears once again. "It breaks my heart that folks assume I don't love Leo. He was—is— the love of my life."

Anne hardly knew what to say. She'd assumed something entirely different.

"Old habits die hard." Bets blew her nose.

Anne couldn't quite make sense of that. "What do you mean?" she asked.

"I mean, we started bickering back in the old days and now I don't know how to stop. It's become an ugly habit." Tears welled up. "You have no idea how much I'd love to just grab that man by the shoulders and plant a kiss on his wrinkled old face." Her cheeks flushed pink. "My, I can't believe I just said that out loud."

"Well, why don't you?" Maggie asked.

"Pride. Stubbornness." She shrugged. "I don't know. Half the time I'm afraid he'll have a heart attack if I kiss him instead of lashing out."

"So you continue to lash out instead?" Maggie fussed with her apron. "I daresay he stands a better chance at having a heart attack over all the arguing than a good kiss. A kiss can heal wounds, not create them."

"At this point, I'm not so sure." She dabbed her eyes. "You have no idea how jealous I am when I see couples in love." She pointed at Anne. "Say you and Jakey, for instance."

"W–what?" Anne took a step back as she absorbed Bets's words.

"Well, sure. Don't tell me you're trying to keep it a secret. It's as obvious as that red flush in your cheeks. You two are so happy... and meant to be together."

"I really don't know what you're referring to."

Bets shrugged. "Well, honey, I'm old and crotchety and my vision's not that good. But even I can see it, plain as day."

"Love is an interesting thing, isn't it?" Maggie slipped her arm around Bets's shoulders. "It causes us to act in strange ways. But I think I know just what needs to be done here, Betsy. I think you need to hightail it back out there and dance with your husband—and not just one dance, but as many as your feet can stand. You know what they say...actions speak louder than words."

"I–I'm not sure I can."

"You can. And you will." Maggie rose and extended her hand, which Bets took.

"I'll do my best." Bets offered the first smile of the day—until she happened to gaze at the garlands that hung just to their right. She took a couple of steps in that direction, gazing at the flowers. "Are these calla lilies?"

Anne's heart quickened.

"Why, yes, I believe they are." Maggie fussed with her hair. "Pretty, aren't they?"

"But I don't know anyone else in town who has this color of callas." Bets looked her way, eyes narrowing.

Maggie patted her on the back. "Now, don't call for the sheriff, Bets. Leo said we could take them."

"He did what?" Her face grew red.

"He said we could take them, and we took them. And here they are, gracing the aisles of a church where people are dancing outside. Don't you see, honey? It was all meant to be. Your flowers. Your dance. This day was meant for you."

Anne wasn't sure how Bets would respond to those words, but in the end, the poor, dear soul flung her arms around her sister's neck and then allowed herself to be pulled out to the dance floor, where she spent the rest of the afternoon kicking up her heels with the love of her life.

Chapter Twenty-Two

. . . .

Summer is upon us, and love is in the air. Fellas, if you're in need of advice on how to woo a lady proper-like, you've come to the right place. Here in the Texas Panhandle, we've conquered the art of courting. I asked my wife to help me put together a list of things a fella could do to catch a lady's eye. First off, learn how to talk to her. Don't bore her with the price of cattle or the latest automobile fad. Make sure you flatter her and call her "darlin'" or "honey." Tell her how pretty that new bonnet is. And pull out her chair for her when you sit down to a meal. Sweep her into your arms and waltz her around the room on occasion. And for heaven's sake, bring home flowers after you've had an argument. I brought home a dozen red roses just last night. —"Tex" Morgan, reporting for the Panhandle Primer

After the dancing came to an end, Jake gathered his four brothers on the church steps. If they couldn't advise him on the art of coaxing Anne to stay in Groom, no one could.

"Fellas, I need to talk to you. I need some advice."

"What sort of advice?" John leaned against the railing and gave Jake a curious look.

"Female advice."

"Ah…female advice." Jeremiah chuckled. "Now we're talkin'. How can we help?" He plopped down on the top step and rested his elbows on his knees.

Jake looked at his brothers. Gathered here on the front porch of the church, they looked like a proper wedding party. Perhaps one day soon they would be.

"You're all married men, so you've figured out how to court a lady. I need advice. I don't want Anne to leave, but it's too soon to ask her to stay. At least, I think it is. I'm not sure. That's the problem. Nothing is clear anymore. I used to think I knew what I was doing, but now I can't even remember if I put my socks on this morning. Do you see my problem?"

"Plain as day," Joseph said. He gave Jake a pensive look. "You're in love."

"Yeah…" Jake sighed and leaned against the railing. "And it's just plain awful."

"Yep." Jedediah drew near and patted him on the shoulder. "Wish I could say there was a cure, but it's terminal."

"Don't really want to recover," Jake said. "Just need to know what to do about it. She's leaving in two days, and I don't want her to."

"Does she know that?" John asked. "Have you told her that you care about her?"

"Well, I've held her hand and comforted her a time or two," he said. He wanted to add, "And planted a few kisses in her hair," but thought they might laugh at him.

"You need to court her proper-like," Jeremiah said. "You've always been loaded with ideas. I would think this would be the perfect time to come up with a few new ones."

"Remember the time you decided we could cut down on our

workload if we would just put ourselves on a schedule?" Jeremiah leaned against the edge of the barn. "You were right."

"And remember when you got that idea—we all thought it was harebrained—to move the cattle to the south pasture because it's more shaded?" John laughed then stopped abruptly. "Turned out you were right."

"Now that I think on it, you've been right most of the time," Jedediah said. "Least when it comes to good ideas."

"So what's stopping you from coming up with an idea to keep Anne here?" John asked. "If anyone could do it, you could."

"Really? You think so?" Jake felt his confidence growing.

"Sure." Joseph grinned. "A-course, you could put a feed sack over her head and throw her over your shoulder like we did to you."

"I don't think so. Not exactly the proper way to win her heart."

"Well, then, what if you work up a few tears?" Jedediah suggested. "I read about a fella who did that once. He blubbered like a baby."

"Did it win him the lady?" Jake asked, considering the idea.

"Nah. She thought he was a big sissy."

"I'm not the cryin' type, anyway." Jake paced the area in front of the church steps.

"There's only one idea that works, Jake." John put his hand on Jake's shoulder. "You're going to have to come out and tell her you care about her."

"Won't be easy," Joseph added. "I remember the first time I told Milly. My palms were sweaty and I thought I was gonna be sick."

"Why didn't you fellas warn me that it was gonna be like this?" Jake asked. "I had no idea love was so difficult."

"Oh, it's difficult all right." Jeremiah sighed. "Just wait till you're married to her for a few years and have a couple of screaming young'uns runnin' around the house. Then you'll know what real love looks like."

"Hmm. How did we jump from telling her that I care about her to being married and having young'uns?" Jake asked.

"Trust me, it's not as big a leap as you might think." Jeremiah grinned and slapped him on the back. "So prepare yourself for the inevitable. If you tell her you love her, you'd best be prepared to show it by walking down the aisle."

"This might be a good time to remind you that I just met her eight days ago." Jake chuckled.

"True, but when you know it's right, there's no point in waiting. Besides, you don't want her to slip away, do you? She's leaving town tomorrow, isn't she?"

"Monday."

"Monday." All four of Jake's brothers spoke the word in unison.

"Doesn't give you much time to come up with something brilliant to say." Joseph's brow wrinkled.

"If you're really asking for help, I know who to call on," John said. Jake perked up at this proclamation. "Who's that?"

"Just a minute." John left and returned with Ruth, Cora, Pauline, and Milly.

"Ladies, my little brother here needs your advice." John gave them a nod. "It's a matter of life and death."

"Life and death?" Cora's eyes widened. "Who's dying?"

"Jake, if he can't convince Anne to stay. So you've got to help him. Tell him what to say to her."

All the ladies began to squeal at once. Jake felt embarrassment wash over him. This wasn't exactly how he'd pictured the conversation going but he listened anyway, just in case any of the women had some good advice.

Before long, Milly got control of the situation. "Now, Jake, you have a seat. We're going to give you some courtin' tips, and I want you to commit them to memory."

As his brothers' wives began to offer their suggestions, Jake found himself overwhelmed. Their ideas were good, no doubt, but he didn't have time to do half the things they mentioned.

He played along, nodding when appropriate, but all the while knowing this really just came down to one thing—courage. He had to work up the courage to tell her. And he would do it today, before they left the church.

* * * * *

When most of the wedding guests had gone, Anne stayed with Maggie, Uncle Bertrand, and a host of others to clean up the mess. Jake and his brothers helped with the big stuff—the tables and so forth. Then they disappeared to the front porch steps to drink lemonade and gab—probably about the weather. The skies overhead had grown heavy. Thank goodness the wedding was behind them. Looked like they had a storm brewing.

Just as she loaded up the last of the dirty tablecloths, a familiar voice sounded from behind her. "Anne, can I ask you a question?"

She turned to face Amaryllis. "Yes, of course. What is it?"

"How do you do it?"

"Do what?" Anne brushed some cake crumbs from her skirt.

"You're just so...perfect."

"W–what?" Anne brought her hand to her chest as she tried to make sense of Amaryllis's words. Was she being serious…or poking fun? Anne could hardly tell.

"Yes. You're one of those girls I'm supposed to hate."

"I don't understand."

Amaryllis took another step toward her. "You remind me so much of a couple of the girls in my class back home. You're so much like them, and yet you're nothing like them. They were beautiful on the outside, like you."

"You—you think I'm beautiful?"

"You don't?" Amaryllis reached to take her hand. "You must be blind! You've got the shiniest hair I've ever seen and the perfect cheekbones. You have no idea what I'd give for your bone structure. And those eyes—they're the color of chocolate!"

Anne shook her head, unable to make sense of any of this.

"Yes, I should hate you, but I can't. You're just too nice. That's what sets you apart from the girls I know. You're pretty inside and out."

How did one go about responding to a comment like that? Should she thank Amaryllis? Anne gave her hand a squeeze and gazed into her flawless face. "Amaryllis, if you had any idea what I've been through in my life, you would know that I'm nothing like the girls you know in New York. I might have been raised in a beautiful house and maybe I had pretty things, but my life these past few years has been filled with not-so-pretty things."

"All I know is this…" Amaryllis's expression shifted to one of great tenderness. "You haven't let whatever has happened to you on the outside destroy the beautiful girl on the inside. I know you've been through several tragedies. You've lost your parents and you had to leave your home. And you've landed in a place where you knew no one."

"Yes." Anne forced back the tears.

"Some people in your position would grow bitter or angry. I just want you to know that it's so obvious you're reacting to tragedy the right way."

"You think so?"

"Yes." Amaryllis sighed. "And I have so much to learn from you. I tend to overreact to the slightest bitty thing. If I break a nail, I cry. If I don't get invited to a social event, I pout. If my dress gets a tear, I think my life has come to an end. It all seems so silly when I look at you."

"Trust me, I've been through those emotions too. I remember the days when my focus was on dresses and parties and hair ribbons—outer things." Anne paused, realizing the beauty of what the Lord had done in her life. "I guess if I've learned anything, it's this: life is fleeting. And material possessions, as lovely as they are, aren't worth a hill of beans in comparison to the people we love. I've already survived losing both parents, as you've said. What difference does it make if I lose my home, my dresses, my jewels?" She paused to finger her tiny cross necklace. "They're nothing in comparison to losing what really matters."

Amaryllis embraced her and whispered, "You're such a brave girl."

"I don't know that I would agree with that." Anne spoke a soft response. "I just know that who I am isn't really wrapped up in those things. Not anymore, anyway. It's a fresh new way to look at life."

Amaryllis took a step back and shook her head. "I can't say I would have responded the same way, but knowing you has made me want to try to be a better person."

"Really?"

"Mm-hmm," Amaryllis said. "And since we're having a heart-to-heart and all, you'd better know something else too."

"What's that?"

"I didn't just want to hate you because you're pretty. And nice. I wanted to hate you because I see the way Jake looks at you whenever you enter the room. He's completely smitten."

Anne felt her cheeks begin to blaze. She opened her mouth to respond but nothing came out. "I—I haven't sought his attention."

"That's just it. You didn't have to. When something is right, it's obvious. And I can no longer deny that he finds you right as rain."

Anne's heart swelled at this revelation. Yes, she certainly knew that Jake had feelings for her. There was no doubt in her mind after yesterday's trip to the canyon. But did he really care about her in the way Amaryllis was suggesting? The words had not been spoken. And with the clock ticking, she wondered if there would be time even if he did speak them.

"Amaryllis, I've only been here a few days, and I'm leaving soon."

"We'll see about that." Amaryllis quirked a brow and giggled.

"No, it's true. My uncle will be driving us to Dallas on Monday morning. And besides, as I said, I've not had any aspirations for love. My devotion is to my sisters. They need a good life, one where they feel safe." Her heart twisted as she spoke these words.

Amaryllis laughed. "According to Emily, they need a life filled with exciting storybook heroes who rescue damsels in distress."

"My sister's head is filled with stuff and nonsense."

"Maybe. Maybe not." Amaryllis fussed with the wrinkles in her skirt. "I only know one thing...the Lord has brought you here. And I've been privileged to meet you...and I do believe in the kind of happily-ever-after stories your sister writes." She sighed. "Even if this particular story hasn't cast me as its heroine." With a nod she turned toward the church.

Anne walked around to the front of the church and found Jake still gabbing with his brothers on the front porch steps. As soon as they saw her, John rose and said something about the weather, leaving in a hurry. So did Joseph, who claimed that Milly needed his help with the children. Jeremiah and Jedediah were the only ones left, but they shot away as soon as Anne approached.

"I see I have quite an effect on your brothers," she said.

Jake smiled and extended his hand. "They just want to give us some time alone. Do you have a minute to sit and talk?"

"Just." She pointed to the skies overhead. "Looks like we're about to have a downpour."

He glanced up and a stunned expression crossed his face. "Go figure. I hadn't even noticed." He looked her way. "Then again, my focus has been on something else entirely. Haven't really been worried about the weather." He gave her hand a squeeze, and her heart fluttered.

See, Anne? He really does care. And he's showing you more and more with each passing day. But what could she do about it? Come Monday morning, she would be packed up and headed to Dallas.

A couple of tiny raindrops fell and hit the back of her hand. "Oh no. It's about to come down."

"I just want to say something before it does." Jake squared his shoulders. "I—I—I think you did a wonderful job with the wedding."

"Thank you."

"I definitely see this as your talent. You are an organizer. A coordinator."

"Thank you. I've been thinking that when I get to Dallas I can—"

She stopped talking because he stared into her eyes. "Make me a promise."

"W–what's that?"

"Don't say another word about Dallas today, okay? This is the perfect day, and I don't want to spoil it by thinking about you moving away."

"All right." She forced back the lump in her throat.

"There's so much I need to tell you...." Jake pulled her into his arms. Just then, a clap of thunder sounded overhead. Off in the distance, Kate let out a scream. Anne pulled away from Jake and turned to find her sister running across the church lawn. Seconds later, the rain began to pour in earnest. Looked like whatever Jake had to say would just have to wait for another day.

Not that she had a lot of days left.

GROOM
1914
TX

Chapter Twenty-Three

....

The Texas Panhandle might not be known for its illustrious hospitals, but we know a thing or two about caring for the sick. Ask anybody's grandmother or aunt and she can fill you in on the proper home remedies for nearly all types of illness. Struggling with heart-related issues? Eat more garlic. Dealing with a gassy stomach? Brew a tea from fresh dandelion leaf. Feeling dizzy? Try a little ginger. Struggling with joint pain? Try a pinch of Epsom salt. Battling a cough? Enjoy a piece of licorice. Itchy with eczema? Use the juice from inside a local cactus plant. Yep, you might have the illness, but we've got the cure. Don't let what ails keep you from enjoying life in the Panhandle. —"Tex" Morgan, reporting for the Panhandle Primer

On Sunday morning, Anne awoke to a flurry of activity outside her bedroom door. She put on her robe and opened the door to find Maggie rushing down the hallway, her red hair looking wilder than ever.

"It's Emily," Maggie said. "I've put in a call to the doctor. She's very ill."

"Ill?" Anne's heart began to race. "But just yesterday she was fine. I can't imagine what happened."

"Maybe something she ate?" Maggie shook her head. "I don't

know. I just know that she's crying out in pain. I've never seen a child in this much anguish."

"Heavens." Anne raced down the hallway and opened the door to Emily's room. She found both of her sisters in the bed, with Kate leaning over Emily. Anne sat on the bed and stared at her sister, who was doubled over.

"Emily. What's happened? Where does it hurt?"

"Everywhere." Emily let out a horrible groaning sound. "Oh, Anne, I'm so sick." She flung her right arm over her head and fell back against the pillows.

Anne reached down and rested her palm against Emily's forehead. "You don't feel feverish. What are your symptoms?"

"My head is aching, and my chest hurts." Emily began to cough then caught her breath. "Oh, do you see what I mean? Can you call for the doctor?"

"Maggie's already done that. He's on his way."

Kate looked on, her eyes growing wide at that pronouncement.

"I'm too sick to go anywhere," Emily said. "I don't believe I can be moved for days. Maybe weeks."

"Mm-hmm." Anne's suspicions kicked in. "Tell me more."

"I think she has dysmantery," Kate said.

"Do you mean dysentery?"

"Yes, dysentery," Kate said with a nod. "That's it."

"I believe dysentery presents with far different symptoms." Anne spoke in her most serious voice. "But I shall wait for the doctor to decide. After he bleeds her out, we will know more."

"B–bleeds me out?" Emily sat up. "Is that really necessary?"

"Perhaps not." Anne shook her head. "He might be persuaded to operate straightaway."

"O–operate?" Emily paled.

"Strange that dysentery would present with symptoms in the chest and throat, though." Anne did her best to hold her voice steady. "Usually it affects a far more...remote region of the body."

"I see." Emily sat up in the bed and rubbed the back of her neck. "I feel a bit woozy, sister. And my throat is..." She coughed again. "Quite terrible. I'm in so much pain. Perhaps it isn't dysentery after all. I believe I must have scarlet fever."

"Ooh, scarlet fever." Anne nodded. "Now that diagnosis makes far more sense. I once read about a character who had scarlet fever."

"Oh?" Emily's expression brightened.

"Yes, she didn't last more than a few weeks." Anne tucked the covers around her younger sister, keeping her expression serious. "And it's quite contagious, so I suppose we'll have to keep Kate from seeing you. Come now, Kate. You'll have to say good-bye to Emily and visit with the adults in the other room."

"Oh, pooh." Kate stood on the bed and began to jump. "Why should I do that? She's not sick anyway."

Emily grabbed Kate by the hand and pulled her down onto the bed, glaring at her. "Why, of course I am. Remember, Kate? We talked about this earlier. I'm quite ill. Far too ill to travel to Dallas just yet."

"So that's it." Anne pulled back the covers, revealing Emily fully dressed and wearing shoes. "You've come up with a story to keep you from going to Uncle Bertrand's house. And you think feigning an illness is the way to go?"

Emily rose and straightened her skirts. She put her hand on her hip and stared at Anne. "Don't tell me you want to go with him, Anne."

"I'm not saying that. I just don't see that we have much choice."

"Oh, but don't you see?" Emily sat on the edge of the bed, and tears rose to cover her lashes. "I feel like we've been given a second chance at life here. It's like we're in heaven. And if we have to go to Uncle Bertrand's, we'll leave heaven and go to—"

Kate's eyes widened and she clapped her hand over her sister's mouth. "Don't say it on a Sunday, Emily."

"Anyway, we'll go to a horrible place with weeping and wailing and gnashing of teeth." Emily's gaze narrowed. "A place of eternal torture and punishment...and all for a crime we did not commit."

"I daresay you've committed a crime or two just since I arrived in the room." Anne sat next to her sister and took her hand. "Though I believe a jury might find you innocent, under the circumstances."

"Any juror worth his weight in salt would find Uncle Bertrand guilty." Emily put her hands on her hips again.

"Of what?" Anne gave her sister a pensive look. "He's just come to give us a ride back to Dallas. That doesn't make him evil. It just makes him..." She couldn't think of how to finish the sentence, so she left it hanging in the air.

"Did I hear someone say my name?"

Anne looked toward the door, stunned to find Uncle Bertrand standing there.

Anne's heart flew into her throat. "Oh, I, well, we..." She shrugged.

"Emily, are you ill? Maggie is quite concerned." He drew near and touched her forehead with his palm. Emily flinched at his touch but eventually rested her head against the pillow and feigned illness. Her eyes fluttered closed.

"I've sent for the doctor," Maggie said, entering the room in a flurry.

"I'll fetch him myself," Uncle Bertrand said. "It won't take me long to get to town in the car."

"No!" Emily sat straight up in bed. "I'm feeling much better, thank you. It's like a miracle, really. Thank you all for praying."

"We never had time to pray, you little tyrant." Anne groaned then looked at her uncle. "You see what you're getting, don't you? She's skilled at storytelling."

"I suspected as much." Uncle Bertrand grinned.

"What gave me away?" Emily asked.

"For one thing, you're fully dressed. If you were genuinely ill, you wouldn't have had the strength to put your clothes on."

"Ah. Good point." She wrinkled her nose. "I'll have to remember that next time."

He nodded. "I, for one, am glad you're well. I stopped by to give you girls a ride to church. Thought you might like to arrive in style in the Cadillac."

"Oh, yes, please!"

Maggie looked back and forth between them, clearly confused. "I guess I should call the doctor back and tell him not to come?"

"That's right." Uncle Bertrand nodded. "Tell him the little minx—er, patient—had a remarkable recovery. He would be better served caring for the real patients."

Maggie nodded and disappeared into the hallway. Seconds later her voice came back, "Breakfast will be served in fifteen minutes. It's our last Sunday morning together, so I'd like to see everyone at the table."

At once, Kate began to cry.

"What's wrong, honey?" Anne asked, sitting next to her on the bed.

"Oh, Anne, she's right. It's our last Sunday here ever. And I was just starting to get used to it."

Anne's heart grew as heavy as lead. She gazed up at Uncle Bertrand, who stood in the doorway with lips pursed. He quickly excused himself.

"We've got to be strong," Anne said, "so dry those eyes. Let's eat some breakfast and enjoy our time with the people we love."

The people we love.

The words came without her even thinking them through. But they were true. Wholly and completely true. She loved these people—every last one of them. And leaving them tomorrow would likely be one more thing in a long line of very difficult things she'd had to do over the past few years.

Still, what choice did she have?

With new resolve, Anne headed off to her room to get ready for the day.

* * * * *

Jake enjoyed every minute of sitting next to Anne in church. He tried not to think about the fact that she would be leaving tomorrow, but those niggling thoughts tormented him despite his best attempts.

When the service ended, her uncle offered them a ride in the Cadillac. Jake took him up on the offer, passing off the family truck to Jeremiah to drive home. Though the others in the vehicle laughed and chatted, he could not. In fact, he felt downright ill. It wasn't a pretend illness, like the one Emily had feigned. No, this was the real deal.

He somehow got through lunch, though he barely touched his food. Afterward, when Anne slipped off to help the girls pack their luggage, he paced the parlor.

His mother approached from behind. "Jake, I don't mean this the way it's probably going to sound, but you look awful."

He turned to face her but couldn't seem to respond.

"Are you ill?"

He shook his head. For a moment, anyway. Then he decided to be honest and offer up a nod. "I think I am."

"It's been a long week. You're probably exhausted. Or maybe you're suffering from allergies. Remember that time you sneezed for a week after eating peanuts?"

"It's not a physical sickness," he said. "I'm…heartsick."

"Ah." His mother drew near and touched his arm. "Because Anne is leaving tomorrow?"

He nodded, doing his best to swallow the giant lump in his throat. It wouldn't budge.

"If you want her to stay, you have to tell her."

"It just seems so complicated. There are more lives involved here than just hers and mine. And besides…" He took a few steps toward the door and then turned back with a sigh. "I'm not good at telling people what I'm thinking. I get tongue-tied."

"Pooh. I see you talking to that mare of yours all the time."

"Well, that's different. She doesn't judge me. Or poke fun at me. And she certainly never twists my words around."

"Tell you what, Jake. You go on out there and pretend you're talking to the woman you love."

"Excuse me?"

"Tell it to Frances."

"You want me to tell my horse that I love her?"

"We all know you love Frances. I'm just saying you might feel better if you take a practice run by acting like she's Anne. Say what's on your heart. Rehearse. There's nothing wrong with that. Might be just the thing to get you over the hurdle. So go on now."

Jake shook his head, understanding how ridiculous that idea sounded and yet how likely his mother was to be right.

She gave him a hug then headed to the kitchen. Jake decided to go for a walk. If he happened by Frances, he might give it a try. Maybe. If his brothers were far, far away, of course.

Seconds later, he strolled out onto the porch. Looking to the right and then the left, he assessed the field. Empty—nothing but wide-open plains. Well, he might as well take a venture out to the pasture. Frances was ready to foal anytime now, after all.

Jake mumbled to himself all the way across the field. He opened the gate to the pasture and was careful to watch his step. Off in the distance, Frances whinnied. She lifted her head and shook it in that playful way of hers, and the weight on his shoulders dropped immediately. Leave it to Frances to make him feel better.

"Happy to see me, girl?" He reached out to run his hand along her neck and then gave her a couple of pats. Afterward, he gave her midsection a feel. "It'll be soon, girl. Not long at all."

She whinnied, as if grateful.

For a couple of minutes Jake stood in silence, just thinking about everything that had happened over the last few days. His entire world had been flipped upside down. Everything he ever thought he knew about falling in love was wrong. And he had to do something about it or die trying.

From the sensation taking hold of his head, he wondered if perhaps dying might not be easier. Getting these words out might just do him in.

He drew in a deep breath and released it before giving Frances a pat on the neck. "Well, girl, Mama says I need to practice my speech on you. How do you feel about that?"

The horse tilted her head, as if she understood every word.

"It's an odd approach, to be sure. But we both know I have an easier time talking to you than anyone. Can't deny that. So let's do it this way. I'll talk out loud as if I'm talking to Anne and you just listen, okay? At the end, you can tell me how I did. One stomp of the foot means I did fine. A whinny means I should try again with something else. Got it?"

Frances nuzzled up against him.

"I know." He raked his fingers through his hair. "I've rendered you speechless. Glad to see I'm not the only one short on words." He swallowed hard, unsure of how to begin. How did a fella go about telling a girl that she consumed his thoughts night and day? That he couldn't seem to think straight when she came around? That he found himself overwhelmed with feelings and emotions he'd never before known?

"Better to just get right to it," he mumbled at last. Jake squared his shoulders, ready to begin. "See, Anne, it's like this. You've dropped into my life like a pebble in that old pond out in the pasture—kind of unexpected-like."

Frances let out a whinny.

"No good, huh?" Jake began to pace, thoughts flying through his head. "Well, what about this...?" He cleared his throat. "Anne, it's a mighty fine day for a walk. The skies are clear and sunny, and you seem to be the sturdy sort. What say we talk a walk through the pasture...for the rest of our lives?"

Frances let out another whinny and he gave her a curious look.

"Either I stink at romancing women or you're just being temperamental. It's hard for me to tell."

She went back to eating, and he struggled to know what to say next.

He decided to give it another try. Squaring his shoulders, he went for it. "I'm not real good with words, Anne. But there's something I've been needin' to tell ya. Call me a coward, but I just can't seem to say it out loud, though my heart says it every time you walk into the room. I suspected it that first night we talked under the stars, but I knew for sure as we looked out over the canyon together.

"I'm crazy about you. There it is. Head-over-heels crazy. And I should tell you. A normal, sane man would tell a girl what he's feeling. But whenever I see you, all the words go flying right out of my head like a star shooting through the heavens and landing who knows where. It's like I completely lose control of my ability to reason correctly when you're around, which frightens me a little but intrigues me even more."

He paused and chuckled. "But who can blame me for losing words when you're around? You're about the prettiest thing I've ever seen. Those beautiful brown eyes, that shiny hair... No fella even in his right mind could think straight—or talk straight—when you're around. Don't you see my problem?"

"I believe I do."

A familiar voice rang out from behind him. He turned to find Anne standing there.

For a moment he couldn't say anything. Finally Jake managed a weak, "H–how long have you been listening?" Heat rose to his face and he felt like running, but he forced himself to keep his feet firmly planted instead. There was no point in playing the coward now.

A lovely smile turned up the edges of her lips. "Long enough to hear you say that I'm pretty."

His gaze shifted to the ground and then back up again. "Well, you are."

Her brow wrinkled. "Do you mind if I ask why you're telling the horse I'm pretty...but not telling me?"

"You must've missed that part." He took a couple of steps in her direction. "Anne, I'm an idiot." *No, don't say that. That wasn't part of your speech.* "Let me take that back. I'm..." He tried to rethink the speech in his head. "There's so much I want to say, but nothing seems to come out right. I want to tell you...."

Her eyes lit up, and she smiled. "Yes, Jake?"

He took another step in her direction.

"I need to tell you..."

"Hmm?" She eased a bit closer to him until he could feel her breath on his cheek.

"Anne, if I don't tell you this, my heart's going to explode." Jake reached out and slipped his arms around her waist and pulled her close. For a moment he thought about diving back into his speech. Then, realizing the words were gone once again, he did the only thing that made sense.

He kissed her.

Yep. He kissed her. Soundly. On the lips. In the pasture. With his horse standing next to him and several of his nieces and nephews whooping and hollering in the distance. He kissed her until he felt sure she understood every word coming from his heart.

Apparently he had a lot to say.

When the kiss finally ended, Anne looked up at him with a shy smile. "Y–you were saying...?" She giggled.

"I think I said it loud and clear. But just in case you missed it..." He kissed her again.

GROOM 1914 TX

Chapter Twenty-Four

....

I must confess, while menfolk in the Panhandle know how to rope cattle, build houses, and raise barns, they're a little weak in the knees when it comes to their women. Sure, they try to act tough, but on the inside they're quivering like their mama's tapioca pudding. And when it comes time to state the obvious, they tend to get a little tongue-tied. If you're wantin' to get a gal to say "I do," you might start by "I don't" to a few things—like spittin', chewin', and chawin'. And for heaven's sake, comb your hair and wear your best shirt. There's nothing that'll turn a girl away faster than an old shirt. More than anything, though, let the words of your heart shine through. If you state them plain and clear, she might even tolerate your worn-out shirt. And if she doesn't? Well, then, she's just not the girl for you. —"Tex" Morgan, reporting for the *Panhandle Primer*

Anne awoke on Monday morning with her thoughts in a whirl. Oh, what a glorious few days she'd experienced. She rolled over in the bed, remembering every detail of Jake's kiss. In that moment she'd known the truth—he didn't just care about her, he loved her.

And she loved him too. She loved the way he smiled when she

walked into a room. She loved the way he treated people with such kindness. And she loved the way he'd swept her family into the fold as if they'd always belonged there.

Thinking about belonging to the O'Farrell family caused Anne's emotions to suddenly spiral downward. How could she possibly leave Groom now?

Those emotions gave way to fear. If she had to leave Jake and head for Dallas, would they ever see each other again? Surely Uncle Bertrand would permit it…wouldn't he? The joy she'd felt only moments before was traded for confusion and then sorrow. For, while she wanted to do the right thing by her family, she suddenly felt as great a desire to stay and pursue her new relationship with Jake.

Lord, You said You would give me the desires of my heart. Father, I've struggled so much. And I've lost so much. Most of my desires have been swept aside while I've tried to meet the needs of my sisters. O God, I don't want to sound selfish, but I love him. I love him, and I want to be here…in Groom. This is where I belong.

Her prayer eventually gave way to tears, and though she tried to summon up the faith to believe that everything would work out for the best, she could not. How many times over the past few years had she hoped for the best, only to be disappointed? Would this be another of those instances? Just another link in the long chain of events leading her from Denver to Dallas?

The tears flowed in earnest now. So many things worked their way to the surface—her mother's death. Her father's struggles. His death. The joy she'd felt during the ceremony yesterday. The peace she felt wrapped in Jake's arms. The contentment that cocooned her every time she walked onto O'Farrell's Honor.

All these feelings spilled out at once, making for a lengthy cry.

At one point someone rapped on the bedroom door. She wanted to respond but could not. Whoever it was eventually gave up.

A short time later, she got control of her emotions and rose to see how much damage she'd done to her appearance. One glance in the mirror spoke more than a thousand words. She dabbed at her face with a wet cloth and took several deep breaths. Just as she regained some of her composure, another rap sounded at the door. She eased it open a few inches and was surprised to find Emily outside.

"Annie, everyone is worried because you're not at breakfast."

Anne dabbed at her eyes. "Tell them not to worry, honey."

Emily gazed up at her with more tenderness than Anne knew the ten-year-old was capable of. "You're going to miss him, aren't you?"

Anne nodded, and the tears started again. "I'm going to miss all of this. The ranch. The people. Jake. All of it."

"I know just how you feel. And I'm sorry to have to tell you this, but you need to get dressed and come out. Uncle Bertrand is here, and he wants to talk to us."

Anne nodded and sighed. So, the moment had come at last. He would give them their last-minute instructions, no doubt. Then luggage would be loaded into his Cadillac and off they would go to Dallas.

As she dressed, Anne did her best to remain hopeful. Surely she and Jake could work this out. They would come up with a plan. And for pity's sake, it wasn't like she was moving to the other side of the country. Dallas was just a hundred miles away. Why, by tonight she'd be sleeping in a bed at Uncle Bertrand's house.

Though still feeling shaky, Anne knew better than to keep her uncle waiting. As soon as she'd made herself presentable, she went into the parlor. She found him seated on the sofa next to Maggie.

He took one look at her and asked if she felt ill.

"No, sir. I'm just…" She shrugged. "Not quite myself today."

"I'm sorry to hear that. But then, you've had a busy weekend. No doubt you've worn yourself out."

"I have." She nodded. "It's been very eventful."

Uncle Bertrand glanced at his pocket watch. "I'm sorry that I can't stay to chat, but I must leave for a while. I have a meeting in town. I just wanted to stop by and let you know that something has come up and I'll be detained."

"Detained?" Anne wasn't sure what he meant.

He rose and reached for his hat. "I won't be able to leave Groom for at least another twenty-four hours. I do hope that doesn't interfere with any of your plans."

"Another twenty-four hours?" Emily let out a whoop, which was followed by a squeal from Kate. "Is it really true?"

"Yes, well, I've got some business to attend to."

"In Groom?" Anne couldn't make sense of his words but didn't argue with him. After all, he'd just offered her a twenty-four-hour reprieve.

Uncle Bertrand nodded. "Nothing to be alarmed about. Rest easy." He reached over and patted her hand. Then, after going to the kitchen to speak to Maggie, he disappeared through the front door.

"Oh, Anne!" Emily rushed her way and threw wide her arms for an embrace. "It's just too good to be true, isn't it?"

"It is." Anne found herself speechless.

"I wish this next day would stretch out forever," Kate said. "I'm going to miss my new friends."

"And this ranch," Emily said. "It's been great fodder for my story."

"And Maggie." Kate's eyes filled with tears. "I think I'm going to miss her most of all."

Anne felt the sting of tears once more. "Well, let's not focus on the negative today, all right? We've got a full day to do as we please. What will you do with it?"

"I was going to dig up my dolls and ask them a host of questions," Emily said. "But now I'm not in the mood. I think I'll play with the other children. Willy's going to teach me how to shoot a gun."

"W–what?" Anne could hardly catch her breath.

"Oh, don't worry. Not a real gun. It's just a piece of wood." Emily giggled. "What are you going to do with this day, Anne?"

"Hopefully spend it with Jake."

Jake. She just realized...this was Monday. He'd probably already left for work.

Anne went into the kitchen and was surprised to find Maggie seated at the table, looking a little misty-eyed. "What's wrong, Maggie?" she asked.

"Oh, fiddlesticks. I hadn't planned for you to see me like this." Maggie swiped at her eyes with the back of her hand. "Sorry, Anne."

"You're upset."

"Yes." She nodded. "I... Well, I don't want you to leave." A lone tear trickled down one of Maggie's cheeks. "It's going to be so quiet around here when you leave. Nothing will be the same. There's going to be a giant hole in my heart. I know because I'm already feeling it and you haven't even left yet." She looked up at Anne. "I've grown to love you...all of you."

"I love you too, Maggie." Anne knelt beside her and allowed herself to be wrapped in Maggie's comforting embrace.

Immediately she was transported back to an instance with her mother, many years ago. She'd arrived home from school with her feelings hurt about something or another and Mama had wrapped her in her arms, just like Maggie was doing now.

The same sense of peace swept over Anne. She rose, knowing in her heart of hearts that everything would work out. If God could stop a train in Groom, Texas, to introduce her to the love of her life, He could certainly give her a sense of direction about what was coming next.

"Would you like some help around the house this morning, Maggie?" Anne asked. "It's the least I can do."

"Not just yet, honey," Maggie said. "My feet are still aching from all the work we did over the weekend. I think I might actually sit on the sofa for a while and read the paper. Why don't you go out for a walk? Check on Frances, if you will. She's due to deliver any day now."

"I'll do that." Anne walked outside, pausing as the fresh aroma of newly cut hay greeted her. Off in the distance, John and the other brothers were baling hay. She watched the process for a moment and then went to check on Frances. She found her in the stall, looking uneasy.

"Won't be long now, girl," Anne said. She stroked the horse's side, noticing at once the tightening there. "Not long at all." Anne waited a couple more minutes and then left the barn, heading back for the house. She'd almost reached the porch when Jake pulled up in the truck. He took one look at her and sprang from it, rushing her way.

For whatever reason, the tears started again the moment she saw him. And try as she might, she couldn't seem to keep them away.

"Anne?" Jake looked concerned as he approached. "Are you all right?"

She didn't even try to hide her tears. What would be the point in hiding her feelings now? "Oh, Jake."

He pulled her into his arms. "Shh, now. No tears. Not today."

"How can we possibly make this work?" Anne asked. "Dallas is several hours from here, and I don't know that Uncle Bertrand would approve of me taking the train back and forth." She paced back and forth, finally turning to him once more. "And the girls... I just don't know that I could leave them to come and go. It would be so hard on them. They've lost so much already. Their parents... their home...everything they held dear. I'd hate to see them hurt again."

Jake brushed a hair out of her face. "I would never expect you to come back and forth without your sisters." He paused. "But, Anne, this doesn't have to be as complicated as all that. If you'll just—"

"I don't see any other way. Yes, Uncle Bertrand has softened. That much is apparent. I daresay he's smitten, both with your mother and this town. But even with that..."

"Anne."

"I honestly don't know, Jake. I've thought about it from every angle, but—"

"Anne."

"Even if I have my uncle's permission to court you, nothing will be the same once I leave." She paused, finally noticing the hopeful glimmer in his eyes.

"That's the very thing I want to talk to you about," he said. "Now, if you don't mind, I have a little something I'd like to say."

* * * * *

Jake felt his excitement grow as he faced Anne. Inside he quivered, but on the outside he managed to hold it together. "I've come up with a plan."

"Are you thinking about making trips to Dallas, then?"

"Anne, I really think that—"

"Because I honestly don't know if my heart could handle it if I don't see you every single day. This whole thing is just too much to take. Too much to think about."

"Then do me a favor and stop thinking."

"W–what?" She looked perplexed.

He paused, mortified by the words he'd just spoken. "I'm sorry. Didn't mean that quite the way it sounded. And if I ever picked a good time to say the wrong thing, it was now. Figures."

"What do you mean?"

"I mean, I have the answer to the problem. It's been the right answer all along, and the only one that makes sense. You're not going anywhere and neither am I."

"I'm not?"

"No." He pulled her close and whispered, "Don't you see? The reason the Lord brought you here wasn't for a temporary visit. And it wasn't so that I could trek back and forth to Dallas. I have no desire to go to Dallas. Never have."

"But…"

"Who was it that once told me the only buts were the ones left behind after a fella finished a good cigar?"

She sighed. "Me. But you're not a smoker."

Emily let out a whistle from the front porch. As they turned to face her, she waved. "Papa used to smoke cigars. Tell him, Anne."

Jake shook his head. "Anne, you're not listening to me. We can stop all of this right here and now and just do the most obvious thing."

"O–oh?"

He knelt and took her by the hand. Emily and Kate began to whoop and holler from the front porch. Anne looked as if she might faint.

"Maggie!" Emily let out an ear-piercing squeal and then yelled, "Maggie, get out here! He's doing it! He's proposing!"

Anne's eyes grew wide. She looked at Jake and whispered, "Is that what you're doing?"

He nodded and gave her a little wink.

"Oh my goodness."

"Please wait just a minute, Jake," Emily called out from the porch. "I want to get my writing tablet so I can take notes. And Maggie's on her way. I can hear her."

"Hurry, if you please," Jake said, shifting to the other knee. "I can't stay in this position forever."

His mother came out to the porch, wiping flour-covered hands on her apron. "What's all the fuss about out here?" She took one look at her son on bent knee and immediately began to weep. "Praise the Lord and pass the potatoes. He's really done it!"

"Not yet," Jake called out. "But I'm trying to."

"Well, don't let me stop you. I'll just sit right here and watch." She waved a hand then took a seat on the swing and pulled Kate next to her.

Emily returned to the porch that same moment with her pad in hand. She began to scribble. "Okay, start over. Say it all again."

"Oh, for pity's sake." Anne slapped herself in the head with her one free hand.

"Have you got a ring?" his mother called out.

Jake shook his head. "No. Didn't think that far ahead."

"Hold that thought. I'll be right back with your great-grandma's opal ring." She looked at Anne. "Will that work for you, honey?"

Anne nodded and gave him a little wink, which sent his heart sailing straight to the clouds.

Seconds later his mother came rushing across the yard with the ring in hand. "Could stand a bit of cleaning, but we'll take care of that later." She passed it to him then went back to the porch.

Jake looked into Anne's eyes, doing his best to keep the focus on the two of them and not their audience. His hand trembled in hers. "I would be honored if you would do me the great honor of becoming my wife."

"I would have posed it as a question," Emily called out. "Don't you want to give her the option of saying yes or no?"

Jake groaned as he turned to Emily. "Give me a chance. I'm not done yet." He gazed into Anne's eyes, and for a moment he was reminded of the first time he'd laid eyes on her, when she was wearing that beautiful lavender dress. She had looked like a princess then. The past ten days had proven that she actually was one. In every conceivable way, she was his Guinevere…a stranger from a foreign land who had been dropped from heaven into his world.

"Annie, I hope you don't think this is too impulsive. I assure you, it is not. I've given it a great deal of thought and even more prayer."

"Prayer is the solution," his mother called out. "It's the only answer for the problems we face in life."

Jake sighed. The only problem he happened to be facing at the moment was the obvious one. If things kept going the way they were now, he might never get this out.

"I've been praying," Anne whispered. She gave his hand a squeeze.

"Me too." He spoke the words, his heart fully alive. "Will you marry me, Anne? Will you live at O'Farrell's Honor in the house I plan to build right over there?" He pointed to the east field.

"You always said you wanted the field west of Joseph's place when you got married," his mother corrected him.

"The west field," he echoed. "Will you? Because if you don't, I'm pretty sure we're going to be written up in that book of Emily's as evil villains. And I'm really, really sure my brothers are never going to let me forget it."

"No doubt." Anne giggled.

"Say yes, Annie!" Emily called out.

Anne's hands trembled in his. She turned to face her sister. "Emily, if you don't mind, I would like to answer this one myself."

"All right, all right," Emily huffed.

Anne turned to face Jake and, with tears streaming down her face, whispered her response to his question. "I can't think of anything I would love more."

With joy flooding his soul, Jake slipped his great-grandmother's opal ring on Anne's finger and rose to kiss her. Though he couldn't be certain—what with his eyes closed and all—Jake was pretty sure his mother and the girls did a little celebratory dance on the porch. He only wished his father could have been there to join them.

GROOM
1914
TX

Chapter Twenty-Five

....

Hoping for a career as a door-to-door salesman? Wishing you owned a mercantile? Interested in carpentry work, or do you have a hankerin' to work for the railroad? Are you ready to take on a slew of children in a classroom? Considering life behind the pulpit? There are jobs aplenty in the Texas Panhandle. No matter which occupation you choose, the Panhandle is the perfect place to begin a new career. Here in Texas's far north corner, we've got both the inner zeal and the encouragement of our friends and neighbors. What more do you need to succeed? —"Tex" Morgan, reporting for the *Panhandle Primer*

After Jake's proposal, Anne's hands trembled so hard that she could barely see the ring. "I...I..."

"It's all right," Jake whispered in her ear. "You don't need to say anything."

"Oh, but I do. This is all too...perfect."

"Yes." He paused and gazed into her eyes. "It's the right thing to do, Annie."

She nodded, unable to think of one intelligent thing to say. Then Anne gestured for her sisters and Maggie to join them in the yard, and before long they were all in a tearful embrace.

"I don't believe it." Maggie dabbed her eyes. "Jake, you really caught me off guard. This is the best news ever."

"Do you know what I think?" Jake turned to face them. "None of this was a coincidence—the track being out, you girls choosing not to go to the hotel with the others, ending up at O'Farrell's Honor.... God has arranged every step of this. How can we ignore the obvious? The Lord couldn't have made it any plainer if He'd written it down for us to read."

"I wrote it down," Emily said. "Every word. And now my story's coming true!"

Anne slipped her arm around Jake's waist. "And I'm so glad… about all of it. Living here in Groom is going to be a chance for all of us to start over." She'd no sooner gotten the words out than she clamped a hand over her mouth. "Oh, Jake."

"What?"

"Uncle Bertrand. You don't suppose he'll try to take the girls back to Dallas with him, do you?" She pulled Emily and Kate close.

"I don't want to go, Annie." Kate began to sniffle.

"I'll bury him in the backyard if he tries to make us." Emily crossed her arms at her chest. "I'll do such a good job of it that no one will ever find his body."

"Now, I don't believe that will be necessary." Maggie patted Emily's shoulder. "God has an answer for all of this, I'm sure. One that won't require a burial."

Jake took Anne's hand. "Don't you think—and I don't mean this in a hurtful way—that he will be relieved?"

"Oh." Anne paused to think about that. "I never really thought about it from that angle before, but maybe you're right. He's never been keen on having children underfoot, and it's clear he's got his own work to keep him busy. Perhaps he will see this as positive news."

Maggie's eyes grew a little misty. "Anne, there's something you need to understand about your uncle. I...well, I've had a few days to get to know him. I know he's a crusty old soul on the outside. I daresay you could take an ice pick to him and chip away for hours without making much of a dent."

"No doubt." Anne nodded. "But what were you going to say?"

"Like most folks who've been wounded, there's the exterior and the interior. And the two don't always match. I can see, upon further examination, that the man on the inside is not as cold or hard."

"What do you mean?"

"Just yesterday we had a marvelous conversation about his store. You did know that he runs a store in Dallas, didn't you?"

"I knew he had a business, but I don't know much about it." She shrugged, unsure of where this conversation was heading.

"Well, he has a store. And he's been thinking of branching out to neighboring counties, and we talked about his plans to do so." Maggie smiled. "Funny thing. When you get a man to talking about his dreams and goals, his eyes light up in a way you wouldn't expect. That's what I wanted to tell you. He might be an old codger on the outside, but on the inside I saw a little boy with dreams. Someone who wanted to make a difference through these department stores of his."

"Department stores?"

"Well, that's what he called them. They're stores with different departments. There's a section for clothes, one for shoes, one for household items.... Like a general store, only much larger."

"Ah. We had a store like that in Denver. I always loved shopping there. Very convenient."

"I don't know about the rest of you, but proposing sure makes a fella hungry. Anyone ready for some food?" Jake took a couple of steps toward the house and then looked back. "What do you think, ladies? A little food to celebrate?"

Maggie paused. "Well, there is this little thing I'd like to discuss before we go inside."

"What's that?"

Maggie faced Annie. "I'm going to be your mother-in-law soon."

"Yes, that's right." Anne smiled. "And I'm so excited."

"Well, I'm wondering if it would be inappropriate...I mean, I don't want to offend you in any way because I know you had a perfectly wonderful mama. But I wonder if you would consider calling me 'Mama Maggie' like my other daughters-in-law do."

"I would be honored."

"What about us?" Emily asked, crowding into the space between them. "Can I call you Mama Maggie too?"

"Me too?" Kate asked.

"Technically, if you're Mama Maggie to her, then you're our Mama Maggie," Emily said. "Because she's our sister. And sisters have the same mama."

Anne's heart began to twist. For a moment—just a moment—an image of her mother's face flashed in front of her. But just as quickly it faded, and then all she could see was the heavenly glow surrounding Maggie's wild red hair.

"What do you think, darlin'?"

"Mama Maggie it is," Anne said. "And we'll all call you that. It will simplify matters. Right, girls?"

"Oh, it's wonderful!" Kate pressed into the spot to Anne's right and did her best to get her arms around Maggie's waist.

Maggie swept Kate up into her arms and gave her a kiss on the cheek. "So there you go, little miss." She turned to Anne. "If you don't mind, I'd like to ask a favor."

"Of course." Anne looked at her future mother-in-law with a smile. "What is it, Maggie?"

"Well, I've been thinking." She ran her fingers through her messy hair.

"Yes?"

"Here are my thoughts." Maggie's eyes sparkled with mischief. "You know that Jakey's my youngest. And he's kept me company all these years since his brothers got married."

"Of course."

"Well, I just love the chatter of voices in the house—all the more since you and your sisters came to live with us. So I got to thinking about a solution that might just work for all of us."

"O–oh?" Anne drew in a deep breath, trying to anticipate the direction of the rest of this conversation. Would Maggie try to talk them into living with her, perhaps? Ask Jake to give up on his dream of building a home on the family property? She glanced his way, and his eyes grew wide. She could almost read the fear in them.

Maggie's nose wrinkled and she put Kate down. "Now, listen, Anne. You know I love my son."

"Well, of course. I love him too." She gave Jake a shy smile, and he returned it with a wink.

"And I know he loves this place." She turned to face him. "Don't you, Jakey?"

He offered a tentative nod.

"It's been his home, well, forever."

"Yes." *Brace yourself, Anne. Here it comes...*

"But to be honest, he's a real mess."

"W–what?" Jake looked stunned. "Mama!"

"Well, it's true." Maggie put her hands on her hips as she faced Anne. "You might as well know, he drags in mud on his boots and eats enough food for two men in spite of his small size."

"Mama!" he said again.

"He wouldn't know how to wash a dish if it jumped up and bit him, and he's never washed an item of clothing in his life. In other words, he's just like every other male I've ever known."

Jake continued to shake his head, but Anne couldn't keep a smile from spreading across her face. "So what are you saying, Maggie?"

"Are you trying to talk her out of marrying me, Mama?" Jake asked.

"No, son. Not at all. I just had an idea that might make everyone happy."

"What's that?"

"You know what I'd really like?" Maggie asked. She gestured to Emily and Kate. "Daughters."

"Daughters!" Emily and Kate spoke the word in unison.

"It's about time, don't you think? The good Lord blessed me with five sons and I tolerated them the best I could."

"Tolerated?" Jake looked stunned.

"Well, loved 'em, of course." She grinned. "But as I said, they're a lot of work and not much help around the house." Maggie paused and her eyes twinkled. "I—well, would it be presumptuous to ask if the girls could stay on in the main house with me? It would give you and Jakey the privacy you need and me the companionship I crave."

A sense of relief flooded over Anne. Still, she didn't know how her sisters would feel about this. She turned to face them. "Girls, what do you think?"

Emily nodded. "I like it here, Annie. In this house. You're going to be a *honeymooner*." She stressed the word and giggled. "If we stay here, I can have my own room...and a writing desk. Imagine the stories I could write in this house!"

Anne fought to keep from rolling her eyes. They'd already had enough stories in one week to fill a half dozen novels. Still, she could well imagine the new chapters Emily could add to her ever-growing story...and she could also imagine the positive influence Maggie would have on Emily's life.

"Oh, Annie, this is too wonderful to be true!" Kate danced a little jig and laughed.

"Hmm." Anne turned to face Jake, who gave her a little shrug. No doubt. This was her decision, after all. She took Maggie's hand. "If Jake and I were going to be living elsewhere, I'm not sure I could have stomached the idea. My sisters and I are so close. But since we're on the same property and I am going to be newly married..." She felt her face heat up. "I suppose it would be all right." She was quick to add, "If Uncle Bertrand approves of all this, I mean."

"Oh, posh, he'll approve." Maggie grinned. "I think I know that man pretty well. And in case you haven't noticed, I'm pretty good at talkin' folks into things. So I think I can handle one skinny little man whose bark is worse than his bite."

Anne had to laugh at that image. However, she had to wonder if she would still be laughing once her uncle got wind of the idea. Sure, everyone else was celebrating, but what about him? Would he offer congratulations—or snatch up the girls and carry them off to Dallas without her? A shiver ran down her spine at that last option.

She quickly pushed it out of her mind and focused on the good. Yes, today the good surely outweighed the bad. And she would enjoy it while it lasted.

* * * * *

Later that afternoon, Jake slipped back out to the barn to check on Frances. Sure enough, things had progressed rapidly for her. Before long, a new colt had made his arrival, standing to his feet almost immediately. Looked like this day was going to be pretty unforgettable on several fronts.

"What've we got there?" John's voice rang out from behind Jake. "Did she deliver?"

"She did."

"Well, now, that's a mighty fine-looking colt." He patted Frances. "You did a terrific job, Frances."

Both Jake and John remained with Frances and the newborn for several minutes, making sure they had everything they needed. Then, as they left the barn, John patted Jake on the back.

"So, I understand congratulations are in order."

Jake nodded. "Yep."

"I'm very happy for you." They stepped outside into the sunlight. Jake took a few steps, but his brother stopped him. "Can I ask you a question, Jake?"

"Of course."

"Were you itchin' to get hitched because of what we did to you the other day?"

"What?"

"That day we wrestled the feed sack over your head. Is that why you did it, because you felt pressured, being the last single fella in Groom?"

Jake shook his head. "If you want the truth of the matter, I really hadn't fretted over not finding a gal. Oh, sure, I got a little rankled at all the jesting. And the attention was embarrassing too. But that didn't make me want to get married."

"I see." John nodded. "Well, I feel better, then. From the minute I got the news, I wondered if our jesting had forced you to rush into something you weren't ready for."

"No. Something happened to change everything inside of me. Or maybe I should say *someone* happened. God brought that perfect someone right to my doorstep. It's pretty miraculous, if you think about it. She came all the way from Denver to a place she'd never even heard of before."

"Definitely sounds like more than a coincidence." John gave him a brotherly pat. "Well, I just want you to know that I'll stop ribbing you once you're married. For the most part, anyway. I'm not sure why we always took such pleasure in getting you riled up. Just started years ago and I didn't know how to stop it. It was like a freight train barreling down the track."

"Only now it's been derailed?" Jake grinned. "Is that what you're telling me?"

"Yep. Ironic."

"Well, do me a favor, oh brother of mine. Don't stop all your joking. I don't think I could take it if it all dried up. Promise?" He extended his hand and John took it.

"I promise."

Jake gave him a nod then led the way to the house.

* * * * *

Anne worked alongside Maggie and her sisters in the kitchen, preparing supper. She tried to pay attention to their conversation, but her thoughts kept shifting back to earlier today. Jake's proposal had swept her off her feet. Oh, that glorious look in his eyes as he'd gazed at her. So tender. So loving. Everything she'd ever dreamed of but didn't think would come true. And then every prayer had been answered in one swift move—*swift* being the key word.

She paused, wondering for the umpteenth time what Uncle Bertrand would think of this. Likely he would call them impulsive or irresponsible. She would need to come up with a compelling argument for that. For, while they had moved quickly, they had moved in the direction of their hearts. No one could deny that.

The door to the kitchen opened and Jake entered. She couldn't quite make out the look on his face. He crossed the kitchen and stood next to Emily.

"Young lady, come with me. We've got a little business to take care of."

"Oh no." Emily almost dropped the dish she was holding. "Did I do something wrong?"

"No, just follow me, please."

From the look on his face, Anne could tell that Jake was up to something...but what? She and her sisters tagged along on Jake's heels. They made their way outside and then across the porch and down the steps.

"What's he doing, Annie?" Kate whispered. "Is she in trouble?"

"I can't imagine she's in trouble." Anne turned to her youngest sister. "Unless she's done something we don't know about." Of course, knowing Emily, that could be just about anything. Anne tried to catch Jake's eye. She wanted to ask him the obvious question—but didn't dare.

When they entered the barn and approached the stalls on the far side, Jake turned to face them. "I have a little present for you, Emily. It's a special thank-you for keeping us entertained with those stories of yours. What I'm about to show you is something very new and exciting. Are you ready?"

Emily nodded and clasped her hands together. "I'm ready."

"All right, then." He led the way around the corner to a stall with a horse inside. "You've already met Frances, my mare."

Emily nodded, and then her gaze shifted downward to the newborn horse standing just behind Frances. "Oh, Jake! Is this my present?"

"It is. He's all yours. If you want him, that is."

"If I want him? If I want him?" Emily's eyes sparkled as she ran her hand across the colt's neck. "Is that a trick question?"

"No trick question."

"Really, truly, he's mine?"

"Yes." Jake nodded. "And I'm pretty sure you've already got him named."

"Oh yes. His name is going to be Copper because of his beautiful color. I've always wanted a horse named Copper." She sighed. "I have never been this happy...ever." She turned to face Anne, tears streaming down her cheeks. "Oh, Annie, we really are staying, aren't we?"

"Well, of course, honey. That's the idea." *As long as Uncle Bertrand doesn't put up a fuss.*

Emily leaned over the little colt and hugged him tight. "Now that I've seen my new baby colt, I can never leave O'Farrell's Honor. It's my home. Nothing can tear me away."

The emotions that filled Anne's heart at the scene were beyond anything she'd ever felt before. In fact, she'd never known such joy existed until now.

They stayed in the barn until it began to grow dark inside. Anne and Jake held hands while they watched the girls play with the colt.

"I think it's time to let our new arrival get some rest," Jake said after awhile. "You can come back in the morning and spend time with him."

"Thank you again, Jake." Emily rushed over to give him an embrace.

She skipped out of the barn with Kate following on her heels. Anne and Jake paused for a little kiss in the doorway of the barn and then walked out to the yard.

"Oh, Jake, look." Anne pointed to the sky. "It's another Panhandle sunset—just magnificent. She linked her fingers through his and they walked together toward the house. Off in the distance she heard the sound of children's voices and realized that more of Maggie's children and grandchildren had arrived. She could hardly wait to tell them her news. She was getting married! Milly and the other girls were likely to squeal with delight.

But just as soon as they reached the porch, Uncle Bertrand's Cadillac pulled up. Anne's heart began to quicken at once. She tried to rehearse a speech in her head...tried to think of something persuasive to say when her uncle got out of his car.... Unfortunately, she found her tongue stuck to the roof of her mouth. She could only hope it would cooperate by the time he reached the house. If it didn't, he would likely have her sisters packed and ready to go to Dallas before she could do a thing about it.

Chapter Twenty-Six

....

Wishing you could travel the high seas? See exotic places you've only read about in books? Why board a ship when the world comes to your door in the Texas Panhandle? For a real sightseeing adventure, visit the towns of Canadian and Memphis. Sip tea in Wellington, nibble on scones in Stratford, and pick four-leaf clovers in Shamrock. Get married in the town of Groom, or practice your archery skills in Spearman. If you're looking for culture and fine living, look no further than the Texas Panhandle, where you can experience society at its finest. —"Tex" Morgan, reporting for the *Panhandle Primer*

Anne forced a smile as her uncle approached and willed her heart to slow its near-frantic pace.

"Anne." He offered an abrupt nod. "Is everyone here?"

"Yes, the whole family. Maggie's made a special dinner." She hesitated, not sure if this was the right time to mention the proposal. How would he take the news?

"Good. Glad everyone's in one place. I need to talk with you."

"O–oh?" She suddenly felt queasy. Would he decide to leave tonight after all? If so, would he expect her and the girls to go with him?

"Yes, let's go inside for a chat. I'd like to meet with you and your sisters." He paused and smiled. "And Maggie. I think she'd like to be in on this too."

"All right." Anne took a few tentative steps toward the house. Once inside, she was met with a flurry of activity.

"Oh, Anne, is it true?" Ruth grabbed her hand. "Emily told us that—"

Anne flashed her a warning look and shook her head.

"Guess I'm getting ahead of myself." Cora giggled.

"It's the best news in the world," Pauline added. "I'm just speechless."

Milly drew near and wrapped her arms around Anne's neck. "We're going to be sisters now," she whispered. "Welcome to the family."

"Sisters?" Uncle Bertrand drew near. "What's this, Anne?"

"Oh, well, I—"

"Bert, you're back." Maggie entered the parlor, fussed with her hair, and untied her apron. "I didn't know if you would be back today or not. I've made a special meal. We're celebrating."

"Can it wait a few minutes? I have something I need to share with the girls."

"Now is fine. Should the rest of us leave the room and give you some privacy?"

"No, please stay. This concerns all of you." He began to pace.

Maggie sat on the sofa and Anne took the spot beside her, feeling a little shaky. Jake stood behind Anne with his hand on her shoulder, as if to say, "We can make it through this, whatever it is."

On the other side of the room Milly, Cora, and the other ladies stood, looking a bit perplexed. Adding to the confusion, Bets and Leo also walked in, holding hands. Behind them came Jake's four brothers, gabbing about the price of feed. Looked like the whole clan had arrived. And just in time, though for what, she could not be sure.

Uncle Bertrand continued to pace the room. He finally came to a stop in front of the window then turned to face them.

"The Texas Panhandle is a booming place," he said.

"Indeed." Maggie nodded.

"A man with a business such as mine would be a fool not to take advantage of a location such as this. Why, Carson County doesn't have one single department store. Did you know that?"

Anne could hardly believe her ears. "Uncle Bertrand, what are you saying?"

"I'm saying, the need for merchandise is great in this area. A man in the department-store business could do well for himself here."

"You're going to open a store here?" Maggie's eyes lit up. "Am I hearing you right?"

"Well, why not." He turned to face her, and the wrinkles in his brow slowly faded. "As I said, it's a great opportunity."

"Yes, it is." She quirked a brow, and Anne realized that there was much more to this story than she'd first imagined.

"Anyway, I was thinking I could stay on here in Groom to oversee the building of the store. For a few months, anyway. And then we can see what happens next." He turned to face Maggie. "How does that sound?"

"Like music to my ears," she whispered.

Everyone let out a collective gasp. At once Emily and Kate began to dance around the room in celebratory style.

Anne felt a wave of relief wash over her. "Oh, Uncle Bertrand. Really?"

"Really."

A lone tear rolled down Maggie's cheek. He approached her.

"Would—would you mind so much, having this old fool around a bit longer?"

"I wouldn't mind a bit." She swiped at her cheek. "In fact, I heard just last week that one of our neighbors, David Koenig, is looking to sell his house. It's near the heart of town."

"Might be a better idea than staying in the hotel, and I like the idea of being in town, close to the new store. There's a lot of work to be done in setting things up."

"I'd love to help." Maggie patted his arm. "Just say the word and I'm there."

"Oh, and so would I, Uncle Bertrand." Anne rose and walked his way. "Folks have been telling me that I have a good eye for decorating and such. Maybe I could help with the layout of the store. What do you think?"

"I think you're the perfect person for the job." He then glanced at Emily. "And I'm pretty sure I know who to turn to when it comes time to do a big write-up for the paper."

"Really, Uncle Bertrand?" Emily flung herself into his arms and then suddenly stepped back, clearly stunned by her outburst. "I mean, I've always dreamed of writing for the paper."

"You'll do a fine job." He paused and looked at Anne and her sisters. "But let's get one thing straight. From this point on, no more of this 'Uncle Bertrand' stuff."

"No?" Anne gave him a curious look.

"No. My name is Bert. So let's stick with that."

"Uncle Bert." Kate giggled. "I like it."

"Well, your timing couldn't be better." Anne reached to touch his arm. "Because I have some news too." She extended her trembling left hand and showed him the ring.

"What is this?"

"I've asked her to marry me, sir." Jake rose and took a few steps toward them. "Perhaps I should have asked your permission first, but I let my emotions get ahead of me."

Uncle Bert's eyes misted over. "Well, if that doesn't beat all. You're getting married, then?" When Anne nodded, he wrapped her in his arms and whispered, "Your father would have been so proud. I'm just sorry he's not here to witness this firsthand."

At this a knot rose in Anne's throat. "Me too."

He gave her a squeeze. "I realize I haven't been a very good father figure to you since he passed on. And I'm truly sorry about that. I've been an old fool."

Anne wanted to respond but couldn't find the words. Was he really apologizing?

"In spite of my past transgressions, I do hope you will give me the honor of giving you away when you marry." He gave her a sheepish grin. "It would be the very least I could do to make things up to you."

"Really?" She practically leaped into his arms. "Oh, Uncle Bertrand—Bert—I'm so happy. That's the nicest gift you could have given me."

Off in the distance, Aunt Bets began to sniffle. "It's all just too much to take," she whispered.

"There's something else, Anne." Uncle Bert gripped her hand. "One of the reasons I was so keen on bringing you girls to Dallas is because I have something for you. Your father—in spite of his many struggles—realized the predicament you girls would be in, should something happen to him. When I visited him last year, he gave me some money to be held in trust for you girls until you married. I invested it, of course, and it has grown a bit. We're not talking about a huge amount of money here, but it's certainly enough to act as a wedding gift for you and Jake and also some for your sisters when it's their time to marry."

Anne's heart began to twist at this new revelation. Papa had left an inheritance after all. Even in his weakened state, he'd cared enough to make sure he provided for his daughters. Why this struck her in such a deep way Anne could not say, but in that moment, the tears began to flow.

"Go ahead, sweet girl. Let it out." Maggie joined the circle, drawing Anne close.

The tears came from a well deep inside of her, a place she'd not visited until now. So many of the things she'd held against her father just floated away on the evening breeze. And as she released them, the most freeing feeling swept over her. Suddenly she felt like dancing, and a melody filled her heart. In that moment, with her eyes closed, she could almost see Papa standing at the pearly gates, joining in. Maybe one day she could dance with him. Right now, Uncle Bertrand would have to do.

No, not "have to do." He'd been sent from heaven too, in spite of his sour ways. And heaven had done its part in transforming him into someone she had grown to love.

Off in the distance, Emily got her attention with a grunt. Anne pulled away from Maggie and Uncle Bert to give her sister a look of curiosity.

"What is it, honey?"

"Oh, nothing." Emily sighed. "It's just that I'll have to dig up the dolls from the backyard."

"What do you mean?"

GROOM
1914
TX

"I buried one that I named Uncle Bertrand. I'll have to dig him up now."

"You buried me in effigy?" The wrinkles reappeared on Uncle Bert's brow.

"I guess it wasn't really you," Emily said with a shrug. "It was the old you. The mean you."

"Well, do me a favor." Maggie placed her hand on Bert's shoulder. "Keep him buried. Let's let the new man live on, shall we?"

"Sounds like a good idea to me." Uncle Bert turned to her with a soft smile. "Some things are worth changing over."

"Indeed, they are." The two paused to gaze into each other's eyes. Jake finally broke the silence in the room by clearing his throat.

Maggie snapped to attention. "There's leftover wedding cake if anyone's interested. Who wants a slice?"

Anne paused, waiting for Aunt Bets to say something about how they shouldn't eat sugar in the middle of the day, but the woman didn't do as expected.

Bets rose and took Leo by the hand. "I've been pining for a piece of that cake since we got here. And I think we need ice cream too. My sister's homemade ice cream is the best in the county, if I do say so myself."

"Why, thank you, Bets." Maggie grinned with obvious pleasure.

"One more thing." Bets turned to face Emily. "I'm going to make an assumption that there's another doll buried out there with my name on it."

Emily's gaze darted away. "I, um, I…"

Bets knelt in front of her. "Do me a favor, child. Let her rest in peace. I think I'd rather start fresh too."

Emily shocked them all by throwing her arms around Bets's neck.

Uncle Leo extended his hand and helped Bets stand. "Anyone want coffee?" she asked. "I can put some on to brew."

"Sounds wonderful." Leo gave her an admiring look as she sashayed from the room. In fact, it almost looked as if his eyes couldn't leave her.

He wasn't the only one having a hard time keeping his eyes off a woman. Uncle Bert had snagged an extra glance at Maggie as well. She'd pretended not to notice, of course, but Anne felt sure she knew exactly what she was doing. Looked like Emily wasn't the only one with acting abilities.

Anne wanted to laugh. No, she wanted to dance a jig—the kind of jig Bets wouldn't have allowed just a few short days ago. The kind she would go on dancing forever in her heart.

* * * * *

Jake watched the goings-on with some degree of humor as everyone made their way into the kitchen. In one day, he'd acquired a bride-to-be, learned that her uncle would be building a store in town, and discovered that his mother had feelings for Bert Denning. Not bad for a day's work.

As he gazed across the sea of people and into the eyes of the woman he loved, a lump rose in his throat. *Don't cry, Jake. They already think you're a mama's boy. You don't want 'em to think you're a sissy too.* He released a slow breath and managed to get his emotions under control just as his four brothers approached.

"Looks like our courtin' advice paid off, little brother." Jeremiah slung an arm around his shoulders. "And I, for one, couldn't be happier."

"Same here," Joseph added.

"Because I'm not gonna be the last single fella in town?" Jake asked.

"No." Jeremiah's expression grew serious. "Because if anyone deserves this, you do."

Jake thought about his brother's words as he glanced Anne's way. She offered him a shy smile as she ran her fingers over the little cross necklace. He'd never seen such a look of contentment on a face before. With a very full heart, he eased his way through the crowd and wrapped her in his arms.

* * * * *

Anne smiled as Jake planted a kiss on her cheek. She held tight to the little necklace, complete peace washing over her.

Uncle Bert drew near and spoke in a soft voice. "I've been noticing your cross for days, Anne, but I keep forgetting to say something about it. Do you know the story behind it?"

"It was my mother's." She smiled as she fingered it.

"Yes, but did you realize it was once my mother's?" he asked.

Anne gasped. "No. I had no idea."

"Yes. My mother passed it down to your father when he married. He, in turn, gave it to his new bride. So I think it's only fitting that she passed it on to you."

"Amazing." Maggie drew near and gave the cross a close look. "And just think, Anne—one day you can pass it to your daughter."

Anne's felt her face grow hot. Heavens. Would she one day have a daughter? Jake pulled her closer and placed a kiss on her temple.

"C'mon, everyone. Let's have some cake and ice cream." Maggie went to work at dishing it up. Anne offered to help, but Maggie wouldn't hear of it. "Not today, honey. This is your day. Yours and Jake's." She gave her son a wink.

Emily approached and embraced Anne. "Isn't it interesting, Annie? My story really is coming true."

"Really?"

"Yes. After we talked the other night, I sat down and rewrote the scary parts. I made them nice." She shrugged. "Well, mostly nice. I did leave in one Indian scalping and added a train derailment. Couldn't leave that out. But don't you see? Much of it actually came true."

"Who could have known?" Anne bent and gave her sister a kiss on the cheek. "But I'll have to agree with Uncle Bert that you were born to write."

"Want to hear about the one I'm writing next?" Emily giggled. "I think you'll like it."

"Sure. Why not. What's happening in your next story?"

"Well, there's a beautiful lady named Annie who marries a handsome cowboy...and they have seven baby girls."

Anne swallowed hard. "Seven?"

"Maybe six. But they all live together on a big ranch in Texas."

"I see." Jake cleared his throat. "And, might I ask, are you patterning your characters off anyone you know in real life?"

She nodded. "Of course. Any writer worth her weight in salt knows there's just a tiny line between fiction and reality."

"And sometimes that line gets a little blurry, I understand." Jake grinned. "Not that I'm complaining."

"Me either." Anne laughed and then looked again at Emily. "What happens after that, honey? Do they all live happily ever after?"

"I dunno." Emily waggled her eyebrows and laughed. "I guess that's up to you."

"I see." Anne gazed at Jake, her heart swelling with joy. "If I get to choose, I'll go with the happily-ever-after ending. Even if it is a little sappy."

"Sappy is good." Jake gave her another kiss on the cheek. "I can live with sappy."

"Good." Anne slipped her arm around his waist in response. "Because I have a rather sappy idea I'd like to pass your way when you have the time to talk it through."

"What's that?"

"Oh, just a little idea I had about opening up a wedding chapel on the road leading to town." She gave him a wink.

"A wedding chapel?" Kate squealed. "Oh, how lovely."

"What a delicious idea!" Emily chimed in.

"This is the town of Groom, after all," Anne said. "It makes sense to have a wedding chapel." Her excitement grew. "I can see it now. People will come from all over the place to get married in Groom. What a novelty it will be. We'll have a beautiful outdoor area with a gazebo...and an inside area, too. What do you think?"

"I think I'd like to be the first groom to walk that aisle," Jake said. "If you like the idea."

"I guess we'd better get busy, then." Maggie laughed and looked toward Bert and her sons. "How long do you think it will take us to put up this chapel she's talking about, boys?"

"I don't know." John shrugged. "Maybe a month or two."

"Maybe less," Joseph added. "If we ask for help from our neighbors."

"I think that's a fine idea." Maggie crossed her arms and appeared to be thinking. "That's just what we'll do. We'll plan it just like the old barn raisings we used to have when I was a child. How does that sound?"

"Perfect." Anne felt the edges of her lips curl up as a satisfied feeling swept over her.

"Anne, what do you think of this?" Uncle Bert's eyes sparkled. "What if we added a department in the new store for bridal needs?"

"Bridal needs?"

"Things like fine china or glassware."

"And silver," Maggie added.

"And table linens and other things of interest to a bride-to-be," Bert continued. "What do you think?"

"We could put it all together in one department?"

"Yes, and you could work there, if you like. Who knows. Maybe you'll drum up customers for the wedding chapel. We could lean on each other."

"Interesting idea. Most of the brides will be from out of state, I suppose." She smiled as something occurred to her. "Now that Jake and I are getting married, there aren't any single men left in Groom."

"Oh, that's right," Jake said as he sliced the cake. "I'd almost forgotten about that."

"I know of one," Emily said as she stuck her spoon into her bowl of ice cream.

"Oh? Who's that?" Anne asked.

She pointed across the table. "Uncle Bert. He's not married, and now that he's planning to stay, he'll be a Groom resident."

"Ooh, Uncle Bert!" Kate clasped her hands together.

They all turned to look at him, and his eyes widened.

"I've decided I'm going to write a romance novel with you as

GROOM
1914
TX

the main character, Uncle Bert." Emily lips turned up in a sly grin. "You can be the hero. How does that sound?"

"Oh, well, I don't know about that," he said. "I've been an old codger far too long to think about adding a love interest to my story."

"Those are the best stories of all," Emily said. "The ones with the surprise endings. In my story, you're going to marry…" She paused and then looked at Maggie with a grin. "A wonderful woman who loves to cook and who has a heart of gold."

Maggie cleared her throat. "Anyone else want coffee? Or cake?" She looked at Bert. "Anything at all?" She clamped a hand over her mouth after she uttered those last words, and she held it there until everyone in the room stopped laughing.

Bert quirked a brow, and his handlebar mustache twitched. Anne almost laughed but quickly swallowed it. No point in bringing further embarrassment. Still, she found it wildly ironic—as Emily would say—that Jake had passed the "last single man in Groom" mantle to her uncle. Wildly ironic, indeed.

About the Author

....

Award-winning author Janice Hanna, who also writes under the name Janice Thompson, has published more than sixty books for the Christian market, crossing genre lines to write cozy mysteries, historicals, romances, nonfiction books, devotionals, children's books, and more. Her passion? Romantic comedies! Janice formerly served as vice president of the Christian Authors Network (christianauthorsnetwork.com) and was named the 2008 Mentor of the Year by the American Christian Fiction Writers organization. She is passionate about her faith and does all she can to share the joy of the Lord with others, which is why she particularly enjoys writing.

Janice lives in Spring, Texas, where she leads a rich life with her family, a host of writing friends, and two mischievous dachshunds. She does her best to keep the Lord at the center of it all.

www.janicehannathompson.com
www.freelancewritingcourses.com

Author's Note

....

Those of us who live in Texas are mighty proud of our state. Our praises are often as exaggerated as her size…and there's no greater place to brag about than the Texas Panhandle. As a child, I visited a cowboy museum in Amarillo, Texas, which is nestled in the heart of the Panhandle not far from Groom. When I grew up, I longed to visit that region once again.

I got my wish in 1990, when our family vacationed at Palo Duro Canyon. I'd never seen anything as breathtaking. The colors of the canyon walls caught me off guard. After all, I'd lived in Texas for most of my life and didn't know such a place existed. My daughters were all in elementary school at the time. I remember pulling our car up to the edge of a low spot at the Red River. The girls got out of the car and walked through the river in their bare feet. I still have the photo…and, yes, the water looks red against that hard, red clay.

I can honestly say that *Love Finds You in Groom, Texas*, has been my favorite historical romance novel to write. I hope readers enjoy both the whimsy and the moments of depth. I also hope they see my passion for sharing the tale of a God who interrupts our ordinary lives to give us extraordinary opportunities—both to love and be loved.

I would be remiss not to thank those who helped with this story: Rachel Meisel, my awesome editor at Summerside; Chip

MacGregor, the wonderful agent who champions my work; Connie Troyer, my delightful copyeditor; Jay O'Brien, who responded to my questions about ranching in the Panhandle; and my wonderful critique partners, Martha Rogers and Janetta Messmer. May God richly bless you all!

Want a peek into local American life—past and present?
The *Love Finds You*™ series published by Summerside Press
features real towns and combines travel, romance,
and faith in one irresistible package!

The novels in the series—uniquely titled after American towns with romantic
or intriguing names—inspire romance and fun. Each fictional story draws on
the compelling history or the unique character of a real place. Stories center on
romances kindled in small towns, old loves lost and found again on the high plains,
and new loves discovered at exciting vacation getaways. Summerside Press plans
to publish at least one novel set in each of the fifty states. Be sure to catch them all!

Now Available

Love Finds You in Miracle, Kentucky
by Andrea Boeshaar
ISBN: 978-1-934770-37-5

Love Finds You in Snowball, Arkansas
by Sandra D. Bricker
ISBN: 978-1-934770-45-0

Love Finds You in Romeo, Colorado
by Gwen Ford Faulkenberry
ISBN: 978-1-934770-46-7

Love Finds You in Valentine, Nebraska
by Irene Brand
ISBN: 978-1-934770-38-2

Love Finds You in Humble, Texas
by Anita Higman
ISBN: 978-1-934770-61-0

*Love Finds You in Last Chance,
California*
by Miralee Ferrell
ISBN: 978-1-934770-39-9

*Love Finds You in
Maiden, North Carolina*
by Tamela Hancock Murray
ISBN: 978-1-934770-65-8

*Love Finds You in
Paradise, Pennsylvania*
by Loree Lough
ISBN: 978-1-934770-66-5

*Love Finds You in
Treasure Island, Florida*
by Debby Mayne
ISBN: 978-1-934770-80-1

Love Finds You in Liberty, Indiana
by Melanie Dobson
ISBN: 978-1-934770-74-0

Love Finds You in Revenge, Ohio
by Lisa Harris
ISBN: 978-1-934770-81-8

Love Finds You in Poetry, Texas
by Janice Hanna
ISBN: 978-1-935416-16-6

Love Finds You in Sisters, Oregon
by Melody Carlson
ISBN: 978-1-935416-18-0

Love Finds You in Charm, Ohio
by Annalisa Daughety
ISBN: 978-1-935416-17-3

Love Finds You in
Bethlehem, New Hampshire
by Lauralee Bliss
ISBN: 978-1-935416-20-3

Love Finds You in North Pole, Alaska
by Loree Lough
ISBN: 978-1-935416-19-7

Love Finds You in Holiday, Florida
by Sandra D. Bricker
ISBN: 978-1-935416-25-8

Love Finds You in
Lonesome Prairie, Montana
by Tricia Goyer and Ocieanna Fleiss
ISBN: 978-1-935416-29-6

Love Finds You in Bridal Veil, Oregon
by Miralee Ferrell
ISBN: 978-1-935416-63-0

Love Finds You in Hershey,
Pennsylvania
by Cerella D. Sechrist
ISBN: 978-1-935416-64-7

Love Finds You in Homestead, Iowa
by Melanie Dobson
ISBN: 978-1-935416-66-1

Love Finds You in Pendleton, Oregon
by Melody Carlson
ISBN: 978-1-935416-84-5

Love Finds You in Golden, New Mexico
by Lena Nelson Dooley
ISBN: 978-1-935416-74-6

Love Finds You in Lahaina, Hawaii
by Bodie Thoene
ISBN: 978-1-935416-78-4

Love Finds You in
Victory Heights, Washington
by Tricia Goyer and Ocieanna Fleiss
ISBN: 978-1-60936-000-9

Love Finds You in Calico, California
by Elizabeth Ludwig
ISBN: 978-1-60936-001-6

Love Finds You in Sugarcreek, Ohio
by Serena B. Miller
ISBN: 978-1-60936-002-3

Love Finds You in
Deadwood, South Dakota
by Tracey Cross
ISBN: 978-1-60936-003-0

Love Finds You in Silver City, Idaho
by Janelle Mowery
ISBN: 978-1-60936-005-4

Love Finds You in
Carmel-by-the-Sea, California
by Sandra D. Bricker
ISBN: 978-1-60936-027-6

Love Finds You Under the Mistletoe
by Irene Brand and Anita Higman
ISBN: 978-1-60936-004-7

Love Finds You in Hope, Kansas
by Pamela Griffin
ISBN: 978-1-60936-007-8

Love Finds You in Sun Valley, Idaho
by Angela Ruth
ISBN: 978-1-60936-008-5

Love Finds You in Camelot, Tennessee
by Janice Hanna
ISBN: 978-1-935416-65-4

Love Finds You in
Martha's Vineyard, Massachusetts
by Melody Carlson
ISBN: 978-1-60936-110-5

Love Finds You in Amana, Iowa
by Melanie Dobson
ISBN: 978-1-60936-135-8

Coming Soon

Love Finds You in
Lancaster County, Pennsylvania
by Annalisa Daughety
ISBN: 97-8-160936-212-6

Love Finds You in Branson, Missouri
by Gwen Ford Faulkenberry
ISBN: 978-1-60936-191-4

Love Finds You in Sundance, Wyoming
by Miralee Ferrell
ISBN: 978-1-60936-277-5

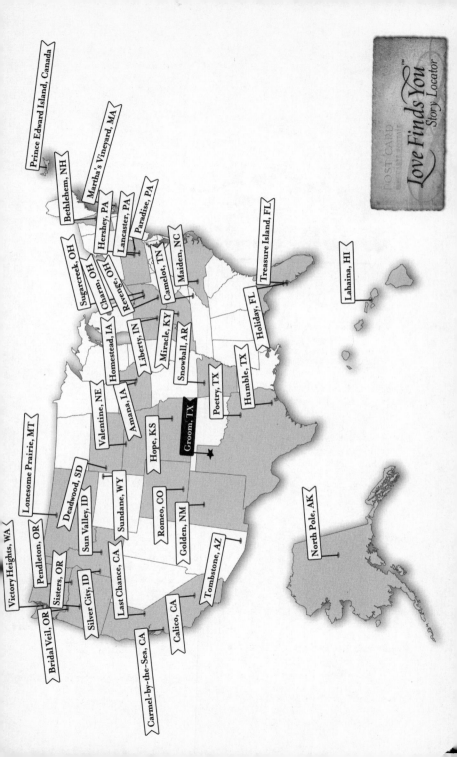

Walla Walla
County Libraries